For Mom, Dad and Diane

Published 2019
Printed in the United States of America
Print ISBN: 978-0-9977220-8-6
EBook ISBN: 978-0-9977220-9-3

Publisher Information:
DartFrog Books
PO Box 867
Manchester, VT 05254

www.DartFrogBooks.com

AS SHE DIED

Even though we would like to believe that in the end there are flashing pictures and brilliant insights, the last thought Mandy had before she let go of the rope swing of life—the very, very last thought that she had—was to wonder whether she had ordered enough scotch.

ONE

THE MAN AND THE PORPOISE
CONNECTICUT 1983

The church was empty and expectant when he entered carrying a canvas bag on his shoulder. It was 8:30 on Saturday morning. He wore a gray sweatshirt, hood up, and strode with purpose down the center aisle. Halfway there, he paused, saw it and slowed. At the altar, he climbed the two stairs and lowered his bag to the floor.

It was there, closed.

He looked around to be sure he was alone and then removed the two identical large sprays of the "In Deepest Sympathy" yellow roses from the top of the coffin and laid them gently on the floor. Then he knelt, rested the side of his face against it, and closed his eyes. With his fingers outstretched, palms flattened, his bony hands moved over the top in wide arcs, caressing the gray metal.

It's like a dolphin or a porpoise, intruded a thought. What's the difference anyway? He rested there, face against the metal, arms draped over the top until he felt ashamed, pushed away, and stood up. His fingers itched with anticipation; he couldn't wait any longer. He felt along the crack of the lid, unhooked the latch, and raised it up so that it fell back on its own weight, hatched and open.

He gasped at the sight.

She wore a headband of tiny flowers and a veil of tulle that fell to her shoulders but did not cover her face. Her head rested on a white, heart-shaped pillow bordered with lace. The lid was adorned with folds of white satin. Inside, her slender arms were bent and her fingers closed to clasp the long stem of a pink rose to her breast.

He recognized the blue chiffon dress with the straps that crossed her bodice to call attention to her breasts. The style was perhaps a bit immodest for a woman of Mandy's age, but he appreciated that it was familiar, not something new.

Resting his hands on the edge, he gazed down at her face thinking that she looked pretty, not overdone; they did a good job on the makeup, maybe even better than she did herself. No frown or weird smirk, perfect pink lipstick, blue eye shadow, a hint of blush on her white cheeks. Even the white wig with bangs and shoulder-length hair in the "flip" almost seemed real. She looked contented and peaceful, the way she would want to appear. Lots of her wrinkles were gone, too. How did they do that?

It felt good to see her. Yes, he'd made the right decision to view her one last time before she was gone. She almost looked like herself (he was relieved about that). Yet, here she was, laid out so still, so perfectly still, and so neat, like a fancy table setting before the meal, not the way she was, not like her at all. She could never be as still as this.

A lone tear dropped onto the bodice of her blue dress, surprising him. He didn't know that about himself—that he felt so strongly. But then again, he was here, wasn't he? Gotta get back to business. He reached out to touch it with his finger but stopped midway. The tear had already seeped into the fabric, leaving a dark spot. There was nothing to be done about it. Too bad. She didn't like to be messy. Better hurry up.

He backed away, crouched over his shoulder bag, and removed the camera and a flash cube that he pushed onto the top. He took one photo after another, close-ups of her face and then backed away to shoot from different angles, replacing the cube to take more. As he was preparing to take a shot from the front of the coffin, he heard a shout from the hallway, "Hey! Hey *you*! What do you think you're doing in there?"

The damned preacher.

In haste, he closed the lid and returned the flowers to the top. All the while, the Reverend Wally Shuttan was marching down the aisle calling out, "You! I said, what do you think you're doing in here?"

The man slung the bag over his shoulder and with his back still turned away from the preacher, waved in half-hearted greeting. He replied more to reassure himself than to be heard and so he spoke softly. "Don't worry. It's all right. She said it was all right."

Then he hurried away.

"What? What did you say?" asked the preacher. But before his last words were out, a door slammed in the choir room, sending a cloud of glittering dust into the sanctuary that tumbled in the sunlight broadcast from the high windows near the crucifixion.

"That's odd," muttered Reverend Wally aloud. "Where'd he go?" After a decade in the sanctuary, much of it time spent alone, no one knew the church and its sounds and the doors leading in and out better than he did. If the man parked in the church lot in back, he needed to drive past the front door.

The reverend sprinted to the lobby with his boat sneakers squealing on the polished linoleum, thrust against the massive front door, and bounded down the steps to the driveway.

He walked down the driveway, shading his eyes from the morning glare to scan the back parking lot for the man. He was too late. It was empty; the guy was gone.

A twirling funnel of sand and brown leaves skittered across the pavement toward him. He stepped aside to watch. Who was that man and who gave him permission to take photos of Mandy Flanagan in her coffin? Always something. People do strange things.

Oh, well. Oh, well.

The reverend went inside.

Across the street, the man started the engine, certain the reverend hadn't noticed him sitting in his car, watching from the bank parking lot. He sucked in his cheeks in a wry smile and drove away.

JAN ARRIVES FROM A WORLD AWAY

As she walked off the plane that same morning, Jan felt buoyant. The soles of her sneakers met the floor in a light-hearted shuffle, happy to be on the ground at last. The midnight takeoff from San Francisco was flawless and she expected to settle down to read a book for the long flight to New York. But turbulence hit midway through, jostling and shaking the passengers. At one jiggling moment, a knapsack of books bounced across the aisle and slid into her shins. A few minutes later, her coffee leapt from her cup like a bullfrog and landed on the yellow golf shirt of the man beside her.

"Actually, I prefer tea," he said, eyes downcast.

When the wheels touched the runway, there were hoots and genuine, grateful applause. With her backpack slung over her shoulder, Jan had the classic look of a Girl Scout leader marching off through the woods. It was the way she walked with long confident strides down the corridors and how she stood erect, her chin fixed while riding the escalator down to the baggage claim to the rental counters.

But there was no reason to rush; the rental car wasn't ready. She leaned forward over the counter into the personal space of the rental agent, a young man dressed in a maroon shirt with gold trim, a logo sewn on the pocket.

"Look. I didn't want to have to mention this, but I need a car right away or I'm going to be late for a funeral."

His face reddened. "Oh?"

He tapped the keyboard and she leaned in toward him, trying to see the screen. "Yeah, it's my Aunt Mandy's funeral and I have to be there to help out. You get that, right? I'll take practically anything you've got. Forget what I ordered. Find me something, anything. I have to get going. My mother will have a *cow* if I'm late."

He smiled.

Jan flicked her tongue into the wide space between her two front teeth, fingered her watch, looked around, shoved her hands into the front pockets of her khakis, took them out, and briefly drummed her fingers on the counter then pushed the suitcase around with her foot.

I'm acting like my mother, she thought.

The clerk stopped tapping and looked up. "We wouldn't want your mother to have a *cow*, now would we? You're in luck. Something just came back."

That "something" was a Chrysler station wagon.

Oh, well, she thought, not cool, but maybe I should get used to a family car.

Driving away, she imagined the long day ahead, the funeral service, the wake, seeing her mother, Uncle Ned and all the relatives. And of course, she would see Terri. Been a while, a very long while.

Calling her yesterday to insist that she go to the funeral hadn't been easy. Had to be done. That's what Aunt Mandy wanted, so that's what she did.

But she felt like a jerk.

"Hi, Terri. It's me, Jan. Got a minute?"

"Who?"

"Jan. Your old friend. Glad I found you at home. I know this is sudden but I need you to go to a funeral with me."

"What, Jan? Really, Jan? It's been a long time."

"I know, I know. Look, I need you to go to a funeral with me."

"I thought that's what you said."

"Aunt Mandy's funeral. On Saturday. I need you to go with me. And there's a wake after at Uncle's Ned's. In Wallingford."

"Wait, wait, you're serious? I haven't seen your aunt in years—or you."

"I *am* serious. It won't take that long."

"But why?"

"Terri, I know this is kind of out of the blue, but I really need you to go with me. Believe me, it's important. I wouldn't be asking you otherwise. Besides, we can catch up, right?"

Quiet. Long quiet.

"Terri? You still there?"

"Ah, well, okay, I guess I can go...but the kids have soccer games Saturday, so I may be late."

"Great. That's okay. It was the smoking."

"The smoking?"

"She wrote it all out in a letter to my mom: what to order for the wake and who to invite. She's a nervous wreck. You know how she is."

"You mean your mother?"

"Oh, yeah, my mother."

"Kind of *intense*. Barbara, right? She must be getting up there, too. How's she doing?"

"My mom? Perfect health."

"Oh, that's good. Where is it?"

"The letter? I don't know where she put it."

"No, no, the service. I need the address if you want me to go."

"Oh, yeah, sorry. St. John's, eleven o'clock. Remember it?"

"Same church we went to that time?"

"Yeah, that's it. Same place. My aunt's church. I'll meet you there. Gotta help my uncle first."

"Like I said, I may be late. Kids have soccer and I just re-membered they have a birthday party, too, but maybe Sam can—"

"Late's not a problem, no problem at all. Hey! I'm really looking forward to seeing you again, lady. It'll be great."

"Jan?"

"What?"

"Well, I sort of wrote you off. Funny hearing from you."

Pause.

"Wrote me off? Well, I guess not yet, huh? Hey, you know I hate to go, but I gotta book my flight. See you soon. You're a real pal."

SO NEATLY PLACED

At 8:30 on the Saturday morning of the funeral, Terri stepped from the shower and felt her hair frizzing into a wild kinky mess. She groped for her glasses on the sink.

Since the phone call, she couldn't think of anything else. Jan moved to San Francisco eight years ago and now, with only a phone call, she agreed to attend the funeral of someone she hardly knew. Bad enough she had to tell Sam. Oddly, he didn't seem to care.

"Long as I don't have to go to the funeral with you, I'm fine. You go. I'll take the kids to soccer."

"And the birthday party."

"And the birthday party."

Of course, she *had* to go; Jan was so insistent. And now she was curious. Was the funeral simply an excuse to get together? But a bigger question was: why had she agreed to go?

But she knew why.

Her old pal Jan had said three little words—words she never heard her say before.

I.

Need.

You.

They were friends.

Good friends who rode on the first exhilarating waves of feminism together, marches and rallies, an exciting time to be in the company of women. But it wasn't enough. Jan split to San Francisco chasing after another friend with stronger tendencies. Everyone seemed to be moving there.

Not her.

There was no warning. No kiss goodbye. When she called Jan's house to ask her out to a movie, her mother Barbara answered.

"Oh, I'm sorry, honey. She didn't tell you, did she? Maybe she didn't want to upset you. Jan's been planning to move to San Francisco all summer. Her Aunt Mandy and I helped her load the car."

That phone call seemed long ago now. So much had happened. It was like a cyclone. Less than a year later, she met and married Sam.

Now they had three kids and a house in the suburbs. She was normal. Average.

Figure that.

Oh, sure, they still exchanged Christmas cards and corny birthday greetings, but the important things between them were left unsaid. Jan skipped the wedding and never asked Terri about Sam, the kids, or her ordinary life, and Terri never asked Jan about her social life.

Why not? Because. Why bother to write about obvious things when the politeness of silence communicates just fine? After all, words in a letter sit flatly on the page, anchored in time, always there, and those cemented sentiments are never wholly the truth. And with so much weight on the words, no wonder they didn't try to explain. Each was busy in their own new lives and they simply weren't that close anymore. Besides, sometimes things work out for the best when you just leave them alone to settle down.

In time, probably one of them would be very late sending out a card.

Or maybe one of them would move and forget to forward the new address.

Or maybe the new address would get lost or misplaced.
Time would stretch out and yawn.

No cards.

No friendship.

It was okay and yet sad that there was no moping about over someone who was once so important. But now you were content to let them slip away into a memory—on purpose.

Perhaps that's just the way it is.

We expect that to happen. It's how things are supposed to go in this busy world. There are too many people to hold onto, too many to hug.

It's like saying goodbye at the airport, putting a friend on a plane. Sure, they might wave, but they don't turn around and they don't come back. They hurry importantly away, down the long aisle to the gate, up the ramp to board the plane, and fly up into the wide sky. Gone, really gone away from you.

You pay the parking ticket at the booth and leave the airport.

At first you're a little melancholy, but the drive home is nice. The solitude is nice. The quiet is nice.

But every so often, sometimes some things and some people so neatly placed in the past return to disrupt your comfortable, predictable life.

SETTING UP FOR THE WAKE AT NED'S

At the church in Wallingford, Aunt Mandy lay there in her coffin, all dressed up in her favorite blue dress, waiting for folks to come and cry. Hey, what else could she do? She was dead. That was her job.

Meanwhile, her brother Ned was sitting at the round kitchen table, still wearing his red plaid duck hat with the long flaps over his ears from his walk to the mailbox. He was a retired toolmaker and continued to wear green work pants and a green work shirt every day without exception, even though this day's activities should have been an exception.

Ned lived alone. He was a bachelor; he liked women but never learned what to do with them or met a woman to show him how. He kept to himself and lived in a neighborhood tract where the houses were all built the same year in the same ranch-style with the sidewalk in front and small square yards in the back. Every house had a concrete driveway on the right side that led to a single car detached garage in the corner of the property. Some of the houses had carports instead of garages. But it was a nice neighborhood. Neighbors strolled around the block, they waved to each other, and dogs, cats, and children roamed freely and no one cared because everyone knew everyone.

Ned was okay. He was that guy who lived alone but had family. He had a routine.

He read two papers a day, one in the morning and one in the evening, and two magazines a week, *National Geographic* and *Time*. When Ned finished reading a newspaper, he'd fold it up and lay it on the top of yesterday's paper; same for the magazines. For forty years, he saved every newspaper and magazine that came to the house. There were stacks six feet high in every room with narrow, maze-like paths between them (the basement had filled long ago).

He was proud of his stacks. Sometimes a neighborhood kid doing research for a term paper would ask him to find an old magazine or newspaper. He knew just where it was and handed it over but was overwhelmed with worry until it was returned to its rightful place in the stack. Sometimes the town librarians admitted they didn't have it but said to go check with Ned Flanagan.

Ned was trying to peer through the half-glasses that had slid to the end of his nose, finish the morning paper, and was about to start his third cup of coffee when there was a polite ding-dong at the front door. But before he could push away from the table, he heard urgent slapping on the front door and then the doorknob jiggled.

"Hold your horses, Barbie, I'm coming, I'm coming. Door's open anyway."

As he stood up, his sister Barbie lunged into the hallway still holding the doorknob. She stood forward, breathless. "I've got everything taken care of! The liquor's in the car and the caterer will be here at noon and the..." her voice trailed off and in that space, the front door slammed shut by the wind.

It was quiet.

She surveyed the rooms, her lips pursed and her right cheek sucked up—a dangerous sign.

"Ned! My God, it's *still* a mess! Where's Jan? She hasn't called?"

"No, not called and she's not here yet, and Barbie she—"

"Well, I can see that! Did she call?"

"No. I said, can't say as she did. But I haven't been—"

"Why on earth haven't you cleaned anything?"

Ned removed his hat, ran his hand over his crewcut, put his hat back on, spoke in his usual slow, careful way with a crooked index finger striking the air for emphasis. "Now don't go gettin' hysterical on me, Barbie. A little dust never hurt anyone. The people won't mind it. I put Mandy's *Extravaganza* picture over on the TV set, see? It's the way she wanted it, see?"

Barbara looked toward the television. At seventy-two, she was older than Ned by two years and taller by three inches. Her tinted red hair was still worn below her shoulders, though this day, it was tied back in a blue ribbon. Dark-framed glasses gave her a serious (scary) and determined look, and she tended to speak loudly, the result of a hearing loss. So that when her anger was fueled and directed (like now) on some poor soul, even her brother Ned could become quite intimidated. Barbara carried this disposition forward from her Boston childhood and into her marriage and mothering. Jan witnessed her mother in this temper many times (as had Ned and Mandy). To them, it was usually no big deal, just Barbara being herself. They knew that after she erupted, it would be over.

Unfortunately, this time she was seething, fueled by the occasion. Poor Ned stood facing her for a moment or two then decided that it just might be prudent to retreat to the kitchen table to wait it out sitting down.

But it was too late.

"Where are you going Ned? The newspapers! You were supposed to get rid of the newspapers!"

"Well, I was, I was, but the—"

"You were supposed to—"

"I was but—"

"The newspapers."

"Well, now, you see, the Boy Scouts... they don't pick 'em up anymore. Next 'cycling pickup is on Tuesday... lady at the town hall said I couldn't put out more than a bag at a time... And I did put out a bag... See, Barbara? See? Used to sit right there near the 'frigerator, see? It's gone."

Barbara was quiet. She wore a look of disgust. But her thoughts were more critical of herself than of Ned. She felt defeated. Why had she ever believed for a moment that she could rely on her worthless brother and her unreliable daughter (who was supposed to have arrived over an hour ago)? What was she thinking?

Ned was Ned, her only brother, always a little off. Ned wasn't going to suddenly rise up and take charge like a man should, even in these trying times.

And Jan, well, they had had their fiery moments. At some undefined point in the last few years, each concluded that it was best to leave a lot of things unsaid, creating a tall, wide dune to traipse around. With so much to avoid, they didn't talk about much that was worth talking about. Was it Jan's preference for women that caused the distance between them? No, it wasn't that. Not anymore. That would be too easy. It was more complicated than that.

Jan and Mandy had been close, and that bothered her. And those two embraced Ned in their little circle, too. She was the one on the outside, always had been. She sighed. Mandy gone, the arrangements—the whole thing was just too much, too much. The responsibilities always fell to her. Why was that? Barbara the doer. She always took charge.

After quarreling with Ned, she really didn't want to be angry with Jan when she arrived—if she arrived. It was going to be a sorrowful, exhausting day as it was. Family. She sighed again.

Newspapers and magazines everywhere. "Ned's library" they called it. Used to be a family joke, funny. Not funny today. The church service would start at noon with the wake here right afterward. How many people would come? How would they all fit in the little house? Was there enough booze? It was already eleven; how could Ned do this to her? She felt her heart quicken and her face redden. She should be on her way to the church by now. She needed to go. Oh, God. Ned, Ned, Ned.

"What about the garage?"

"Can't do that. Nope."

"Why not Ned? Why on earth can't we move some of this *junk* to the garage!"

"Garage is full, Barbie."

"Full of what?"

"Oh, newspapers, from the forties, some fifties, too. Um, there's some bottles and *Reader's Digest* out there, too. Don't get it delivered anymore, read it at the library."

She removed her coat, folded it in half and laid it on a stack near the door. Then she set off heavy-footed down the narrow hallway going from room to room. Barbara's tan skirt fell below her knees and wagged from side to side as she slammed doors, clicked her tongue, and sighed in exasperation.

Meanwhile, Ned sat at the kitchen table with his skinny legs crossed, slowly peeling the newspaper pages, pretending to read. He was silent. No sense getting her all riled up again, he reasoned; stay out of the way. Stay out of her God damned way. Not my favorite sister, he thought. No. Not by a long shot. No. No siree Bob. He turned the pages without reading them and jiggled his foot. He hadn't noticed his niece entering the house, so it was a surprise when she kissed him on the cheek and stood by his chair just as Barbara came down the hall.

"Jan!" Tearful, Barbara rushed to embrace her daughter then stood back to admonish. "I am so glad you're here. But where have you been? Did you miss your flight?"

"No, they didn't have a car ready at the rental."

"No car? Oh. Well, you should have called to let me know. Then I wouldn't have worried. This place is a mess and you pick today of all times to be late."

"Not my fault. Hey, Mom, look, I'm here now. Calm down. Everything will be fine. I'll roll up my sleeves and get started. We'll take care of everything, won't we Uncle Ned?

Ned nodded.

"Mom, you go ahead, go. We'll do it."

Barbara looked between them and sighed. "Well... okay. I'm glad you're here, honey. I know I can rely on you. I'm sorry. I'm a nervous wreck. I just want it to be the way she wanted it to be."

"Mom, I know. I do, too."

"Me, too," said Ned.

Barbara leaned toward Jan. "Give me a hug. I need a hug, a good one."

GOD DOESN'T CARE
WHAT YOU WEAR TO CHURCH

Ned sat in the very last pew on the left side while his sister Barbara sat in the front row on the right side, nearest Mandy's coffin. She turned around to glare at him a few times. He was supposed to sit up front, next to her, all the family together. At this, Ned turned to the short dark man beside him and whispered, "You know Mandy was my favorite sister." The man smiled, nodded.

The church murmured with low conversations. It was a good crowd for an old lady's funeral with about thirty people politely scattered in the pews: relatives, neighbors, old friends and a family with four young children.

Terri sat on the left side, a few empty rows behind the organist, in front of the family. She crossed and uncrossed her legs then tried to push her black curls into place, frizzed-out from the rain in a wild triangle tangle from her shoulders. She glanced down at her watch again and pushed her glasses back up her nose.

Jan was late.

Just like the old days.

The fat angels on the ceiling looked familiar. Eight years ago, she had come with Jan to this very same church. After the service, they went to Mandy's house in Wallingford for dinner. Back then, she remembered thinking how conspicuous it felt to sit beside her lesbian lover in a church that surely did not approve of their relationship. After the service, Aunt Mandy beamed and clearly enjoyed introducing them around, maybe even rubbing it in to her churchy pals. She liked her for that.

"Have you met Jan, my niece, and her *special* friend, Terri?"

People were cordial but stiff. "No, I haven't. Welcome."

And, "How nice for you," grinning, looking them over.

Even now, attending a church like this was never a comfortable experience for her. The problem was that she couldn't stop wondering about all the good, pious people in the pews and whether they were quite different in the world outside. Perhaps they acted the same in or out of church.

Who's to know? Who's to judge?

God.

(If there is one.)

Terri felt a little guilty.

She and Sam agreed that a spiritual compass was necessary for their children. He was a lapsed Jew and she was a lapsed Catholic, so it had to be a different religion altogether. Pauly, their oldest, was almost six and they still hadn't visited any of the local churches to try them out.

And now, here she was, eight years later, at the last church she remembered attending, sitting in the pew, staring ahead at the coffin of Jan's Aunt Mandy.

Funny that. Life was strange, no doubt about it.

And after the service, she would go to the house of Jan's Uncle Ned, have a drink or two, express her condolences, and leave. She looked at her watch again. It was already after twelve. The service was about to start; still no Jan.

Barbara turned to look and nod in greeting and appreciation as people came in and sat. And did Barbara just wink at her?

Yes, she did. Barbara actually winked at her.

Gawd.

And there it was—the closed coffin. Terri berated herself. Why, oh why, did I have to sit so close to the front? Now it was too late to move. Now she had to look at it and imagine the contents inside. She couldn't stop herself from thinking.

Did the undertaker bother with a bra? Were her toenails still pink? Was she wearing eye shadow the way she used to do, lavender or midnight blue? What kind of day was it when Aunt Mandy wrote to her sister Barbara to describe the outfit she would wear today?

Of course, most people never get the chance to plan anything before they die. It's too sudden. Or by the time they realize they're dying, they're too decrepit to care, mind gone. Perhaps if you do have the stamina and time, it might be fun to plan every little detail of your demise to make up for the shock and thrust of birth, your disappointed parents, your unfulfilled accomplishments, your pathetic life, your unrequited love...

Terri stared ahead mesmerized and thought, Aunt Mandy is in that box, that box *right there*.

Aunt Mandy in-the-box.

Sounds like a kid's snack. "Kids just *love* Aunt Mandy's In The Box!"

But her odd thoughts were interrupted when an old man slid down the pew, coming to rest right beside her. He smiled. He wore a camel hair jacket too large for his small frame and a toupee rested on his head like a black glove. Otherwise, he resembled a short, aged Clark Gable, with wide ears and a mustache. She tried not to stare.

The music seemed to grow loud and insistent. Had it been playing the entire time she was seated and she just noticed it now? The organist, short and quite plump, had an especially big derriere that stood out majestically from the rest of her body. She covered this feature with white stretch pants pulled up high above her waist, making her cheeks appear like two giant powder donuts standing side-by-side. She swayed and played with a lagging, loud left bass-hand whenever she leaned to reach up with her right hand to pull out an organ stop. When her hand plopped back in place, it first slurred over a few wrong keys on the way to the intended chords of the composer, making Terri and the man beside her wince in unison. What was she trying to play?

The organist glanced over her shoulder. Seeing the Reverend Shuttan standing at the back of the sanctuary, she rushed to the end of the anthem, tripping and skating over the keys to an abrupt premature finish that ended in a low, fog-horn honk that caught everyone gasping, "Oh!"

Of course, the music was supposed to end gently, timed with the preacher at the pulpit so that he had a moment to review his notes and look out serenely at his flock before speaking. That was the way he had always done it–service after service–and that was the way it was *supposed* to be done now. But alas, this was a substitute organist. Golly gee. And he was still way at the back of the church, way back. Not. There. Yet.

Like most preachers, Reverend Shuttan liked order–supreme and worldly. When the organist stopped playing, the silence grew louder and folks turned to look about but the reverend was in the back, not quite ready to appear.

Timing is everything. Behind Terri, a young boy put his hand under his armpit and began to crank away, making impolite fleshy noises to entertain his older brother, two little sisters, and the entire church. Of course, this entertainment didn't last long. He felt a firm hand seize his arm in mid-crank. "Ow!" His mother held fast, as an amused murmur rose from the pews.

It was during this diversion that the good reverend finally started his unhurried walk down the center aisle with an open Bible lying in his palms. He wore pennies in his loafers, brown dress pants, and a green satin, knee-length liturgical robe with pleated bell sleeves and a white satin collar.

This was the uniform of his job.

Seeing his shoes, Terri smirked, then felt ashamed but only for a very brief moment.

Church.

Now she was off, her mind racing this way and that, distracted by every little thing. Must be the tall ceilings. She had to admit that church was more entertaining than she remembered. They should be able to find a church for the kids to attend.

But where was Jan? Why was she here at all?

Reverend Shuttan looked out over the heads of the parishioners toward some distant apparition, closed his eyes, and grasped the pulpit. Then his eyes popped open and his voice boomed and bounced off the tall ceilings so everyone was alert and paying attention.

"Mandy Flanagan! Now, *this, this* was a fine woman! She lived a simple life. Attended church regularly and was always very generous with her pocketbook. She was a fine Christian woman. A fine woman." After that, he seemed to run out of words and calmly shuffled through the notes his wife had written, at last finding his place.

"Mandy Flanagan grew up in Irish Boston. Her father was a longshoreman and she was the oldest of six children. A family of five girls and one boy. Lucky fellow that boy! Ha, ha. And it was a *hard* life, but Mandy was a *good* child. At the age of seventeen, she married and moved to New York City. Many of us did not know that our Mandy worked in the entertainment business most of her adult life in New York. She starred in *The Extravaganza* and many, many other theatrical performances. She was well-known and well-loved. And she helped with the war effort. Yes. World War Two, that is, not the... not the one that was World War

One...so! And when she retired, she moved from New York to Connecticut. So there you have it! Her entire life and how she became a member of our little congregation.

"Even though Mandy was the oldest child, she was pre-deceased by two sisters. Unfortunately, her sister Nelly is hospitalized and could not make the long trip from Chicago. Today, Mandy Flanagan will be greatly missed by her niece, Jan, who has flown here from far away San Francisco, her only brother, Ned, and her devoted sister, Barbara, who lives in Somerville, Massachusetts.

"But Mandy also had many, many friends. She is remembered here today for her generosity of spirit and her love of life. She was a happy, caring person. She especially loved children, so I am reminded of a story about Jesus that is no doubt familiar to you all. In a crowd of followers, when one of his disciples tried to pull the children away from Jesus, Jesus said, 'No, let the little children come to me.' And so it was with our beloved Mandy. Like Jesus, she also loved the little children.

"Some of you have asked–and yes, it is unusual–but Mandy wished to be cremated and her ashes saved for later... ah, pouring?...ah, no, scattering. For later, anyway. I'm not sure we know where, now do we? So there will not be a burial today. But! I have been told to invite *all* of you to a get-together after the service at the home of Mandy's brother, Ned. She wanted you to attend.

"Will it be an Irish wake, Ned? Heh, heh. Ned lives only three blocks away on Maple. So, please, join the family at this time of remembrance. It was Mandy's last wish that you should all come together at Ned's house and celebrate her life. Ned will be in the lobby after the service to give you printed directions to his house for those of you from out of town.

"Mandy Flanagan will be sorely missed. She was a *fine* woman. And now, we will recite the Lord's prayer. Let us bow our heads and pray. Our Father who ..."

With the service almost over and no sign of Jan, Terri figured she could skip going to Ned's house and safely go home to salvage her Saturday. But just as she was eyeing the door, planning her escape, there was a startling smack, like a broom handle falling on the hard floor, followed by, "Oh!"

It was a cane falling to the floor and it belonged to the very white, elderly gentleman sitting diagonally across from her. He had a white mustache and silver hair, and looked distinguished in a nicely tailored blue suit, crisp white shirt, and tie. He leaned down to retrieve it from under the pew and placed it beside him on the bench. Then he turned to the black man in the yellow turtle neck and tweed jacket to his right and yelled, "Did you know Mandy when she was young? She was a *beautiful, beautiful* girl!"

"...Thy will be done. On earth..."

The man continued, "I should know! But she played around, yup! Yes-she-did! Right from the start, mind you. Yup! And the boys were all over her! That girl couldn't help herself. Nope! But what a girl, Mandy was! Gives me the chills just thinking about her."

The unfortunate recipient of those remarks glanced about before replying, "I hear ya, I hear ya. And the whole place can hear ya, too. Don't you know this is a *funeral* service! Have some respect, man."

"For thine is the kingdom, the power and the glory. Amen. And now, please stand as you are able and join me as we read Psalm 22, found in the blue hymnals on page 532."

He began to sob and wail, "Oh, Mandy, I was *such* a dope!"

People turned. People stared.

"..my rod and my staff they comfort me..."

He was very loud. "I loved that girl better than my second wife. Better! Yup! Mandy! Mandy! What a girl! She was the best! The best!"

"Amen to that," said the Reverend.

A long, Dracula-like chord blared from the organ.

"Oh!" said everyone.

And like that, the service ended.

Terri stood up and tried to hurry toward the door but was caught in the center aisle behind a slow crowd bunching around Barbara. That's why she clearly heard the gentleman in the yellow turtle neck say to his loud neighbor, "Oh, I know who you are! Didn't recognize you at first–you must be Henry."

"Yes, yes, that's right. And who, who might you be...sir?"

"Me? Oh. I'm Robert Jones, but Mandy called me Bobby. Mandy and I... Mandy and I were friends. It was long time ago. Good friends."

"Friends?" puzzled Henry. Then he muttered, "But why should I know you? I know hardly anyone."

"Say again? I'm a little hard of hearing," said Bobby.

Henry looked at him straight on. "I'll always think of Mandy the way she was, the way I knew her when she was a pretty young thing. And when I was a young man."

Bobby nodded. "Probably for the best."

"Why? You know something?" asked Henry.

"Me? No, no. She made a big impression on me, though. But I'm married. We haven't kept in touch."

"Me too, or at least I used to be married. My second wife passed last year. But I have to know what happened to Mandy–what she did with her life, whether she was happy."

"Yes, fill in the blanks. That's why I came."

TWO

WHEN HENRY FELL
CRAZY IN LOVE WITH MANDY
BOSTON 1924

A bouquet of red roses lay beside his derby on the middle stair of the stoop. His hands moved to straighten his bow tie. Then he worked to smooth down his auburn hair, parted in the middle, Rudolph Valentino style. He took off his glasses and rubbed the lenses with his handkerchief. He looked at his watch and tugged at his sleeves muttering, "It's okay to be early. Mandy doesn't mind."

Henry was a half hour early for their date.

The brownstone looked like all the other buildings on the street: reddish brown, solid and square with rectangle window eyes. But to Henry it was special. This was Mandy's house in the South End in the Irish neighborhood. It was a nice warm Saturday in June.

Up the block, four girls played hopscotch on the sidewalk while boys in knickers chased after hoops rolling down the street, dodging the clip-clopping horse carriages of the vendors yelling and selling pots and pans, ice, and vegetables.

On the corner, the fish man banged on a pot hanging from his wagon, calling out, "Freeeesh fish! Freeeeeesh Cod! Sss-melts! Sss-melts!"

Henry looked at his watch again. When the girls started up the sidewalk toward him, he decided it was time to go in and stood to dust off his pants.

Thin as he was, he seemed tall when he bent low to retrieve his hat and the bouquet. He climbed the two steps and stood before the door, contemplating. Meanwhile, the girls had skipped up the sidewalk and now stood at the bottom of the stairs, smiling, gawking up at the well-dressed man carrying flowers standing at the door. "Hey, mister. Who the flowers for? You have a sweetheart?" When he turned around and tipped his hat, they giggled.

There were two bells. The girls watched as he rang the top one. Inside was the clamor of a child methodically hopping down the wooden stairs with a final jump to the landing. The door opened.

"You here to see Mandy?"

"Sure am, Ned."

The boy turned his back to Henry to shout up the stairs, "Ma! That rich guy is here to see Mandy again!"

"Are you rich, mister?" asked one the girls from the sidewalk.

Ned leaned out past Henry. "None of your beeswax Marjorie-dargery." He turned to Henry. "She's not ready yet. But Ma says it's all right if you want to come up and wait in the parlor."

The girls left as the door closed. Henry followed behind the boy, trudging up the stairs to the second floor where Mrs. Flanagan stood in the open door to the apartment. He removed his hat.

"So, are you bein' in good health this lovely day, Mr. Henry Russell? We have had such a bit of rain now, haven't we? Oh, what lovely, lovely flowers."

"These are for you."

"Oh, they're dandy. I shouldn't take them, but I will." You could tell she liked Henry. Polite was not easy for her.

"I am doing fine today, Mrs. Flanagan, thank you for inquiring."

She looked out the window to the alley below.

"Oh, so I see you have taken your father's automobile today. Mandy will like that, of course. But she's a funny girl. She sometimes fancies a walk down the avenue to a ride in a motor car. Can you imagine that? Tsk. Won't you have a seat in the parlor until Mandy appears?"

While Henry waited on the red velvet settee, Ned sat on the floor in the hallway, pretending to draw in the dust with his fingers while keeping an eye on Henry. Because Mrs. Flanagan had not taken his hat, he placed it on his on lap and began to slide the felt brim through his hands, twirling it round and round.

The parlor was furnished with dark chairs and the walls were crowded with the oval portraits of stern, stocky relatives. The windows were open, but the smell of frying chicken seeped upstairs from the apartment below. Opposite him along the wall sat the black upright piano, polished shiny, keyboard open. He heard a clock ticking from a shelf and wondered why he hadn't noticed it until now since he'd sat on the same sofa three times before, waiting for Mandy. He hardly noticed the smell of boiling potatoes, onions, and cabbage.

There were six children in the Flanagan household from Mandy the oldest at sixteen to the baby who was nine months. Today was unusually quiet.

"Where's the rest of the family, Mrs. Flanagan?"

"Oh! It is lovely, isn't it? What I wouldn't give for an hour of peace like this every day. Mr. Flanagan has taken the children downtown on the streetcar. Seems the circus has come in at the station and they went to see the elephants deport. Poor Ned here isn't feeling so well, now are we?"

"I could have gone. I don't feel that bad. I could still catch up. I know the way."

"Oh, what have I started. The child had a fever last night and his leaning over the bedside into a pail kept me up to all hours. You are still not fit to ride that streetcar, young man. Your father will make it up to you. So now, I don't want to be hearing another word of it."

Ned smirked and then made a great show of stomping off through the kitchen to the back door and out to the fire escape where he sat and sulked.

Mrs. Flanagan went to the hall closet and retrieved a small coat. "If you're going to sit out there mister, you will need to wear your coat. No sass. Put it on." She threw the coat at him.

"But it's June!"

"Put it on young man or I'll send you to bed."

Henry continued to twirl his hat. This was the only time he had ever been alone with Mrs. Flanagan or had seen her in a mostly calm mood. She spoke to him from the kitchen. "It is so quiet I can almost hear the ghosts talking. You'll have to excuse me."

Henry smiled awkwardly. He had no idea what she was talking about and hoped Mandy would arrive soon. Where was she anyway? Next time, he would bring a book or a newspaper.

Mrs. Flanagan busied herself at the sink, peeling carrots, aware that Henry sat facing her profile. But she preferred this to making a conversation with him. Pale, thin, and freckled, she wore her black hair parted in the middle, braided and pinned up. She always looked tired. Wisps of hair flew about her face making her look a bit crazed, and the lines that spoked across her temple made her look older than thirty-five. And yet, Mary Flanagan's eyes were a startling azure color, same as Mandy's. That feature made her a beauty despite all.

Henry thought she had too many children and worked too hard.

We'll have one or two. And a maid, of course. Mandy won't be like her mother.

When he last visited three days earlier, Mrs. Flanagan was rattling to herself about cleaning, cooking, and cuffing someone's ear. She'd hardly noticed him at all. He never knew what to expect. Each time a new household argument seemed to be brewing. And yet she was always polite to him, even though she might be chasing a child around with a wooden spoon.

That wasn't all.

Mandy disclosed that her mother had the habit of a daily pint or two. Most nights, one of the children would skip to the basement brewery down the street carrying a pail to fetch the frothy ale. And woe to them that spilled a drop of Mother's beer!

On Saturday nights, the neighbors gathered around the Flanagan's piano. After a few pints, the ballads would begin.

One night after a date, when Henry returned Mandy to the flat, they heard a chorus from the street with Mary Flanagan leading the rest in an alto of strength and distinction that carried just the right waiver of sincerity. Henry was enthralled. "Is that your mother, Mandy? Why, she's marvelous! Let's join in, shall we? I don't know the words, but I am a solid tenor."

Before she could stop him, Henry charged up the stairs and squeezed into the parlor. He leaned against the wall and grinned at the spectacle of Mary Flanagan, cheeks ablaze with passion and pints. Men were crying.

Mandy hustled him away. "No, we shan't be joining in." She was ashamed and sensitive to the ways of her family, particularly this fun-loving, musical aspect. After that, she kept Henry away on Saturday nights.

Jack, Mandy's father, loaded trucks down at the dock. He had his clever wife to thank for his employment and never tired of telling the story. They were young, new arrivals from a little town in Ireland near the notorious Silvermines. Mary Flanagan was six months pregnant with Mandy when she met someone who knew the ward boss who knew someone's cousin at city hall. She elbowed her way past the "Employees

Only" sign behind the tall counter and into the office of the bewildered City Manager, where she took a seat.

"My husband Jack must have a job. We are Americans now. He must work like everyone else. Such a God-fearing man needs to put his hands to work and soon we will have another mouth to feed. And did you not know that Ann from the bakery is a very good friend to your sister Molly who is soon to be her unborn child's godmother? Oh, you did not know? Tsk. Why, that must be why my Jack hasn't gotten a job like all the other blokes. Oh, but you say there *is* a vacancy? A job that has very recently opened up? On the docks, you say? Yes, that would be grand. Tomorrow, you say? That would be grand. Jack will be so pleased. And it was such a pleasure meeting your acquaintance. You must come round to see us. Have a wonderful day."

"My Mary," Jack would say, "God love her." Then he would turn to the children. "Where would we be without your mother? Where would we be, the lot of us?"

But Mr. Jack Flanagan was not quite as welcoming of Henry as his wife. He distrusted all Protestants on principle (good Catholic that he was) and he distrusted the well-to-do (good Irishman that he was). Jack had to meet Henry only once to know that there was "something wrong with a man that was so polite." He didn't approve of Henry dating his lovely daughter Mandy.

That's why Mary Flanagan conspired with her daughter to discreetly arrange Henry's visits while her husband was away. She wanted to encourage Henry's advances. After all, he had an automobile. She felt Henry was better than the local "honest" working-class blokes her husband preferred for his daughter. With Henry, Mandy had a chance to move up in society and maybe lift them up, too. Why else live in America if not for the opportunity to better oneself?

And Mary Flanagan also believed that Henry genuinely cared about her daughter.

In time, Mandy might learn to care for Henry. Not love, that was too much to expect. But perhaps she might grow fond of having him around. Or perhaps when they had children (and they should have them), she would appreciate being cared for by an affluent man and give up her foolish ambitions.

As it was, Mandy had skipped two grades and finished her education early, so she needed to get married soon. That was all there was to it. Grandchildren? Mary Flanagan hoped not—not so soon, not like herself. Let there be some quiet in the house for a change, let there be peace and no babies. Could her daughter be that old? Yes, she was at the marrying age of sixteen, almost seventeen. Better to get married soon and get that over with before the babies started coming and then have to rush into it.

Finally, Mandy appeared at the parlor door. She wore little heels and a stringy green flapper's dress, the new one from New York. It was short—very short. And on her head was the matching beaded cap, hiding her auburn hair so that only her bangs showed, like in the magazines. Henry smiled at her ankles, her knees, her face white against her very rouged red lips and her azure eyes.

He felt something move.

"You are not to be stepping one *toe* out of this house with that dress on! Where on earth did you get such a thing?"

She rolled her eyes and lied. "Oh, Ma, I borrowed it from one of the girls."

Of course, Mandy had gotten "that thing" from Henry as Mary Flanagan suspected. How else would she get it? Mandy didn't have money of her own and neither did her friends.

From an open window they heard the craggy voice of Jack Flanagan: "Barbara, now let your little sister be the leader this time. Be fair. It's her turn."

Mary Flanagan began to panic. "Oh, Lord, do forgive me. Now you two had better be going right fast before your father sees you in that dress. Go down the back way. And at least *wear* your coat over the dress for your mother's sake so you won't be arrested for indecency, won't you? This is Boston, girl, not New York. Now hurry, I hear them coming up the front stairs.

"And Mr. Russell, if you would please, do try to start your automobile in a quiet way so my husband doesn't come running after you."

"I'll roll down the street," said Henry.

"And don't stay out past ten o'clock! Now go, go!"

Mandy gave her mother a peck on the cheek and led the way down the wooden staircase to the alley, the green strings of her dress swaying. They peered around the front of the building, Mandy giggling. Henry covered her mouth and took her hand. They ran across the alley and to the car. She went around and hopped in while he cranked down the window and took off the break and jumped out to push. It began rolling down toward the intersection and this was when he would open the door and jump in.

Not this time.

It gained speed, quickly rolling down the hill ahead of him.

When she yelled out the window, "Henry? Henry!" an old women carrying groceries stopped to gawk at them, and two boys pointed and laughed.

He huffed, "Don't worry, honey. I'll. Catch. Up." He caught the handle and it pulled him along running until he couldn't keep up. Being dragged, he let go, falling hard to the street.

Mandy applied the brake and the car rolled to a stop. She opened the door and looked back at him.

"Get in, silly."

Henry pushed up, dusted off his pants, climbed in, closed the door, started the motor, and off they went.

THAT DAY AT THE BEACH

The green stringy dress was made to do the Charleston at a speakeasy, not to be worn to the beach, and particularly not a beach in Puritan-leaning Boston. But that is where Henry drove that clear spring day—to the wide white beach in Lynn.

"Lynn, Lynn the city of sin, you're never the same as the way you went in," Mandy sang as they drove up Lynn Boulevard.

"Really? What an amusing lyric," said Henry.

"I didn't make it up; everyone says that."

"Well, I never heard that before."

He turned up a long driveway.

"I've never been to this part before," she said.

"You'll like it. Very pretty. Like you."

Henry parked the car in a field, turned the motor off, and started to open the door.

"No, wait," she said. "And don't look."

"Oh, of course." He turned away.

She had to remove her heels and stockings. While her coat provided some modesty from Henry, he did take a peek.

Turning from front to back, she unhooked the garters from the right stocking and rolled it down her leg before doing the left stocking. This was her first pair, a birthday present from her mother. She was careful to place the right stocking into the right shoe and the left stocking into the left shoe before stowing them safely under the seat.

"Okay, you can look now." She opened the door, jumped out, then slammed it shut.

"Mandy, wait! Wait!"

Henry raced to catch her hand. They trotted down the dune and crossed the beach.

At the water's edge, she let go to prance in the bubbling sand, daring the waves to roll over her feet.

Henry watched, very pleased.

He adored her and they were alone. No one was strolling the beach looking for shells and it was too early for bathers.

This was the quiet, private end of the beach, farthest from the public side and the public's view. This was the beach Henry visited as a child, the only one he knew. But Mandy had never been, had never dared to disobey her parents, to wander up the beach to the snooty, private side. Here, steep dunes led to a rocky surf that only determined swimmers braved.

The day was quite windy and her hem kept flying up to reveal her garters and panties.

"Oh, dear. It's so windy!" she exclaimed in mock innocence, for Mandy knew what was showing and she knew that Henry was appreciative.

The naughty ocean breeze flattened the little dress against her body, revealing her small high breasts and then rudely rushed up inside her dress, across her stomach, over her ribs and between her breasts, and out the short sleeves, blowing the strings every which way in delight.

She pulled away from him to wade into the water. Henry couldn't stop smiling. He followed along, baggy pants billowing, getting wet in the surf. His eyes teared. The waves teased, gently rolling then slapping him. When he neared her, she splashed further out, to her knees, close to the hemline and stood legs spread, arms stretched to the heavens, eyes closed.

He thought she could be a beacon for sailors, anchored against the wind and the sea, except that he was sure the men would want to come closer to see for themselves the wild green tassels blowing on her dress, enticing them like a siren, power swirling around her.

She felt the deep heaving, surging, pull her toward the wave breaking curl and crash. In the water below, her feet kept sinking into the sand, burying her ankles. Above, long trail of shiny green—a seaweed barge—floated near.

"Honey, you're going to get all wet!" He grabbed her wrists and pulled her laughing from the water, across the tide line, over the hot sand, and into the dunes.

He pulled her down and lay beside her.

It was calm. It was quiet. The sand was warm. He bent slowly over her face, staring into her eyes. She wrapped her arms around his neck as he asked, "Mandy is it okay now, is it okay? I can't wait any more. Mandy, I love you so. Please Mandy, please."

"Yes," she whispered.

And a sudden rude wind blew the strings on her dress, blew them crazily. Her ears were cold and her hair was tangled when he unzipped his pants and pulled down her panties.

The sand stuck to her bottom and coated her legs. She thought it was getting late as she lay back to stare at the sky.

WHY SHE MARRIED HIM

Of all her suitors, only Henry encouraged her dreams, so Mandy encouraged his advances. As inexperienced as he was, when they "went all the way" that day, he felt his manhood rising, his guilt and obligation deepening, and he decided right then and there that he wanted to do it again.

Henry dared not brag, but he wanted to—to every man, every boy, to every old coot that would listen to his exaggerated exploits. Instead, he smiled to himself, he laughed to himself, he winked in the mirror and his stride was a bit more confident. He thrilled to think of her and for the rest of his life, every beach and salty sea smell would remind him of that day and of Mandy in the green stringy dress.

That summer, Henry's family was invited to a number of social gatherings outside the city, at the summer cottages and estates of their friends in the country or at the shore. Although Henry's family had not arrived on the Mayflower or been deeded property from the king as other Boston Brahmin families were, they had nonetheless established themselves among that Beacon Street tier through respectable marriages, landholdings, shipping fortunes (insuring slave ships), and links to Harvard—which all young Protestant men of stature attended.

It was a particularly warm beginning to summer, so the Russells were very pleased to receive an invitation to a party at a friend's summer estate, said to be an architectural wonder, somewhat resembling Mark Twain's Hartford home.

The estate was located down a long driveway, in a forested compound that featured houses for both sons in full view of a pretty lake and the green woods beyond. The Russells had never visited the estate and had only recently become acquainted with the owners through a mutual friend at their club. They hoped to meet the entire Brewster family and their important friends, so they were eager to attend. That, and everyone would be there: the Stevens, the Emersons, the Choates, the Fullers, the Boylstons, the Delanos, the Brooks, and many more of the best sort of families they had come to know as "their kind." Still, they wanted to make an impression.

They didn't know everyone there was to know or everyone they should know.

Also, they had a daughter, Elizabeth, to marry off, and there was Henry.

Looking out onto the lawn and the long driveway from the veranda, the conversation naturally drifted to discussion about the design and construction cost of such an impressive house with all its porches and veranda and the upkeep of so much land. That, and the usual comments about the hordes of Irish arriving nearly every day along with the Scottish girls from Nova Scotia and Prince Edward Island.

"Yes, they are handy as maids and with the children. I wouldn't have one as a cook, mind you, but they were taking over, moving in, and something needed to be done."

"Limit their stay? Prevent them from establishing citizenship? What should we do, build a wall?"

"That's impractical."

"Well, what is to be done about all the immigrants arriving every day?"

"Some are very good tradesmen, you can't ignore that. A fellow showed up on our doorstep saying he was a carpenter. I don't know what I was thinking, but I opened the door. We have a wonderful old table that is sagging and marred. That man made it new again. And he built a brand new hutch with inlaid filigree. Italian man. Very reasonable. I shall hire him again."

"I need to learn that fellow's name!"

"Too true, but they need to go back, to return to where they came from. We have too many."

"I quite agree that the city is filling up with all sorts, even speaking languages so foreign it smites the ears. Yesterday I heard a language that was so strange I had to ask someone. Know what it was? Yugoslavian. What an odd language."

"Not heard that one."

"I think we need to make a place for them. Move over and let them fill the working class so the country can grow."

"You Unitarians are too liberal in your opinions, Jack. They'll take over the nation and then where will we be?"

"And let's not forget the textile workers. Who do they think they are trying to make a *union*?"

"I'm sorry, John. Please. Let's not discuss that today. I need a respite from that conversation."

"Oh, yes, I quite understand, sorry. Is that your girl playing croquet? She's quite a looker."

And so the conversation went around, buoyed by beverages and a bright June sky.

That day, Henry had a date with Mandy so he would arrive on his own to the party rather than disappoint his parents by not arriving at all. Everyone was dressed in white or tan summer wear. All the ladies wore hats. Most of the guests were seated on the enormous porch or under the trees and some strolled to the lake to sit on blankets beside the water. As they chatted and sipped tea and lemonade, the young people played croquet and badminton.

Oren, Henry's father, noticed a particularly fetching young woman with blond hair and hoped that Henry would arrive soon to notice her. It was such a pleasant afternoon. That is until Henry arrived, with Mandy.

"Hello Mother. Look who's here; I've brought along Mandy."

Constance Russell gasped. Oren Russell sputtered and tried to make the best of it. "Well, what a surprise. Hello, Mandy."

Oren turned to Mrs. Bradford sitting next to him to explain. "This is Mandy, Henry's friend from out of town."

Old Mr. Stevens extended his hand, smiled, and asked graciously, "I'm so sorry young lady, I didn't hear the introduction. What is your name?"

"Oh. I am Mandy Flanagan. From out of town, yes. The south part of Boston to be exact."

He continued to smile. "Well, that's very nice that you've been able to travel here from so far away, Mandy Flanagan."

"Yes. This is such a lovely house."

"It is. And now, I must visit with other guests. Will you excuse me?"

"Of course," Mandy replied.

Henry kept smiling at Mandy and didn't notice the raised eyebrows and sideways glances. He was buoyant. "We're off to explore the lake, Father."

"Yes, you do that," his father replied.

But Henry hadn't heard. He had already rushed off, gleeful that Mandy was on his arm, anxious to show her off, waving to the fellows playing croquet.

An hour later, after taking the rowboat to the middle of the lake, smooching and returning to shore, Henry and Mandy returned to the manor house. But the Russell family had left the party early, too embarrassed and chagrined to stay.

Less than a week later, Henry proposed to Mandy and she accepted. When he announced to his parents, "Mandy has consented to marry me. I am the most fortunate man in the world!" they were stunned.

"Henry, she is uncommonly pretty, I grant you that, but don't you see? She is common all the same–and an Irish Catholic at that," said his father with a stab of his pipe. "It will never work, Son, never. What will you talk about? She probably doesn't even read. She is beneath your station."

"Of course she reads, Father! And she plays piano. She is a delight. You don't know her like I do," Henry retorted.

"And I think that she is entirely too young for matrimony," said his mother. "I can't imagine that her parents have agreed."

"We haven't told them yet."

"You haven't *told* them, Henry? How so? Even in the lower classes, doesn't one *ask* permission to marry?"

Henry stomped from the library. "I am marrying her and you need to accept that. It's done."

His father called out, "Henry, please. Let's discuss this further. She is fun, yes. But seriously, you want to *marry* that girl?"

If Henry considered his father's words for a moment, it was a very slim moment. He wanted to be with Mandy and that meant marriage. There was no other way. Yes, they were young (which is always a wonderful excuse for any sort of errant behavior that would not otherwise be excusable), but Henry was not that young. He was nearly twenty-one and she was nearly seventeen. And for the most part, her exploits were harmless social diversions without serious intent or consequence. He imagined that her reputation was spotless and that he was probably her first. However, his father was right about one thing: she was fun.

Henry thought of himself as a bore. And he was. He was stiff and out of step with his peers, even the proper young men from the country club. Henry had spent too many sunny afternoons of his life reading page after page, book after book in a comfortable plaid club chair with his mother, father, and sister reading their books in a very quiet room.

Ironically, it was on one of those evenings that Henry's father turned to him and said, "Now, Henry, I think you should go out with some of your college chums once in a while."

"Perhaps. I will consider that advice, Father, once I have finished this book."

A week later, Henry went out with his chums.

That very same night, Mandy and her best friend Lorna traveled downtown to the Parker House. Of course, they didn't go *in* the Parker House. How could they—two young, unaccompanied girls? No, they perched on wooden crates across the street, commenting on the well-heeled patrons arriving for dinner.

"I'm going to dine here, too. You'll see, Lorna. That will be me someday."

"You are a very silly goose and I don't know why I let you take me here. If my mother knew what you we were up to."

"But she doesn't know, does she, Lorna? And I know about a terrific place called Charley's, down the street, around the corner and down the stairs."

"A *speakeasy!*"

"No, we can't go to a speakeasy, Lorna. We don't look old enough. But they dance and play music."

Harvard men went to Charley's to mingle with the local girls, rumored to be easy (or at least friendly) and they were good dancers. It was a fine place to practice. Charley's was nothing more than a dark basement below a grocery store.

But you never knew who might show up.

Mandy was certainly not a shy girl. She seemed to have a natural talent for putting men at ease, and there was a little game she played to amuse Lorna.

That particular night, a lanky guy with glasses leaned against the wall trying to look at ease, as though he came there all the time.

Soon after they arrived, Mandy tugged on Lorna's sleeve. "Him," she pointed.

"That one? Why *him*?"

"He's alone and he has a nice coat."

"That's all? You are such a silly girl."

"You say 'silly' too much Lorna. Watch me."

Henry eyed the dancers. They did the shimmy and the Charleston and the black bottom. He could only waltz; he didn't know how to do the modern fast dances, but he wanted to try. That's how you get a girl. You have to dance.

He noticed a lovely girl with brown hair and blue eyes right in front of him who seemed to have stopped dancing altogether. Her eyes were closed, and she had slipped into a lazy, dreamy sway, much slower than the frantic music called for. She ignored her dance partner and so he pulled another young miss onto the dance floor beside him.

Meanwhile, the girl in front of Henry hugged herself, rubbed her legs, stretched her arms high in a seductive fashion, and pursed her lips as though puckering for a kiss. When the song ended, she opened her eyes and said directly to Henry, "Thank you, oh-so much," as though *he* was her dance partner.

Henry was infatuated.

And he didn't even have to dance.

She was slender, almost petite, and had chestnut-colored hair worn in a bob and red pouty lips set against a clear porcelain complexion. Her eyebrows were arched in pencil in the stylish way that highlighted her dazzling blue eyes. She was young, not quite a woman, a girl really. It didn't matter. She was perfect.

"I, ah, you are so welcome. Miss..."

"Mandy. Mandy Flanagan. And you?"

"Me? Oh, Henry Russell."

"Well, it's very nice to meet you, Mr. Henry Russell. I am so parched."

"Would you like a lemonade?"

"Yes, that would be very kind of you."

Mandy looked over her shoulder, winked at Lorna.

And so it began.

Fortunately, Henry would never know that the very day he proposed to her, only a skinny hour had passed from a liaison between Mandy and another fellah. It was not that Mandy was so careless of Henry's feelings, she honestly did *like* him. But she also did not want to disappoint or hurt the feelings of any boy out of knickers by denying him her company. Why not brighten his day?

Only a few people knew of Mandy's dreams to leave Boston, her family, the familiar neighborhood, and the swan boats going round and round at the garden.

She dreamed of New York City.

She would be a star.

It was all the rage. Everyone was going there. Oh, the glamour, the parties, and the clothes she would wear, her name on the marquee!

But wait.

She only had two dollars in birthday money. Not enough.

And yet she was better off than most Boston Irish girls her age. For as the oldest Flanagan daughter, one would expect that she would be saddled with childcare and chores. But no. Mary Flanagan wanted a better life for her daughter than being poor, pregnant, and married by fifteen. No. Her daughters would do better.

As the oldest daughter, Mandy glowed with her mother's ambition. They adored the picture magazines, the glamorous stars, Broadway, and talked about what it must be like to be on stage. And so Mandy's head swelled. She would be a star. Why not?

The stage lights hot on her face, the audience applauded wildly then stood to give her a standing ovation. She heard "Bravo! Bravo!" and as each flower bouquet was tossed to the stage, she bent to fold it into her arms, curtseyed and smiled. How they loved her! Alas, it was time to go. She blew kisses to the crowd and left the stage.

Just before she opened the bathroom door, Mandy winked at herself in the mirror.

As usual, she found her little brother Ned sitting cross-legged on the floor, just outside the door. "You're always in there a *long* time. What are you doing? Girly stuff?"

"None of your business."

"Well, it's about time you came out. I really have to go."

THE RUSSELLS OF BEACON STREET

Henry lived with his family in a lovely ten room colonial on Beacon Hill. On most nights, the Russell family–Mr. Oren Russell, Mrs. Constance Tate Russell and their two children, Elizabeth and Henry–sat in oversized armchairs and read. Henry was so well read that he graduated early from Harvard. However, there was no rush for Henry to find serious employment. Like other prominent Boston families, the Russells had inherited wealth, land, and income granted to their ancestors and carried forward from the old world into colonial America. Oren's great-grandfather was a merchant with investments in the East India Company and he traded in silver and metals. Constance's family was deeded land beside the rivers in Massachusetts and Connecticut that would later power family-owned textile mills. The Russell family (and those like them) were the educated elite. The young men attended Harvard and the young women attended finishing schools like Miss Porter's School in Connecticut. When Henry was ready, doors would open and he would stroll in and sit at a large desk. He might enter politics, study law and carry the torch against integration and immigration, and of course he was sure to marry a suitable woman from his caste.

It was not unusual for two or three hours to pass in their parlor without any conversation at all. Sometimes they listened to the radio but not often. In the winter, Henry and his father stirred the fireplace logs. When Mrs. Russell remarked, "Henry, please bring me a warm blanket to wrap my legs, there is such a draft," it was time for Oren to remark, "What you really need, my dear, is a hot toddy to warm you up. I'll go fetch one."

Mrs. Russell, lady that she was, would never directly speak her mind, not even for a simple cup of tea with a kick of bourbon.

The clock on the mantle ticked and Mr. Russell puffed on his pipe, filling the room with a cherry tobacco scent. It was cozy. Only the family. It was always only the family. They had few visitors, because it was too inconvenient, and what would they do with them anyway? Even among the dwindling hierarchy of the Boston Brahmin, the insular lifestyle of the Russell family was unusual.

That's why Henry did not know how to socialize or dance.

THEY ELOPED

Just before they left, Mandy said, "Ma, you look pretty."

"Me? Why I don't think you have ever paid my looks much attention, young lady. You must be sweetening me up for some favor, now what could that be?"

"Oh, but you do look pretty." She kissed her mother's cheek and seeing her surprise, kissed her again.

"Two kisses? Now whatever is that for?"

Henry rested his hand on Mandy's shoulder. "We best be moving on, sweetheart, or we'll be late for the picture show."

"He is right, of course. Go off you two and have a good time, then. Go."

And that is exactly what they intended to do.

Once in the auto, Mandy stared out the window at her building until it dropped from sight as they rounded the corner. Henry reached across the seat to pat her thigh. "It'll be all right, honey, you'll see."

"Oh, I'm okay. I just wish there was another way to do it. There isn't another way, is there?"

"No, not with your father and my family all against us. What else can we do? But don't worry. When we have a baby, they'll come round. You'll see. Don't you think they'll come round if we have a baby, honey?"

She didn't want a baby for a very long time; it would spoil her plans and she certainly didn't want to have one just for Henry's sake. So she didn't answer, bit her lip, looked out the window and was quiet for most of the ride to New York.

Henry worried. She could have anyone, but she chose him. Did he say something wrong?

Mandy left the note on her pillow in an envelope propped up between the knees of her Raggedy Ann doll. It would go unnoticed by her younger sisters already sleeping in the bed nearby. She knew her father would find it first. He always waited for her return from a date, sitting in the parlor chair reading Dylan or Burns. His eyes peered over the top of the book. "Well, do you know what time it is, young lady? I should hope you at least had a grand time of it, making me worry as I do."

She felt the red bristles on her lips as she kissed him. "Yes, Pa, we had a wonderful time. Now go to bed. You have to be up early." She copied her mother's bossy tone. He closed his book with a clap and went to bed.

This night, Jack Flanagan pulled the fob of his pocket watch and laid it in his palm, snapping open the cover. He did this twice. At midnight he stood up to look in her room and there he found the note.

> *Pa and Ma,*
> *Henry and I have gone to New York to be married and to pursue my career. I know you would never approve. Please forgive us. I will write soon.*
> *Love to all,*
> *Mandy*

Jack cried out, woke his wife and she cried too, and followed him to the parlor where they sat together on the piano bench, his arm around her, both fretting loudly, not listening to the other.

She said, "Oh, my Mandy, oh. Too young, you don't know, you don't know about life. You could have stayed in Boston and dated Henry longer, had a proper engagement and then marry. We would have warmed to him. But you had to go, and what will I do now? What will I do?"

He shook his head saying, "I never should have let him cross the threshold, never. He turned her head. He did. He was trouble. I knew that right from the beginning. I should have stopped them from dating. I should have. It is all my fault; I drove her to it, didn't I, luv?"

Ned and little Joan woke up and wandered in to see what their parents were fussing about. Mary was quick to warn them away.

"You two, back to bed! It's very late. You have school tomorrow."

Joan protested, "But Mandy's not in the bed, Ma. She hasn't come home yet. Where is she?"

"Out having a fine time of it. There is nothing to worry about it. Now, return to bed. You too, Ned."

"Listen to your Ma and go to bed this instant."

That night in bed Mary would try to comfort her husband. "You cannot stop love, Jack. They were bound to do it. Henry is a good man, you know that. And he loves her. Would you have her run off by herself to New York–all alone–to chase her dreams? She would, you know. Think of what a tragedy that would be. Mandy is better with Henry who has income. Poor bloke doesn't know what he's in for. Don't blame him, he's just a young man and it was bound to happen. We are hardly a good example. We will have to pray for the best. That's all we can do. Pray for the both of them."

"I know you're right, Mary, but I could have–"

"No. You could not. Now go to sleep. What's done is done. We have other children to worry about."

Jack Flanagan would always blame himself for not keeping Henry away. Can't trust a man with a fancy auto, he'll steal your daughter and drive away.

Henry was sure that his note wouldn't be found until the next morning. He enjoyed writing it, enjoyed imagining the ruckus it would cause.

"So there!" he said and placed the envelope addressed to "Mother and Father" on his desk.

> *My Dearest Parents,*
> *We have eloped because you have left us no choice.*
> *I know you have disinherited me. You fail to understand that it simply doesn't matter. I love her.*
> *We will be in New York. I will contact you soon. It is all for the best. Please don't worry.*
> *Your loving son,*
> *Henry*

As usual, his mother went to his bedroom to call him to breakfast; she found the letter, read it, and ran from room to room wailing. "He's gone! Henry's eloped with that Irish trollop! Oh, he's gone, he's gone, he's gone! My boy has *gone!*"

Mr. Russell lit his pipe and puffed. "Don't worry, dear, Henry will back. Just you wait. She's just a little gold digger, that one. Have faith in our son. He'll come round. You'll see."

"How can you be so confident?"

"Because Henry was raised to know better. We must trust that he will come to his senses in time. We must be patient. Henry has always been such a dear boy; he has no experience in life outside of this house. His behavior is only the impetuous nature of his youth. Remember that girl from Newport I had a whirl with? It was a summer fling, only a summer fling. My parents knew that and they waited it out. They knew you were the right one. So, have..."

"But Henry's... Henry's *married*! He..."

"Dear, have some faith. Really. Don't sell our boy short. Mark my words, Henry will see the error of his ways soon enough."

Mrs. Russell was quiet for her husband's words did comfort her and she believed them because she chose to. Yes, he would return. She would wait for Henry to come home.

They never discussed welcoming Mandy to the Russell family, because they could not imagine such a thing. Consequently, it never occurred to them that they might have a responsible hand in Henry's elopement to New York.

Henry's sister Elizabeth thought that her father should go look for him and convince him to come home.

"But where would I look, dear heart? New York City is a big place."

"But we *must do* something Daddy!"

"We *are* doing something, Elizabeth, we are waiting. Henry will come home when he is ready. It is a good experience for him."

Constance was not happy to wait either. "Oren, how can you say such a thing? When he's *married*! I always *dreamed* of a church wedding and the *lovely* reception we'd have. And, oh, now...I can't...I just can't." She wandered away to lie down in the bedroom. It was just too much.

As the days passed, Mrs. Russell continued to put aside books she thought Henry might like to read. They left Henry's room exactly as it was the day he left and told their friends that he was away with school chums in Europe. And they waited.

NEW IN NEW YORK CITY

That night, tired from the journey, they checked into a small hotel pretending to be husband and wife even though the clerk didn't ask. It was across the street from a produce warehouse. There was no elevator and their room was on the sixth floor, shabby but clean. The springs of the small bed sagged almost to the floor. Henry continued to be chatty, trying to cheer her. They were careful and unusually polite, trying to mask the obvious concern and realization that they really didn't know each other very well. In New York, with everything unfamiliar, they also felt unfamiliar with each other.

Mandy lay down on the small bed in her slip and pulled the sheet and thin blanket over one shoulder. Looking down, Henry could see the small mounds of her breasts but not quite her nipples. He hurried to undress, but he still wore his undershirt and boxer shorts as he lifted the sheet to slide in beside her. She turned her head and barely brushed her lips across his lips before she rolled over to face the wall, yawning as she spoke, "I really am tired. I could sleep for years, simply years. Aren't you tired, Henry?"

"Well, yes, I suppose so but..."

"But what?"

"Oh, nothing, nothing at all. You go to sleep, honey."

He was disappointed. Although he was tired, too, Henry had hoped for a release from the emotion of the day and anticipated a frenzied, exuberant celebration of their first night away.

Instead, gentleman that he was, his thoughts turned to the unfamiliar humbleness of their surroundings and he was glad it was dark. The excitement of the day was over and within minutes his eyes closed and he fell asleep, exhaling deep sighs.

She lay awake beside him, listening to his breathing, the sounds from the room next door, and the city at night. She was disappointed that Henry was such a gentleman when he gave up so easily. She thought more would happen that night. He should have tried.

At dawn, they awoke to parades of horses clip-clopping in the street below and the sounds of men shouting and whistling and loud slaps of wooden boxes being dropped onto the open wooden carriages of street vendors. She went to the window and tried to open it to shout to the men below. "Henry, let's get some fruit. We can have breakfast in bed."

"Yes, Madame. I shall return with breakfast!" Delighted that she was at last animated, he struggled to pull on his pants, hopping from the room to the hall.

She watched from the window. Disheveled hair, bare chest, he looked cute.

Back in the room, an armful of bananas and oranges tumbled onto the bed.

"Look what I brought you."

"Henry, it's lovely."

"And so are you my love."

They ate with abandon, played at snatching the fruit, laughing.

"Mandy?"

"Yes?"

"Will you marry me?"

"Yes, of course."

"What about today?"

"Today?"

"Yes, love, today."

"Well, why not? Yes, let's do it! Let's get married today."

She wore her blue, double-breasted suit with the white anchor buttons and Henry wore his best navy suit and tie and polished his shoes.

They took the subway. She was quiet during the journey, prompting Henry to ask, "Honey, you haven't changed your mind, have you? I mean, you still want to get married, don't you?"

"Shush. Of course I do, silly," she said looking around, hoping no one had overheard.

"Good."

But the passengers near them had heard. When Mandy glanced around, she found them all smiling back at her, some nodding.

They completed the forms, watched another couple marry, and then it was their turn. It was over in a flash; there was nothing to it. Henry placed a sloppy kiss on her lips saying, "Mandy I love you and I'll do anything for you. Someday we'll have a real wedding, I promise."

He stood back and seemed to be waiting for a reciprocal sentiment.

Instead she smiled and said, "Boy am I glad that's over with. Let's get some ice cream. It's so unbearably hot in here." She dashed down the long corridor with Henry gawking after her.

The clerk ordered, "Well, get going young man! She's your wife now."

"Yes, yes, that's right, isn't it?" Henry sprinted down the hall calling out, "Mandy, Mandy! Wait up."

It seemed like he was always trying to catch up with her.

Henry bought a newspaper and in the afternoon they found an apartment in a brownstone on a dead-end street. It was on the East Side, two rooms on the third floor, just off

Amsterdam Avenue in a quiet neighborhood where people sat on the front steps just as they did in Boston.

"How lucky we are," said Henry several times, "and it's so breezy."

After scrubbing the floor, the landlord opened the windows to air it out. The apartment was available only because the last tenant, an elderly man, was dead. The neighbors complained about an odor, a smell like rotten cabbage. Of course it wasn't that. They found him on the floor beside his bed, stiff, long dead of a heart attack or pneumonia or the flu or something else, no one knew for sure.

In their impetuous move, Henry and Mandy hadn't thought to bring any household items. They were fortunate that a table and chair, one pot, a knife, a fork and one plate had not been taken by the landlord or the neighbors. Henry kept muttering, "Don't worry, honey, it's only temporary. I'll get a job. Don't worry. Don't you worry about a thing. Yessiree, don't you worry about a thing."

Finally she shouted, "Henry stop! I'm *not* worried. Really I'm not. It's *you* who's worried. Don't forget why we're here."

"I know we're going to get..."

"I can't *wait* to see Broadway. It's so exciting. Don't you see? This is the start of my career. I'm finally *here*! I'm finally *in* New York."

He was heartened by her ambitious words. Maybe it would be all right. And he was even more relieved when they did make love that night, on the floor, on their coats. The passion was of the short and fierce kind, he being so eager that his youth betrayed him as he exploded too soon, warning, "I'm going to come! I'm going to come!"

There were a few grunts after that, he stiffened and it was over. He lay atop her like a corpse almost on the very spot the former tenant grew stiff and cold.

In response, she said evenly, "It's all right. It's okay."

He didn't understand what she was comforting him about. It never occurred to him that his lovemaking was a tad short and greedy, and that he should apologize and do better next time. Like most men his age, Henry had little experience in lovemaking. He learned on the job—the job of marriage.

Mandy had much more experience in that department. She thought that he should have apologized. Why did she say that it was *all right* when it wasn't? But then again, she hadn't married Henry for that.

"Oh, I do love you," he professed, kissing her mouth. He would repeat that every time they made love.

He felt very heavy. "Get me a drink of water, will you?" she asked.

When he returned, she curled on her side and pretended to be asleep.

Henry slept beside her and was the first one to fall asleep again.

Within a week Henry secured a position as a clerk in a public accounting firm downtown. At first he was enthusiastic but his job quickly assumed a tedious route for he added columns of numbers every day, all day long, sitting on a tall stool in the back of a windowless office. The facts were plain. The owner had five sons, all employed at the firm, all ahead of Henry in rank.

As a Harvard graduate, he expected that he wouldn't have to work very hard and would tell others what to do. It was unlikely he would ever rise above his current station. He was an ambitious young man, one who was used to being singled out as "promising" or "bright" throughout his privileged schooling. But Henry was not allowed to post his entries to the books, not allowed to review the audits of clients or speak with clients directly, not allowed to read the financial news, and he was not even allowed to act as a courier to deliver statements to clients. His only diversion was his lunch break, sharpening his pencils and dreaming of Mandy and the fun they would have later.

They settled in with enthusiasm, every day a new adventure; life was whirling and taking them along. Their timing couldn't have been better. The "War to End All Wars" had ended a few years earlier and life in the city had resumed with fervor, optimism, and just having fun. No need to worry about the future. No time to stop for thoughtful introspection or regret the heartbreak they left behind in Boston.

Now shoes felt tight, socks become holey, and blisters blossomed exploring the neighborhood. Mandy learned where to shop and how to cook supper in one pot. Henry was fond of the "ping"–the sound of a dime dropped in a glass jar. They were saving for a bed.

While he worked, she snuck into auditions for shows and plays to observe the actors and performers and learn about the casting process. Most times, she was ousted. "Young lady, if you're not going to audition, you can't be in here. Only performers."

"Oh, I will. I'm just not ready yet."

"Please move along."

She also told Henry, "I'm not ready yet." Wisely, he didn't probe further. He was content with their life as it was. Like most men, he expected to arrive home and there she would be, supper waiting. But he was married now, not the boyfriend who would say or do anything for a kiss, encouraging, "Why, of course you can be a star on Broadway. You're a natural!"

But it might not be good to encourage her now that they were here. What talent did she really have? And she might fail, become unhappy, and blame him. So he praised her household accomplishments and was careful not to inquire about her meandering about in theaters and dance halls.

Henry was accustomed to the confidence of wealth. It didn't matter that they slept on the floor. He would be wealthy again; this was a temporary situation.

Some nights they went downtown, peered into store windows, and argued over whether to buy the sofa and chairs with the gold tapestry or the green satin brocade as though Henry's billfold was fat with currency. He didn't like the canopy bed. "You still like the dark mahogany one on Sixth, don't you?" Mandy scolded. And Henry agreed that yes, she should have the silver tea set with the dainty sugar cube tongs. "I suppose you'll need that for entertaining, won't you?"

Mandy wrote weekly letters to her mother and to Lorna that were filled with exclamation points. She hoped to show that she was indeed happy and had made the right choice to elope with Henry. Her father read her letters but refused to reply with letters of his own or even to sign his name to the letters his wife penned.

Mary Flanagan also sent letters on her own that her husband did not know about. In these, she lied that he was warming up to Henry and that a visit home was sure to reconcile the two.

Mandy suspected otherwise. If her pa had softened, he would sign the letters and write one of his own. Stubborn, prideful Irishman! He was still angry. Henry never asked permission to marry. Of course he still worried about his wayward daughter. And if they visited, and Henry apologized to Jack, Mary knew all would be forgiven.

But her daughter wasn't ready yet. Mandy didn't want to return home until she was successful and they were rich.

Henry sent only one short note to his family.

Dearest Father, Mother and Sister,
We are married and doing fine. There is no need
for concern. I have obtained a respectable position
in finance at a reputable firm. I shall write again.
Yours Truly,
Henry

He meant to imply that he didn't need them or their money and didn't miss home. This was not entirely honest.

Henry missed the stack of books waiting to be read and the big plaid club chair in the quiet darkened room where he would lose himself in words. He couldn't afford to buy books and the New York Public Library had a long wait list for the books by popular authors.

His mother, Constance, maintained a list of books the family should purchase, read, and discuss. Oh, how he wanted to see that list! It would be a wonderful gesture if she sent the list without him having to ask. Even better would be a wedding gift of new books. Yes, that would be grand! In his next letter, he would ask for her list. That way, she would be comforted knowing that they were reading the same books. Or was it that *he* would be comforted?

Henry did not know that his family knew quite a lot about his New York life and that he could not afford to buy a new book. At his wife's urging, Oren Russell had hired a private detective; he knew about Henry's job, where it was, and how much he was paid. They knew that Mandy went to auditions nearly every day but did not try out. They knew what groceries she bought and they even knew that Henry and Mandy didn't have a bed to sleep in and that the car was safely parked on the street in front of their building, perhaps in need of service. They were heartened to learn that their son was not destitute but safe and indeed did find respectable employment.

But Oren wasn't satisfied. To be reassured, he needed to see Henry for himself. One day, he endured a long train ride from South Street Boston to Grand Central New York, walked two blocks, and checked into the Roosevelt Hotel. The next day, he sat in a taxicab across the street from Henry's apartment building, watching. He followed Henry to work. He followed him home. The next day he followed Mandy but lost her in a crowd. She did not appear to be pregnant so that wasn't it. Constance would be relieved. He returned home.

"Henry looked fine, perhaps even happy. Unfortunately, our boy is still infatuated with her," he told his wife. "But don't worry. It won't last long. Henry will learn. Yes, he will come back. We must be patient. We must have faith in the boy and in her. Yes, his sweetheart will disappoint him, all right. He will return to Boston without her, just wait and see. We must be patient, dear."

HOW LORNA MET HER HUSBAND JAMES

Mandy's best friend Lorna was Italian and two years younger than Mandy. The two were inseparable having grown up on the same block in apartments in identical buildings three doors apart. But when they went out dancing, Lorna hung back in the shadows to watch. Sometimes a boy would ask her to dance and she would demur, "No, thank you."

The morning after her daughter eloped, Mary Flanagan strode down the block to the Santorelli flat.

Michela opened the door. "Mary, how nice to see you."

"I need your help, Michela. Mandy has eloped."

"Aeeee!" Michela screamed.

"Yes. Is Lorna home?"

"Lorna! Come here–*now!*"

Lorna appeared. "Oh, Mrs. Flanagan."

"I have a few questions to ask you, Lorna."

"Yes, she have questions. It's so terrible. You tell her," said Michela.

Lorna knew that Mandy had planned to go to New York months ago with Tom Delaney, a local boy who got cold feet and didn't show up.

"Lorna, Mandy has eloped to New York."

"She did? With Tom? When did she go?"

"Tom? Tom? Who's *Tom?*"

"Tom Delaney. With the red hair? Lost his nerve last time, didn't show up. Mandy was furious."

"That ruffian. When was that, pray tell?"

"Three weeks ago, maybe four?"

"Well, no. It was not to be Tom Delaney this time she eloped with Lorna but with Henry Russell, in his automobile. You did not know her plans?"

"No, not this time, Mrs. Flanagan. I swear to God." Lorna crossed herself in the Catholic way and her mother did the same.

Both looked expectantly at Mary.

"When did she go, Mrs. Flanagan?"

Mary heaved, teared up. "She did not return home last night. Her Pa waited for her to return from the movies and then found her note. As you can imagine, he is stricken."

Michela nodded sympathetically, touched Mary's shoulder.

"I wish she had told me, Mrs. Flanagan. Maybe I could have changed her mind."

"That is probably why she kept it from you Lorna, and from us. Please, you'll be letting me know if you should hear from Mandy, won't you? Any word at all. Her Pa is heartsick with worry."

"Of course I will, Mrs. Flanagan. She has broken my heart as well."

"I am surprised that she did not tell you her plans."

"I knew she liked him well enough and wanted to go to New York to be a star, of course. Talked about it all the time. But she didn't tell me this time. Not a word. I shall never forgive her."

"Well, it's not your fault Lorna. I only wished for a proper wedding after all. I have been saving since she was born. I never had one. She is my first. And now..." Mary wiped her sleeve under her nose and turned to go.

"And I was supposed to be her *bridesmaid*."

"You would be lovely dearie, and the wedding, it would be so grand. She surely broke my heart. I must be going. The children are alone; they need me."

Trying to comfort her, Michela said, "Mary, I am so sorry. Hey, maybe Mandy give you grandbabies, eh? Maybe she have many children?"

To Michela's dismay, her words of comfort only served to distress Mary who pulled up the skirt of her dress to blow her nose before hurrying out the door in tears.

Michela asked her daughter, "Why more children no good? I no make more babies, one only you, my Lorna." She frowned, shook her fist at Lorna. "You must have a wedding! A big wed-ding! I *kill* you if no wedding. You no go away, like Mandy. Poor Mary, I feel so sorry. Heart broke."

"Oh, Ma. You're so dramatic. I don't even have a boyfriend."

"You marry in a church in a bea-u-ti-ful dress I make. I do it! My one child. Go away, lika Mandy, I say I kill you. Your own mother, kill you."

"Oh, Ma."

Two weeks later, Lorna received a postcard of the Statue of Liberty.

Dear Lorna,
I am married! We are here in New York and it is so exciting. I will write again soon when we are settled.
Your good friend,
Mandy

Lorna hated that Mandy sounded so happy when her own life was dull and miserable. She did not want to return to high school in the fall without Mandy. She did not have another best friend. Short in stature, buxom, with long brown hair, brown eyes, and an easy smile of perfect teeth, Lorna was a nice girl and perfect for the glove department at the downtown Jordon Marsh department store.

Two months after Mandy left, it was her good fortune to be working the day a lanky, shy man with blond hair appeared at her counter Christmas shopping.

His name was James Bates Cooke. He was twenty years older than Lorna and had just become the president of his father's bank. Like Lorna, he was an only child and had never married.

Right off, he liked the way Lorna smiled. She was adorable. Right off, Lorna liked him, but she didn't know why. He seemed nice enough.

The glass case displayed a variety of leather gloves and Lorna showed him nearly every pair, trying them on, stroking the leather, and marveling at their quality. "See how soft these are? Kid leather. Imported from Italy. Wonderful. And look at this one, lined with rabbit fur. Your mother would love these. I wish someone would buy me such a lovely pair."

While she was showing Mr. Cooke the gloves, another customer waited for Lorna to finish. But Lorna ignored her. "You have other customers, young lady. I only want to try on this one pair and that pair," she scolded.

"By all means, do help the lady and I'll step aside," said Mr. Cooke.

"No sir, you were here first. I'm sorry, ma'am. I need to finish with this customer and then I will be happy to help you with your purchase."

"I think the store will be closed before you'll be done with him," the woman sneered, leaving in a huff.

"It's my fault that you lost that customer."

"Oh, no, don't go. Let me show you some others."

At that moment, he realized that the pretty clerk might be flirting with him. She might actually *like* him. He smiled stupidly and gave a little laugh at everything she said. "Ha-ha" or "Oh, yes, ha-ha" or "Ha-ha. That will do."

He bought three pairs of gloves (more than his mother needed). When the transaction was over and the paper bundle tied with string was handed to him, he was crestfallen. What could he say to her now? He missed his opportunity. Now that the sale was complete, there was no need to linger, nothing to say; he had to leave.

But Lorna implored, "Promise me you'll come back tomorrow. We have a new order of fancy gloves coming in. I know you'll like them. Can you come back tomorrow?"

He almost blundered but recovered his sanity. "Ah, no, I have a... why yes! Yes, that seems like a very good idea. I still have more gifts to buy. I'll just buy gloves for everyone."

Then he heard his own voice say so clearly and eagerly that it hardly sounded like him at all, "What hour will you be here... so that I can look them over?"

She could have replied that any clerk could help him, but Lorna was too savvy for that. "I'll be here from nine-thirty until six tomorrow and on Saturday, too. But Saturday will be crowded and my supervisor will be in. I won't be able to give you the special attention you need. It's better for you to come by tomorrow, if you can."

He walked away smiling, replaying the way she said "special attention." She was so young, so pretty, so cute. She seemed to like him. Would she like him tomorrow? Maybe he misread her. Maybe she was on commission and said things like that to all the customers.

But he dwelled on it, kept on hearing her words, imagined the gloves she would try on and stroke. Maybe he was being taken for a ride. Maybe she was just a flirt. But he would certainly return tomorrow to get special attention.

He returned to her counter three days in a row, but the new gloves never came in. Each time she would check behind the counter, pulling out this box or that box repeating, "I'm so sorry. They should have been in by now. You'll just have to come back. Is it still raining?"

Thank God for the weather, he thought.

Then on the third day, figuring he just could not go through their charade once again, he bravely stated as casually as possible, "You seem to have a knack for fashion. Would you mind—if it were convenient—would you consider—if you have a free moment—ah, helping me with my Christmas shopping?"

She replied without hesitation, "I'd love to."

Startled by her response, mouth open, he gulped air and felt a cold streak run from his heels through his groin up to his shoulders, giving his whole body a visible tremor.

"When would be convenient for you? I mean, I'll arrange my schedule."

"Wednesday at one o'clock. I have the afternoon off. By the way, my name is Lorna Santorelli. What's yours?"

"My name? Oh. James Cooke. James Bates Cooke. But just call me James, if you please."

"I will do that, James. And I will see you Wednesday."

On Wednesday he actually had an important closing. But it didn't matter, he'd postpone. He rehearsed his excuse to the client as he left the store. "I'm sorry we just don't have the paperwork ready. Would Thursday be convenient for you?"

During their excursion on Wednesday, he was recognized by an old friend from grade school, Eddy Johanson, a government worker. Eddy was out with his wife, a rather tall, thin woman. After a hearty handshake, Eddy whispered in James' ear, "Boy, she's a looker!" grinned and conspired with a wink.

That had never happened to him. James was elated. He was proud. Someone had seen him out with a woman. A *pretty* woman!

And so, Mr. James Bates Cooke courted Lorna Santorelli. And James became less awkward and braver still. Lorna began to fall for him as he became more confident in his ways.

Unlike the reception Mandy had received from Henry's parents, Horatio and Marion Cooke were thrilled that their son James was dating anyone at all. The Cooke family had grown stale and sullen. After all, banking was a rather dull business. James' parents thought their world would not change. James was a loner; he only liked to work. Their lives would be small and quiet. Their last days would roll out like a flat, blank roll of paper until the end. Lorna woke them up to life again. It didn't matter that she was Italian. They adored her. For they could see only one thing: grandchildren. She was young. She was healthy. She was perfect.

Marion Cooke, James' mother, was so enthralled that she invited herself over to the Santorelli house unannounced only one week after James introduced them to Lorna. Even though Lorna's mother, Michela, was not perfectly fluent in English, she knew perfectly well what was going on. The two women laughed and joked, looked at pictures of Lorna as a baby, and they plotted.

Mr. Horatio Cooke waited for his wife in their motor car downstairs. Soon Rosario Santorelli, Lorna's father, a short dark man with a mustache, arrived home from work in his Model T Ford. Horatio introduced himself and was delighted to learn that Rosario was an auto mechanic, a highly-skilled, respectable occupation. From then on, the two men enjoyed endless conversations about motor cars. And baseball. They liked that, too.

Three months and twelve pairs of gloves later, James and Lorna were married.

MANDY'S CAREER

She bought the newspaper every day and circled the audition announcements, eager to tell Henry of her plans. "First, I take the E Street line and go to the Paramount. Then, I have lunch and go uptown to the Arcade. Then..."

After about a month of watching auditions from the back row, she surprised him by actually trying out.

Right from the outset, it was clear that she didn't know what she was doing. That's why she went to every casting call regardless of what the show was about or what talent they needed.

Did Mandy have any stage talent?

No.

She had never appeared on a stage or sang in public. She never took dance lessons, neither tap nor ballet, never studied acting or read plays.

She could play a little piano and sing a little.

What did it matter? How hard could performing be? She read in the magazines how other girls had "made it" and so she would do it, too.

There was one other thing.

Even though she didn't have training or talent, she was fortunate to *look* like she had talent.

It was the cheek bones and the chin atop skinny legs.

The routine of the casting calls was always the same. First, there was the sign-up with the assistant and then he gave you a number. If the assistant was a man, Mandy thought it helped to flirt a little to make a favorable impression. Then you had to wait backstage or in one of the theater seats until they got to your number. Sometimes they auditioned at a studio. She always got the "nervous nellies" and had to go to the bathroom at least twice before her name was called.

In the beginning, she loved standing in line with the other girls, all of them young, all of them pretty. There seemed to be a sisterly camaraderie even though they were competitors. Stories were whispered about auditions, shows, directors, and boyfriends. None of the girls were over thirty and some girls were younger than fifteen but everyone agreed that they were "well developed" and "mature for their age."

After several auditions, she became friendly with a tall, boney girl with freckles and frizzy orange hair who was always chewing gum. Her name was Henrietta-Ann Hackett, but she preferred her stage name, "Cheri Sweet."

Cheri came to New York from Georgia when she was only sixteen after becoming the runner-up in the Miss Pecan beauty contest twice. Someone told her that she belonged on the Broadway stage and so she left the very next day. Three years later, Cheri was a veteran and Mandy welcomed her sage advice. She told Mandy, "Sweetie, you got to put rags down your blouse like this. Make them stand out and say 'Hi!' See? Way up high like this, honey. You got little titties, they're already high. That's what those boys like to see. Right out front, uh-huh, that's right. Way up high, where they belong."

At her musical auditions, Mandy sang, "Ain't she Sweet" because it was a popular song of the time and a popular audition tune. After dozens of auditions, she had yet to receive a callback. And the last time, she was almost turned away as the director yelled, "No! No! No! Not that again! Didn't you hear the last girl sing it? Golly! Can't you girls use a little more imagination? Next!"

"But I've been waiting hours!"

"What else you got?"

She hadn't brought any other sheet music. All she could think of were Irish songs, the old ones her mother sang around their piano. Without piano accompaniment, she sang, "Oh, Danny Boy," her voice a sweet and on-key soprano, young and unwavering but not stage-strong like the other girls.

She had only sung a few verses when she was interrupted by the director, Mr. O'Leary, who shouted, "Stop! Stop! Very refreshing! You're in, honey, by God, you're in! Very nice! Yes, very nice. Next!"

After almost forty auditions, she had finally landed her first show.

She was in the chorus and sang in seven songs. It was a new musical about a woman who falls for a traveling salesman instead of the honest fireman that loves her. When the fireman almost dies, she discovers her mistake. All she had to do was dress in a costume and walk around a bit.

"It's so easy," she told Henry. "Mostly we just stand there; there's nothing to it."

The critics and the audiences thought so, too. Why no tap dancing? It was just a musical review. The show bombed and closed after ten performances. Mandy was devastated.

Most shows wanted tap dancers. Mandy could do the popular speakeasy dances: the waltz, the foxtrot, the Charleston and the black-bottom, but she couldn't tap dance or fake it.

Like a young child on shore watching their pals frolicking in the lake, believing that all there is to the art of swimming is the courage of a leap, Mandy figured she could get by the dance audition even though she had never studied dance. After all, it didn't look so hard and she would wear her brand new tap shoes, the ones she'd bought the day before.

When her name was called, she carefully stepped from the wings with her arms out for balance, only to lose complete control at center stage, sliding on her tap shoe heels into a wide, clumsy split on the floor. Backstage the girls cackled, hyenas all of them, and she was mortified and pathetic, trying to stand, regretfully saying, "Sure is slippery. Whoops, gee. This never happened to me before. They must've waxed the floor."

Everyone laughed, even the casting director who had to wipe his eyes with a handkerchief before he ordered, "Sorry girlie, we need dancers, not comedians. That was good though. Made my day. Sorry about the slippery floor. Move on now, girlie."

At the next audition the girls weren't so nice. Someone snickered, "They must've waxed the floor!" Mandy left, tearful and humiliated. If the audition included a dance routine, she didn't have a chance and Henry didn't earn enough to pay for lessons.

Two weeks later, she returned to the auditions with a new plan. It worked three times. To avoid dancing at the auditions, Mandy told the production assistant that she couldn't do her routine because one of her taps had fallen off. Then she smiled sweetly, leaned toward him, and whispered that she was "willing to do a little work backstage if he'd do a little favor for her." Then she stepped aside and waited for the production assistant or the casting director or both to return and say, "Come on, I got five minutes" or just nod at her to follow him.

Cheri Sweet taught her that you need something *extra* to make it. Mandy was convinced that others girls did it when they were starting out, too. Everyone was talented and pretty.

It happened backstage, in a locked dressing room or an office or costume shop. Usually, she got down on her knees to satisfy the man and avoided her reflection in the dressing room mirror. She never fantasized about Henry or other men. Instead, she thought about the silly things she had to do, like writing Lorna a letter or sewing on a button or making dinner. But most of the time she thought about nothing at all except getting it over. She just wanted to be in the show, right? She rushed. More than once the man complained, "You got to do better than that, girlie, if you want on the show. Put a little feeling into it, will ya?"

She didn't enjoy what she was doing, but she wasn't ashamed and didn't regret her actions later. Business was business. It was only a few minutes, she reasoned. That's all. A few minutes and then it's over. Sometimes you had to do things to get ahead. This was show business. Talent wasn't enough. Everyone knew that.

Henry would never understand what she was doing. She had to be careful. It was just for her career in show business and nothing more. She was cast onto four shows this way and in all four she only lasted until the first rehearsal when it was discovered that she couldn't dance and was fired. Sometimes she told Henry that she quit because she had a good chance at a bigger part in another show. Sometimes she told him that she hated the director or that the show was awful. She never told him the truth.

It ended badly. At the next audition, her pal Cheri forewarned the casting director as Mandy stood before him to sign up for an audition. "She can't dance, mister! But boy, she sure can do other things! Right, girls?" And Cheri ran her tongue around her lips and made smacking sounds to the catcalls, hoots, and whistles of the other girls.

The casting director winked at Cheri and said, "Okay, girls, I got the picture. Sorry, honey. I gotta listen to the girls. This show don't need that kinda talent. You're out."

Betrayed, Mandy retorted, "But you do it too, Cheri! I *know* you do!"

"Well, even if I *did* do it once or twice, at least I can dance, right girls?" Cheri teased. They ganged up on her, cajoled and snickered, smirked, and stabbed with their eyes.

"They must have waxed the floor!"

"It's so slippery!"

"Hey mister, I got talent! Let's go backstage."

Before she left, Mandy stuck out her tongue at the lot of them. On the long subway ride home, she told herself that the other girls had done the same thing to get in shows. Probably when you were a veteran, you didn't have to do it anymore. So why were they picking on her? Because she was new? Or pretty? They were jealous, that's all. They were just jealous.

She wrote Lorna. Her letters were usually merry embellishments, but this one was different. She wrote that many of the girls lacked talent but got on the shows anyway by sleeping around. "That makes it difficult for the rest of us," she wrote. "Sometimes they are so jealous of me I don't know what to do. Show business is tough."

Her eyes were red so often that Henry knew it wasn't going well. Still, he was afraid to bring up the subject, because he didn't want to comfort her, he didn't want to encourage her. So he was quiet. And when she was moody and dinner was nothing but potatoes and onions, he said nothing.

Her reputation followed her around like a long shadow. She never lasted more than two or three rehearsals until she was fired.

But what Mandy lacked in talent, she made up for in perseverance, showing up and hanging around, being there when there was no one else to pick. That's the other way to make it. And so she was finally cast in a variety show, one that was also the most glamorous show of her short career,

The Extravaganza. She didn't make the cut on the first call or the second and it was a very large cast. But she was on the backup list if someone became sick and had to leave the show. With that scant encouragement, she decided to hang around backstage through the first week of performances, acting as though she was supposed to be there. And when it happened that several girls got the flu, she was ecstatic. They were desperate, they had to use her; she was on the show.

Of course her three routines in *The Extravaganza* were far simpler than the intricate tap dancing numbers of the other girls. All she had to do was kick high, stay in line, show some cheek, and follow the girl in front of her taking long leggy strides. The difficulty was the hectic costume changes and balancing the heavy headdress.

At the first performance, when she lingered too long in front of the mirror fussing with her makeup, she was bumped aside by another dancer.

"My turn now. You gotta share, honey. Besides, they ain't lookin' at your face."

GOING UP WITH GUIDO AT THE RITZ

On the occasion of the opening of *The Extravaganza*, Lorna happened to be staying in New York with James, her new husband. They were staying at the Ritz Carlton. Mandy and Henry could hardly afford coffee at the Ritz, never mind staying there. Their fortunes were not fortunes at all, just Henry's measly paycheck that barely covered rent and potatoes.

Even though James was a bank president, he was not as stingy as one might expect. He enjoyed displaying his success by adorning his wife. That meant furs, clothing, and jewelry. Even though it wasn't in Henry's nature to be frugal, there was nothing to be done about it but to look forward to better times. Henry provided Mandy with a small weekly allowance that she spent on clothes and expenses for her potential show business career. *The Extravaganza* would be her first professional engagement, and her first paycheck. They planned to buy wine, go out to dinner, and celebrate.

Lorna was proud, too. She was pregnant and would enjoy surprising her old friend. She'd wired: "Mandy, come to the hotel. It will be wonderful to see you again! Please invite Henry and we'll have a party and order room service. We have so much to talk about!"

But on Saturday afternoon, Henry was stuck at his desk, trying to find an error that either he made or another accountant had made, adding columns of numbers from a set of ledger books. The total was off by just one penny and so he could not reconcile the numbers in the account, close the books, and go home. Every accountant knows that an error of any amount must be found and fixed to uphold their own reputation and that of the firm. For what might be just a penny this time, could be a dollar the next time or who knows, one hundred or one thousand another time. The numbers had to reconcile. That was his job.

Mandy planned to visit Lorna between performances of the matinee and the evening show. It was against policy to wear the costume on the street and she could be fired if caught but that is what she planned to do. Why not? It was worth it. She wanted to dazzle Lorna, show off that she was on her way to making it in New York. Besides, it was practical. She didn't have enough time to visit and change before the next show.

It was a very dark night. She left right after the afternoon show, tip-toed into the alley, crossed to the next block, and hailed a taxi hoping no one from the cast was watching.

She thought the driver of the cab was very nice. After she placed a small tip in his hand, he hung from the window and shouted after her, "I'm the one that should be giving you the tip, miss."

She would replay his remark in her head every time she took a cab.

When she neared the hotel, men in uniforms of red and black with brass buttons smiled and held the door open.

"Where's the front desk?" she asked.

"Just keep going straight that way, Miss."

"Oh, over *there*. Silly me. Thanks a bunch."

They watched, smiled, and winked.

The red headdress was heavy with feathered plumes. The dress, too, was deep red, flamboyant, a no-doubt-about-it *fiery* red. A red that was so red, her Boston Irish-Catholic mother would certainly remark that "only one kind of girl" ever wore that kind of red. It was the red that said: look, look, look, sex, sex, sex. It made men smile.

Her dress had a long, feathered bustle that fell to the floor, bunched absurdly on her derriere for a coquettish effect. In front, the dress was mostly missing on the bottom, the better to highlight the fishnet stockings encasing her legs up to her thighs and down to her startling gold tap shoes just ready for a dance. On top, the dress had a daring v-neck with a clever push-up bra that exaggerated even Mandy's small breasts into smooth little pillows. She strode forward with a wiggle and held a frilly red and black parasol in black lace gloves. Long, spidery eyelashes adorned her aqua lids. Even though the performance had ended an hour earlier, her lips were still painted a deep red, her cheeks streaked in orange rouge, all on a backdrop of ivory-colored pancake makeup.

She just wanted Lorna to see her, to show her that she had made it to Broadway. Wanted Lorna to see that she was a success in show business, maybe not a star yet, but close, very close.

As so maybe she strode through the lobby knowing everyone watched, going tap, tap, tap for the hotel staff and the guests who pointed and smiled. "Oh, look, a showgirl!"

She was quite a spectacle–clearly the most exciting event in the lobby–and she enjoyed every moment of adoration, slightly bowing, acknowledging her admirers. Wagging her bustle from side to side, she tap, tap, tapped her way across the lobby to the marble counter of the front desk.

"Hello. Where can I find Mrs. Lorna Bates Cooke?"

When she approached the desk clerk had his back to her, but when he turned and saw Mandy, he smiled, took his time, knowing others were watching.

"Why, let's see if we can find out for you! Mrs. Cooke. Mrs. Cooke. Yes. Yes, here it is. Staying with her husband in room 906. Should I ring her for you or do you want to surprise her?"

"Oh, I think I'll go up and surprise her," she said with a wink.

"Of course." He gave the bell a deliberate two-slap, ding-ding. "Please follow the bellboy, Miss. He'll show you up."

She strutted across the lobby tap, tap, tapping, still enjoying the gaze of all who eyed her, following the bellboy into the elevator, smiling, happy with herself, pleased that she could turn heads. Such fun. She felt the headdress slip to one side.

When the elevator doors closed, the bellhop turned to ogle. "I've never seen a chorus girl up close before. Boy, you sure are pretty. Did ya come from a show?"

"The show's tonight." She tried to right the headdress with her gloved hand.

The bellhop was a small man, perhaps under five feet. From the back, she thought that he was a schoolboy. Looking closer, she saw the mustache. No, he was a fully grown man with dark Mediterranean eyes and ears that stuck out a bit. Mandy thought he looked somewhat like Buster Keaton but short.

"Looks like your hat is going to fall off. You oughta fix it. Want me to fix it for you?"

She knew that the feathered headdress was slipping clumsily to one side, ruining her glamorous appearance. It was her fault. She had walked out of the theater in such a hurry, worried about getting caught, that she didn't take enough hairpins. They were always coming loose.

"Fix it? How could *you* fix it?" she dared.

The elevator stopped at the fifth floor. The doors opened, but no one was waiting to get on. The doors closed and it started up again.

"My dad worked in a millinery shop. Taught me about ladies' hats. You just need it clipped right there to get it balanced."

"Really?"

"Sure. I can fix it for you, but what'll you give me if I do?"

Taken aback she asked, "Come on, out with it, what is it you want?"

"Oh, I just want a kiss, that's all. A kiss."

She thought a kiss doesn't matter so much. It doesn't mean anything. Well, why not? "Okay, mister bellhop. Fix my hat."

He stopped the elevator.

"You have to turn around and squat down so I can reach it," he said.

Mandy gathered her skirt and squatted down in front of him. She hoped that the elevator door wouldn't open. He straightened the headdress and then tapped it until it fell to the right.

"Aha! What'd I say? It's not balanced. It's not balanced right at all."

"But it didn't do this in rehearsal."

"You're missing one of the big clips right here. Probably fell out. Do you have any extra?"

"No. Nothing."

"Well, I'll have to give you one of mine. But you won't tell anyone where it came from, okay, sweetie?"

"You wear hair clips?"

"We all do. Part of the job, wearing a stupid hat. I wouldn't be caught dead wearing an elastic band under my chin. Been here seven years, might be manager this year, and then I finally get rid of it."

"Really? Manager of the hotel?"

"No. Manager of guest services, boss of all the bell hops. By the way, honey, my name's Guido." He pulled a long thin hairpin from the side of his pill box hat and slipped it slowly into her headdress.

"Okay. That should do it. Try it now." He started the elevator.

She stood up and wagged her head from side to side. "It worked. Thank you so much. You really are a dear."

He grinned. The elevator began moving, going up again.

"Wait, this is my floor next. Isn't it number six?"

When it stopped, the doors began to open and Guido the bellhop said, "Here you are, darling. But where's my kiss?"

She stepped out of the elevator as neatly as the couple that stepped into the elevator, the man and woman smirking, having heard the bellhop's request.

Mandy faced Guido as the doors closed, teasing, "Well, that'll just have to wait, won't it?"

She started down the hall in the wrong direction, humming a song from the show. The room numbers were going up so she turned and went the other direction down the long corridor. But Lorna's room wasn't there either.

She hurried toward a maid leaving a room. "Miss? Oh, Miss. You must help me. I am so lost. I can't find 609. Just point me in the right direction, will you?"

"There ain't no 609 on this floor, honey. Where 609 is supposed to be is a linen closet. You sure it's not 906? There is a room 906, three floors up, fancy room. People mix them numbers up all the time."

"Well, gee, now that you mention it, maybe it is 906. Darn! I got off on the wrong floor."

"Just go back up on the elevator or the stairs are over there. By the way, Miss, I like your costume, so fancy and red. You must be in a show, huh?"

"Yes, I am and I better hurry up or I'll be late. Thank you so much."

"You're very welcome." She unlocked a door and went in.

Mandy stared at the door to the stairs. She couldn't do it, couldn't use the stairs, not by herself. Not here. There was something about doors and stairs that made her anxious. And the costume would surely get in the way.

There was nothing to be done about it. She had to go down the hall and wait for the elevator to take her up.

Only a few minutes had passed but her mistake made it seem later. Would she be able to sneak in the stage door without being noticed?

She was so lost in her worry that she didn't notice Guido leaning in the elevator doorway, waiting for her. "Going up, Miss?" he asked.

"You *are* so terrible! Why didn't you tell me I was on the wrong floor?"

"Well, I figured if I was halfway lucky you'd come back right about the same time those people got let out at the lobby and then I would go back up and there you'd be. And I did get lucky, didn't I, sweetheart?"

"What if I had used the stairs? You didn't think of that, did you?"

"Oh, no, you wouldn't do that. A lady doesn't take the stairs, now does she?"

Mandy softened. "Well, I guess you're right about that." She reasoned, well, if he insists, what's a kiss? I did promise. A kiss isn't so bad.

So, she got back in.

As the doors closed and the elevator began to go up, he lunged, grasped her head between his hands, and fully wrapped her mouth with his lips, wagging side-to-side, deep and adoring. Her eyes fluttered; she was captivated and aroused.

When the elevator came to a stop on the ninth floor, they were still entwined as the doors opened on a large, unshaven, bald man dressed in a maroon, silk bathrobe.

"Is that you, Mandy?" he asked.

Like a waltz, when Guido released his endeavor, she wiped her lips with the back of her hand, straightened up, righted the headdress, stepped into the hallway, and the elevator doors closed.

Guido the bellhop was gone.

She looked up to face James, Lorna's husband, and felt like a naughty child, the weight of the headdress pressing her down, shrinking her.

"Tell me it wasn't what it looked like, Mandy. Tell me that you weren't kissing the *bellhop*. I can't believe you'd do that! I can't believe that you'd do that to Henry. A bellhop! My gawd."

"No, no, James. It was nothing, really. Just a game. He was ..."

He started off down the hall. Mandy trotted behind. She was disappointed that he hadn't said anything about her costume.

"A game? No, no, I don't want to know what game you were playing. I can't imagine. If I ever, *ever* caught Lorna doing such... oh, I just can't fathom... this is too much. Too much. You are a terrible influence on Lorna, but I don't have the *heart* to tell Henry. You know he told me about some of your exploits, but I could hardly believe it, now I do. And this time—"

"When did Henry talk with you?"

"Never mind that. His family is a client, that's all."

"But—"

"I hope you learned your lesson, Mandy, I really do. Lorna is so fond of you and..."

James continued his rant as they rounded a corner. She kept quiet in penitence but also because she was still distracted at the misfortune and coincidence of his interruption. That and she could not stop replaying that thin glance at him, when she saw James as just a man, a merry voyeur, watching them, enjoying their passion–until he was stricken and ugly when he recognized her and she recognized him.

And there was another distraction. She was preoccupied with the encounter and bemused with the revelation that a scrawny man wearing a pillbox hat had given her the best kiss of her life.

Maybe little men know how to do it better.

Maybe they have to.

Henry never kissed her like that. He didn't know how.

So James was right. She had learned a lesson.

Meanwhile, James continued his banter. "Really, now. Lorna is so looking forward to seeing you. Of course, she'll adore your costume. But when I saw you carrying on like that–I just don't know if I should allow Lorna to continue to see you. And Henry, oh, what a saint you married! He adores you. He deserves better, Mandy, he really does. You–"

When James turned around, he saw that she was forlorn and contrite, and this broke his vehement indignation. "Well, all right then. It looks as if you're a little bit sorry. We won't talk about this anymore. Now perk up. Lorna has been waiting all afternoon for you. Just wait till she sees your costume. But wait till you see *her!*" he winked.

She didn't understand what James was alluding to and he never did volunteer the reason why he was still in his bathrobe in the middle of the day. He seemed so much larger and balder than six months earlier when Henry and Mandy had attended their wedding. Years later, Lorna confided that when James was on vacation, he had the habit of smoking stinky cigars, drinking excessive amounts of brandy, cursing, walking around naked, and he refused to shave or bathe. Except for that, he was a perfect husband. Bankers got tired of wearing pinstripe suits, it seemed.

James came to a halt before room 906. "Lor-na? She's here!" He rapped on the door, fumbled for the key in his pocket, and called through the closed door. "Wait till you see her. Just open the door, it's me."

Mandy wasn't sure whether he was talking about her or about Lorna.

The knob turned and the door opened.

There was Lorna: six months pregnant Lorna.

Mandy felt the red headdress slip to one side.

DISAPPOINTMENT

The *Extravaganza*. Even Henry came to three performances. It was the red costume from this show that Mandy proudly displayed for Lorna at the Ritz. Though she was never caught wearing the costume at the hotel, her glory didn't last. The day she displayed her scant costume to Lorna at the Ritz there was an October fog. It felt like the breath of some hissing prehistoric reptile, the air something between day and night, dead and alive. Within a few days, she developed a cold that led to a sore throat that developed into a fever and delirium. "I have to get ready for the show. Help me up, Henry. I need to get ready. Go get my mother. Ma, come help me get ready. Ma. Go get her, Henry." She fell back exhausted and closed her eyes.

Henry was terrified. A doctor was called. He touched her forehead, stood back. "It's the fever. Try cool compresses and soup. No visitors. You'll know in a day or two."

"Know what?"

"If she's going to make it."

"Make it? Can't you do anything for her? Take her to the hospital? Prescribe something?"

"No room at the hospital. She's better off here. Try to keep her strength up and wipe her forehead, keep her cool. She's young. She needs to fight it off."

People were dying all over the city.

"And young man, you had better be careful that you don't catch it. It's everywhere. In fact, I have another stop in this building. The apartment above you. Their new baby and the four year old."

Henry gasped. "Thank you for coming, doctor."

Two days later, when the fever broke, Mandy woke up to realize that she'd missed three performances and began to cry. Henry could not console her. *The Extravaganza* was her big break and she had only been in ten shows. After a week, she returned to the theatre, and attended every rehearsal for three weeks hoping to rejoin the cast. But it was no use. No one left the show and it closed after a six week run.

After her illness, she decided to concentrate on musicals but discovered that there was more competition among the young women trying out for singing roles than there had been for the dancing shows. And although Mandy had a sweet, clear voice, she was no match for the exuberant, trained voices at the auditions, voices you could hear in the last row. In an entire year of auditions, she had obtained only two small roles.

This fact did bother her. And as her desperation grew, she needed to bolster her chances the only way she knew how: through the attention of men. At about this time, Henry noticed a change in their sex life. It went from mildly interesting to creative and then to downright daring.

He was as surprised as any husband would be and eagerly returned home each day.

She began to wear her slip around the house, beckoning, inviting. She bent over him from behind so that her firm little breasts nudged the side of his face as she poured his morning coffee. She took the ostrich feathers from her hats, tied them together, and tickled the crack between his buttocks and his inner thighs. In the bathroom down the hall, she gave him a bath, dried him off slowly from top to bottom and later in bed, combed his pubic hair with her tortoise shell comb. But best of all, she went to bed naked.

Henry was delighted and heartened. He thought that because her Broadway successes had been so few, she was finally beginning to accept her shortcomings and was naturally inclining her attentions to him and their neglected home life. Yes, she was finally coming round. They would have a family after all. Mother would be so pleased.

Henry was wrong.

WHEN HENRY PROTESTED

He opened the front door and then slammed it. Henry was angry. Mandy's playmate slid off the couch to the floor with an untidy "ugh." He was just a young man of about fifteen or sixteen, very tall, all knees and elbows with unkempt, straight sandy-brown hair that fell over one eye. A simple boy, he tossed his whole head to shake the errant strands from his sight.

"Sorry, mister. I didn't mean nothin' by it. Nothin' happened. I swear, nothin' happened!"

"Get out!"

The boy's shirt was still unbuttoned as he hastened toward the door and said a sorrowful, "Bye, Mandy," as the door closed.

She had to explain again. Make something up. Convince Henry of her innocence. Secretly, Mandy enjoyed the challenge, the drama, and the passion of his attention. This was a common trait among theater people. She liked to perform offstage before a small audience almost as much as she liked to perform onstage to a packed house.

That, and she didn't take his anger seriously.

"I can explain everything, Henry. Henry, *please!* We were just rehearsing for the new show. You know the kissing scene in the folly thing? He's the new understudy for Sam. Henry, oh Henry, please, just listen to me."

When Henry was angry, he scolded with a pointing finger. When he was very angry, he acted like a child having a tantrum. The blood rose to his face, his voice became shrill, and he charged about flailing his arms.

"You're *not* going to get me to believe another one of your stories. I won't believe it! You just can't get me to believe another one of your *lies*!"

She looked up, forcing instant tears from her forlorn blue eyes. Her little red lips pursed in feigned hurt. She shook her head sadly.

"Henry, Henry, you know it's not like that! We were just rehearsing. Call the theater. Ask Mona. Mona knows. He has to learn his lines. He's so young. How could you *possibly* think something of it? He's so stiff and if Sam got sick again—well, Allan suggested that we rehearse—"

"Stop! Stop! Stop! I won't listen to another word! You can't expect me to believe that. It's just a... a *community* theater production! Not even Broadway, Mandy."

"Even if it's not Broadway, Henry, it's the truth. Sweetheart, I'm innocent. Come here, come here. Let me make it up to you. I haven't been paying enough attention to you, have I? Did you have a rough day at the office? Is that it?"

She walked toward him and began touching his face with both hands. He softened immediately—couldn't help it, just as he always did—which is why Mandy did not take his outbursts seriously.

He stopped shouting. "You can't expect me to believe that, Mandy. Why should I? And in our *own* apartment. I can't trust you! Why do you carry on so? Why, why, why? Don't I do the best I can for you? Don't I... what *is* that noise?"

"Oh, that's just that old lady banging on the pipes again."

Henry quieted. "Oh, that. Honey, you don't have to be doing this stage thing. It's not right. You should be thinking about having a family, having children. You shouldn't be working at all."

She held his face in her hands. "Now, Henry, you know why we came to New York. You promised that you'd support me. Don't be so cruel. You must let me pursue my career. I need to rehearse, to learn the lines, so if someone gets sick, I'm prepared when they call me. You must understand that by now."

She began unbuttoning his shirt, distracting his argument, dismantling his objections, redirecting his anger to other topics.

"Henry, you know I wouldn't do anything to hurt you. Let me make it better..."

But his voice was clear, loud and shrill. "Mandy, this *can't* go on! You *can't* sleep around like this! I pro-test! I most certainly pro-test! I..." Then he broke away from her, went to the window of the fire escape, opened it wide, leaned out, and shouted down, "Shut up you old hag!"

"Henry!"

"Mandy it just isn't decent! Don't you *know* that it's wrong? How many times have we talked about this? You're my wife, for God's sake! You can't sleep with other men."

"I know that, Henry. But it's show business. We've discussed this. It's really all right, it's all right."

"Well, you've got to learn to say no! No! No! No! Are you listening to what I'm saying? You've got to... no... don't try..."

His words faded as she kissed him gently on the mouth, gently on the forehead, gently on his cheek. He grew silent. He didn't protest. She kissed him gently on his neck and brushed her lips along his chest. She unbuttoned his shirt and pulled it off his arms to drop to the floor. He stood there silently, wishing he wasn't so weak. He stood there obediently while she pulled his undershirt over his head.

She kissed him gently on his shoulders, on his hairy arms, on the inside of his elbows.

She undid his belt then whipped it off with a crack in a deliberate show.

She undid the top button on his pants and then slowly unzipped his front zipper.

She pulled his pants down over his hips; it fell to the floor around his feet.

She pulled his boxer shorts to the floor.

She dropped to her knees.

She kissed him on his thighs. He stood silently, obediently in his white shirt and bow tie.

She went around to his back and kissed his cheeks.

She licked the crack of his buttocks.

She kissed him on his thighs and licked him on the inside of his thighs.

She moved to the front and licked his bellybutton.

She placed her hands on his thighs.

She kissed him on his curly brown hair.

She kissed him on his penis.

She kissed it again.

She licked it. He did not protest.

THE AFFAIR IN NEW HAVEN

I t was only four or five city blocks from the train station to the green. Mandy had to keep her eyes to the ground, tiptoeing and hopscotching between the puddles and the mud, carrying her red coat over her arm, clutching a wicker suitcase. She carried a bag of chestnuts in the other, a present for Henry that she bought from a street vendor near the station.

The snow banks and ice patches along the streets and sidewalks trickled glistening streams of melt beneath a dazzling sun. For just one day it was spring in February. The world was simple, friendly and sweet, the air clean and buoyant; butterflies might flit by; it was lovely and civilized. Gentleman tipped their hats, ladies smiled and nodded.

Grateful that she hadn't taken a major spill in the mud along the way, she arrived at the familiar park bench by the flag pole, sat down, and soon found herself smiling at a policeman walking by twirling his night stick.

She was anxious to tell Henry that she'd rented a new apartment on Amsterdam Avenue with lovely windows. She was also impatient simply to see him. Her weekdays in the city were uneventful and the auditions were tough. She looked forward to the carefree weekends with Henry when he enjoyed spoiling her.

They had been meeting on Saturdays in New Haven for weeks now, going to the Shubert and to dinner. They usually stayed at the grand Taft Hotel checking in as husband

and wife, which was nearly true. Six months earlier, his let-ter had arrived. "How are you? How are you getting along? Can't we just have a friendly talk in the park? I have business to attend to in the morning."

He wanted to see her. He still cared.

And so they met. Mandy had always believed that Henry would return, that he would call on her again and they'd start over. And he did. She also believed that Henry had never really stopped loving her. And she was right about that, too. She blamed Henry's mother for their divorce, not herself. Even now, it was surprising how quickly their mar-riage had ended until Henry disclosed that the judge was a friend of the family.

Nine months had passed since their divorce. She did have some regrets. Perhaps she had been too silent and too welcoming of her freedom. Perhaps she should have tried harder to keep him from leaving. Perhaps she should have made a fuss and not let him walk out so easily. Then again, at the time, she was convinced that Henry was holding her back. And she also thought that he didn't have the *guts* to really leave, because he had threatened it so many times before. He hated his job and Mandy was the only audience he had to hear his complaints. Not just that, he resented that she was going off to theaters every day—without any success to show for it. Mandy thought that Henry's attitude was a distraction and that it eroded her confidence. It was Henry's fault that she did so poorly at auditions. He just didn't understand that in show business, sometimes you had to do little *personal* things to get ahead. It was *who* you knew, not what you knew. That was the way show business worked. Everybody knew that.

Mandy and Henry fought. Their arguments became more frequent and ended only when the neighbors pound-ed on the pipes or the ceiling with broomstick handles or confronted them at the door. It became so bad that the landlord threatened to evict them. Gone were the neighborly chats on the stoop with the other tenants that they had enjoyed so much.

Henry hated his job. He wanted to quit but couldn't. He expected that Mandy would grow tired of the stage and want babies. When he left in the morning, Mandy was still asleep. He usually returned home to an empty flat. At the very least, he expected that she would leave dinner to reheat or a note of explanation, saying where she was and when she'd return. She thought Henry had become accustomed to her late nights and her show business friends and that leaving a note was simply superfluous.

She was young and just wanted to be out having fun.

Before they married, Henry was entertained by her escapades and infatuated with her stories. "You did what?" he would ask incredulously. But after they were married, things changed. Henry took everything far too seriously. Even worse, he had no sense of humor, especially concerning her theater friends.

One Tuesday night, Henry went too far. In the thick of a heated volley, he said outright that maybe she "just wasn't good enough for Broadway" and that maybe it was "time to face the music that she just wasn't talented enough."

It was a horrid thing to say, a dagger to her soul. She walked out, slamming the door behind her and stayed out all night, going from club to club, making new friends, waking up at a strange man's apartment in Queens.

She might not have loved Henry when they married, but she was always comforted that he believed in her talent and would stand by her and support her on the way to the top. After all, that was why she married him over the other fellows; he believed that her goals were realistic. But now, with those devastating words spoken, Henry's love for her meant nothing, nothing at all and she doubted everything about him and the first crack of doubt about her own talent began to spread and grow. She hated him for it and that grew, too.

When he came home from work that night, she was in bed asleep. He sat beside her and roughly pulled the covers back to wake her. "Where were you last night?" he demanded. She awoke with a start, still hungover. She could hardly bear to look at his face; his hateful words still echoed in her head–that she had no talent and that it was time to give up. She could not, would not talk to him. She rose from bed, used the toilet, and washed her face while Henry shouted through the door, "You can't do this to me anymore, Mandy. I'm leaving. This time I'll be gone for good! You'll be sorry. I'm leaving you, Mandy."

He began slowly, hesitatingly to pack up his things into the suitcase, expecting that she would beg him to stay. But she did not rush to his side; she ignored him. She took cigarettes and the open wine bottle from her coat and went onto the fire escape in her nightgown, joining an orange cat lounging on a stair above. She smoked cigarettes, exhaled long dramatic smoke streams into the dreary brick courtyard, and drank glass after glass.

Henry mucked about, muttering to himself, because he really didn't want to go; soon he was sobbing.

It wasn't like that for her. With each swallow she was more convinced. Yes, she would be better off without him. Yes, she would show him he was wrong. He would be sorry someday that he didn't stick around.

Yes, she didn't need him, he was in the way.

Gradually Henry realized that she was not going to implore him to stay, not this time. Feebly, he beseeched her, "Mandy, last night... I, I, didn't mean it. Of course you have talent... Honey, look, if I go this time I'll be gone for good. Do you hear me? I'm leaving... I'm going out the door... I'm not coming back... Say something, will you? Okay be like that." He stood at the door a moment, looking down at his shoes or at nothing, turned the knob and said softly, "Goodbye, Mandy."

The door closed.

That next day without Henry was difficult, not because he was gone, but because the apartment was so quiet. She played the radio loudly and busied herself by washing all the dishes in the cabinet. She didn't go anywhere, just bought magazines, sat and read. When the next day passed without Henry's return, she began to worry.

She had never been alone and now she was alone in New York and she was just eighteen.

Although they were separated, Henry was an honorable man. He sent money every week for rent, food, and her usual allowance. Two months later, they were divorced. Actually, the legal papers she signed called it an annulment because a lawyer friend of the family had found a trivial error on the marriage license. Mandy's middle name was misspelled. She told the clerk it was *Anne* not *Ann* as her birth certificate stated. What did it matter? So when Mandy received the legal papers in the mail along with a check for two thousand dollars, she smiled. Two thousand dollars. She should have divorced Henry long ago.

But as the months went by, she missed him, boring as he was. She decided to forgive his harsh words. He really didn't mean it. He had said so. He had apologized. And she wanted to accept his apology and wanted to believe that he didn't mean it. And Mandy decided that she might even love Henry a little bit, though she wasn't quite sure.

It didn't matter that Henry remarried within six months of their breakup. Mandy knew that he'd come back to her one day. And it was just two months into his new marriage when he sent her a postcard. She knew he would, of course he would, he still loved her and always would. He couldn't possibly stay away; he'd apologize again and she'd forgive him. Things weren't over yet. No, not yet.

And so they met in New Haven as lovers.

It didn't matter that he was married. She never inquired about his wife.

She looked at her watch, just 12:00, right on time. The train from the city to New Haven had come in early. But Henry was late. She would tease him.

A matronly woman wearing a large brimmed hat with a mink stole over a black coat sat down at the bench across the sidewalk from her. The woman tossed popcorn to the ground and soon pigeons flocked around her bobbing, pecking, and cooing. They flew in from all sides of the green, landing with a "whoosh" of their gray, feathered wings on their little birdie legs.

"I don't have any. Go over there, see? Scat!" Mandy distrusted the pigeons and put her hands over her head like a child. She feared they might land on her, their little birdie toes and claws digging sharply into her scalp, beaks pecking her head, pulling out strands of her hair to pillow their nests.

The old woman gave her an amused but not a kindly kind of look. *What do you expect? She's a pigeon lady,* Mandy thought. Henry would be so amused.

"Now you let your little friend have some, Blacky! You've got to share, Blacky. Now Blacky, don't be a pig," the old woman scolded.

Mandy looked at her watch: 12:35. Maybe his meeting was running late. He'd never been late before.

After a while, the bird woman shook the last of her sack of popcorn to the ground saying, "That's it for today, friends." Without a backward glance at Mandy, she left the bench and waddled up the sidewalk. She watched as the old woman crossed Chapel Street and disappeared behind a baby carriage. Even the pigeons left, flocking to a group of children on the far side of the green near the band shell.

Mandy looked at her watch again: 1:30. Something was wrong; maybe he was not coming. The air cooled, she felt a breeze, and the light dimmed until it seemed almost night-like from the shadow of cloud rolling over the green, spreading out over New Haven. Gone was the robin's egg sky. Gone was the squinting sun. February was back. She buttoned her coat and turned up the collar.

The same policeman walked up the sidewalk toward her. She felt conspicuous, still waiting there on the bench. She avoided his stare and pretended to be searching for something, fumbling with her chestnut bag and suitcase. He passed without a word, but she knew he would come back; he was watching her. She hated being embarrassed and could not tolerate waiting for anyone or anything. Where was Henry? Where *was* he?

It took all her fortitude to stay for another ten minutes. But he didn't show up. I should be at the hotel with Henry by now, she thought.

The weather changed. A gloomy dampness blew in under an oppressed sky crowded with clouds, deep, dark and low. It would rain soon, there was no doubt, and she was unprepared, hadn't carried an umbrella because the day had started with the optimism of a blazing sun.

Gathering her belongings, she hurried down the sidewalk toward Chapel Street. At the corner, she slid on leaves and mud (or something else) and the bag of chestnuts flew from her hand and landed in the street. She stared at the chestnuts a moment, thinking what a bother they were to carry, and hurried on. A bent-over man in an odd black coat dashed into the street to retrieve them. He followed her and tugged at her sleeve, hand outstretched. She shook her head and went on her way.

At the train station, she found a telephone booth and called Lorna in Boston. "You should see this cute little hat I just bought. I'm in New Haven."

"Is that why you're calling me, all the way from New Haven, because you bought a new *hat*?" Lorna asked incredulously.

"Well, no, not exactly. Henry didn't show."

There was a pause as Lorna created the sad scene in her head. "Oh, Mandy. I'm *so* sorry. But you knew it was bound to happen someday. He's got his new wife to think of."

"Oh, no, *that* can't be it. He told me he didn't love her," she said without pause.

"Why not? Don't you know his wife just had a baby? He really ought to be with her, settle down, and leave you alone. It's only right."

"A *baby*? How do you know that? Henry didn't say anything about a b*a*by."

"The birth announcement was in the newspaper last week, in the *Herald*, I think it was. A little boy. Henry's probably busting at the seams, handing out cigars."

When she didn't reply, Lorna asked, "Mandy, are you still there? Mandy?"

"Oh hey, Lorna, here's the train. I have to run. Talk to you later. Bye-bye."

Of course she didn't know whether the train had arrived, she just wanted to stop listening to Lorna. The conversation ended with the stabbing of truth. She died listening to it. Worse, it was delivered from Lorna, her best friend now sympathetic with Henry's new wife–simply because she was a mother. That hurt almost as much as Henry's no-show.

It was a terrible day. And for Mandy, the truth-telling by Lorna, her best friend, left a bloody mark she could not ignore. It would take time to heal. It would have been better to read the news herself. She felt Lorna's pity all the way from Boston over the wires and into the booth at the New

Haven train station. She couldn't think of what it meant that Henry was a father; she could only resent not knowing.

She wandered into the great hall eyeing the rows of tall-backed, wooden benches. She found a space to sit and stared ahead at the entrance to track five, sobbing, but not aware that she was, that people were looking.

"Are you all right, ma'am?" a freckled sailor inquired.

Strangers leaned in, stared in concern.

"Oh, I'm fine, I'm fine. Just a little lonesome, that's all," she said lightly.

"I'm a little lonesome myself, ma'am. Just finished shore leave. Yeah, I was home for two whole weeks and now I'm going back. It was too short. I hardly even know–"

She cut him off. "Oh, I see, you too, huh? Well, thank you so much for your concern. But I have to go now." She stood up, gathered her things, and dashed down the cavernous passageway to the platform. There it was: the New York train, horn whistling a final time, ready to depart. And yet, it didn't feel like she needed to hurry. The train was waiting just for her, beckoning, "Come on now, get on board. You don't belong here anymore."

As she stepped on, the door closed and started up with a chug. She was grateful to find an empty seat beside a little boy in the same car. She settled down, looked out the window, and then realized that she had sat in the wrong seat after all.

She was going backwards.

Mandy hated going backwards.

Gathering her things, she stood up, and charged down the aisle, looking this way and that, hunting for a seat facing the forward direction of the train. The car swayed and she fell against a young woman. "I'm so sorry."

"That's alright."

She left the gentle syncopation of the inside and pushed on the door so it opened to cross to the next car and was jolted, nearly falling, her suitcase tumbling over. She was outside, stopped, and found herself mesmerized by the noise and the movement of the primitive mechanics around her, the open air, and that she could see that it was just a platform over the coupling, just iron wheels on iron tracks screeching at corners. But the weight and pull of it all was daunting. A person could die here, be tossed off or fall between and no one would know. The train would keep moving. She rushed to push open the door and entered the next car.

Polite men usually gave up their seats for women. Not this time. She was on her own and felt invisible, perhaps not pretty enough to be taken care of and not pretty enough to be noticed. This was a new experience and it brought on the revelation that without a husband, she was truly on her own and needed to care for herself.

She hurried through the car and deftly traversed over the coupling to the next car and the next car, men looking away, indifferent to her plight as she searched for a seat, until there weren't any more cars to search.

She was at the end of the train.

It was full, at least for now. Passengers would get off in Bridgeport, so she would search again later. That was her plan. Instead, she stayed at the far end of the last car, sitting on her suitcase, eyes closed, and leaned against the wall in the corner by the door for the entire ride back to Grand Central.

At least I'm not going backward, she thought.

CAREFREE

The day after Henry didn't show in New Haven, the stock market crashed and there were screaming headlines of financial ruin. When she read about the crash it didn't touch her because she didn't have any stocks and didn't quite know what they were.

But in the weeks that followed, long lines formed of tired, angry men. Some reminded her of Pa, waiting for bread or work or a handout, and she softened and grew as worried as everyone else. Wasn't there enough food or work? What was wrong? Why didn't they just feed everyone until things got better?

She had no idea how the world worked and so she didn't know what was happening. Henry sometimes tried to explain business but she scoffed at its importance. Now that she was on her own, she bought the newspaper and began to learn just how serious it was.

Other things worried her. In the last six months, there had been only a handful of new productions. Business was bad. Even so, it didn't matter since she was living off the large settlement from her divorce. But after a year and half of buying clothes, furnishing her new apartment, and eating out whenever she wanted to, only two hundred dollars remained. There were only a few auditions and they were so crowded with hundreds of hopefuls, that many producers began to hold invitation-only, unadvertised auditions and selected only the veterans of previous shows. The phone in the hallway on her floor never rang for her.

She looked back fondly on her first months in the city with Henry when she was a fresh face, new to theater and didn't know anything. She never had to worry about money; Henry took care of her. She was so confident that her career would be successful. But now that the affair with Henry was over and she was running out of money, she needed a new plan. In three years, she was cast in fewer than a dozen shows. Of those, she was fired from nine performances for tardiness, illness, lack of dancing ability, forgetting her place, smiling during sad numbers, and her worst offense—upstaging the star. The other three shows all closed within a week of opening. She considered acting but was truly afraid that she would forget her lines. Her doubts about her career were fueled by the knowledge that she had made only $142 in three years. Without the financial support from Henry or someone, she couldn't go on living in New York.

Asking her parents for a loan was out of the question. She hadn't even told them she was divorced and alone. She couldn't. But Mary Flanagan learned about it anyway—same as Lorna—from the birth announcement that mentioned Henry as the proud father in the *Boston Herald*. And just how did they see that particular notice? Someone had left a copy of the newspaper at their doorstep, the birth announcement circled in pencil, a hint from a neighbor or a friend too timid to tell them face-to-face. They never learned who left it.

Mary Flanagan had enough to worry about and now Mandy was divorced and alone in New York. She should have said something. Men were losing their jobs at the dock. Jack could be next and lately he was wheezing, needing to rest coming up the stairs. He was only forty-five but two years older than his dear Pa when he dropped dead in front of seven children.

Jack buried his face in his hands after reading the birth announcement and then looked up to his wife. "What on earth is this? For the love of God, weren't they married as husband and wife? Mary, how could he be married to this other woman and to Mandy, too, answer me that? I knew he was a bad sort! I should have stopped them. And where is Mandy now? On her own in the city? What shall we do? Scoundrel probably not giving her a penny. Oh, what shall we do with our wayward daughter, Mary, what shall we do?"

"I will write her a letter," she said.

Of course Mandy couldn't go back to Boston. She still wrote her mom exaggerated reports of her success. Contacting Henry for more money wouldn't do. She was through with him. It was over.

And although the idea was repugnant at first, she gradually came to accept that she needed to get a job. There was nothing else to do. But what job? Where? Would she be like all those men waiting in line, begging for work, for bread?

RUDY AND ROSALIND

B ecause of a slight bump on the table, the pool ball hooked into the side pocket with ease, as if pulled by a string. And it was like that for Mandy when she met Rudy. She was invited by someone who knew someone who knew someone who was going to a farewell party in Forest Hills for a young writer and his friends moving to Hollywood. It seemed like everyone in the New York theater scene was going out west to Hollywood and beyond, hoping to turn around their fortunes. But that was never a consideration for her. She had no money and didn't want to be so far from her family in Boston. A week had passed and she still hadn't replied to her mother. She needed some positive news to leverage the explanation her mother demanded. It wasn't the divorce from Henry that was so bad, it was that she hadn't told them about it.

She arrived alone at the party, but it was almost midnight and it didn't seem to matter. When the door to the apartment opened, she was happy to see that it was so crowded she could easily slip in unnoticed. And everyone was already drunk (which is what she predicted). Even so, the first half hour she felt like an interloper and was ready with the poor urchin excuse, "I'm lost! I don't know where my friends are. They must be here some place." But no one asked. Instead, a tall young man looking very preppy in a white cardigan offered, "You look thirsty, doll. Go get yourself a drink in the kitchen."

And that's where she first encountered Rudy. He smiled at her but quickly left with a sloshing glass.

Rudy was a very big man in his fifties with full white whiskers and a wheezy voice. He owned a few business-es and several restaurants and he had even produced Broadway shows. But on the very day of the party, no one knew that he had just lost nearly his entire fortune in the stock market. Rudy also didn't have the courage to tell his dear wife, Rosalind, sitting on the couch in her blue tailored suit, fingering her pearls, drinking gin. She was amused by the crowd of young men and women singing around the piano, Mandy among them. Meanwhile, her husband Rudy had gone to the kitchen for a double whiskey when she saw him veer off into the bedroom filled with coats.

Rosalind tolerated her husband's escapades. It began seven years earlier, after they lost their only child, a daugh-ter, to a virus when she was almost ten years old. At first, she confronted Rudy about each tryst and he would tear-fully confess. But after a while, she realized that he need-ed something to cover the sadness and tedium of their lives, and she was worn out. They had no children and so they would have no grandchildren. But she still loved him. He had always been a generous man and after each affair ended, Rosalind received a present. She learned to call it her "guilt" jewelry just as her girlfriends called gifts from their husbands. By this time in their marriage, she had quite a collection of baubles.

Mandy downed her punch–something pink and alcohol-ic from the big bowl in the kitchen. Then she stood by the piano, happily singing with the others. But in the middle of the refrain, "Five foot two, eyes of blue, has anybody seen my gal?" her nose began to drip in an embarrassing way. Was she getting sick? She retreated to the bedroom to pull a handkerchief from her coat pocket. As the door closed behind her, she glimpsed the enormous rear-end and legs of a large man dressed in a suit clumsily pulling himself out of the window and onto the narrow snowy ledge.

Aghast, Mandy rushed over to the window. He stood on the ledge no wider than his own shoe with his back and palms pressed against the brick building. The snow blew in flocks of heavy flakes, this way and that and already a soft cascade rested on his head and shoulders. She stuck out her head, asking the man incredulously, "What are you *doing* out there?"

Rudy looked back at her. "You scared me half to death, young lady! You were just in the kitchen. And if you don't mind, I prefer to die in the fall, yes, I do. So go away, please-shoo! I thought I locked the door."

"You can't do that; I won't let you! Why would you do such a thing?"

"Because I'm broke, that's why! Not that it's any business of yours. And my poor wife's out there. I can't tell her! She deserves better than me, she expects more... I'm all washed up! Nothing left! It's all gone! Poof!"

"Let me go get her."

"No, no you won't! You do that and I'll... I'll jump that's what I'll do. I'll jump!"

She was silent a moment but then decided it best to keep him distracted from his objective. "You're really a very selfish man, you know that? How do you think your wife will feel if you do this?"

"Oh, she'll be better off. I'm convinced of it. And yes, I am a selfish man. I only have a couple of the businesses left, nothing like it used to be. No, those days are gone. We're very poor now, actually," he said calmly.

He peered down beyond his shoes, down the ten stories to the icy pavement, and she worried about what to do next. She was afraid to leave him. Even if he did change his mind about jumping, it was so icy on the ledge that he just might slip and fall anyway, right in front of her. She had the strange thought that maybe other people had accidentally fallen after they had changed their minds about suicide as if fate yanked at their pant legs. How terribly sad. No one would know it had been an accident after all and not a suicide. We've all had regrets and a change of heart. But who would know? There had to be a witness, a witness to their thoughts and last words. If he fell, she would have to tell everyone what had happened. It would be awful, just awful. Her life would never be the same.

"Look, I don't have any money either, but you don't see me killing myself, not yet anyway. Hey, maybe I should! I need a job. Maybe I should just join you out there." She pretended to be hoisting herself through the window.

"No! No! Don't do that! You're too young!"

"But I need a job! I'm all alone. My husband left me!" she cried.

"But you can't jump just because of that! Go away! This is my ledge!"

"Here! Here's a nickel. Let's toss. Heads you go first, tails, I go first. Okay? Now call it."

"Call it? Call it? You can't be serious! I'll do no such thing! I won't have your blood on my hands! You just back right away from me! Get back in the room! Get back!"

"I need a job!"

"All right, all right, all right! What...what...what kind of a job do you need?"

"I don't know... I... I... was in show business but there are no shows! I don't know what to do anymore." The tears covered her cheeks.

"Husband?" he spat.

"No. No husband. He *left* me."

"Oh yeah, right. Can you sing?"

"Yes. Yes, I can sing and I can–"

Then Rosalind shouted through the closed door, "Rudy! Rudy! I know you're in there with that girl! Don't make me come in and embarrass you in front of all these people. I'm coming in! You've been in there long enough. It's time to go home! Now, open up the door! Everyone's leaving..."

"Just a minute, sweetheart, just a minute. Oh my God! How do I get back in? You've got to help me."

"Give me your hand!"

"I can't! I'll fall!"

"Rudy! I'm coming in!"

"Squat down!"

His feet landed on the floor just as Rosalind opened the door.

"Roz! I was just offering to help this young lady find a job singing at the station. She has a wonderful voice and–"

Rosalind looked at Mandy and grinned. "I bet she does, a regular songbird. Now come on honey, it's time to go home."

"Wait a minute, Roz. This young woman just saved my life–"

"They all do that, Rudy."

"No, no, this time you've got it all wrong. What's your name, honey?"

"Mandy Flanagan."

"Mandy, you be at my radio station, you know, 'the people of New York' station,WPNY, on Monday at eight o'clock in the morning. Tell them Rudy sent you. Ask for Sam. Got that?"

"That's your station? I thought you said you–"

"Never mind, never mind... Don't worry, honey, it's okay."

"Oh, thank you, thank you, thank you! A job! I got a job!"

"Yes, you do and–"

"Rudy," implored Rosalind. "It's late and I'm tired. Come on."

"All right, all right. We'll go."

As Mandy stood in the foyer adjusting her winter hat to leave the party, the front door to the apartment was open just a sliver and she overheard Rudy and Rosalind in the hallway. She said, "Now Rudy, you didn't go out on the ledge again, did you? What did you say to that poor girl? And don't give me any more jewelry. We can't afford that now."

"You know me sweetheart. I–"

The elevator door closed and they were gone.

THE FORGOTTEN STORY ABOUT BOBBY

On the subway one day, Mandy was jostled by a sudden braking in a tunnel and her bag of oranges burst open. When the lights came back on and the train started up again, her oranges rolled under the seats in every direction as though they were not just rolling away but running away.

Everyone in the car bent over to pick up the oranges near them but there was still one of the nine oranges missing. "Did you get them all, dear?" someone asked. She hadn't. There was one missing. She looked under the seats once again, but it wasn't there. Then she spotted it. There it was, sitting in the nest of a colored man's crotch in the corner of the car, three seats away. How on earth had it gotten *there*? What to do?

He was asleep, that much was sure. It looked like a music case that lay beside him, a horn of some sort. His mouth was wide open. His head was back and his hat sat over his eyes. Should she reach down and grab it? What if he woke up? What if she touched something (by mistake, of course)?

The orange jiggled a little with the swagger of the train. She found herself staring at it. Embarrassed, she looked away just in time to catch the grin of the older woman beside her who had just asked if she'd found them all. So, the old woman knew where the orange went the whole time! It seemed as though the whole train was smiling at her in amusement, winking at her predicament, speaking in foreign languages about the lady and the orange. Even the woman in the sari across from her was telling the story to her daughter, gesturing with her hands, wiggling her fingers, girlishly cupping her mouth in amusement, laughing with her eyes.

Composing herself to ignore the stares, Mandy carefully arranged the bag on her lap to sit more comfortably, to give the appearance that she was unconcerned about the lost orange. Then she settled into the familiar blank gaze of a subway traveler while the car rocked to and fro from darkness to light with the loud metal sound of the wheels on the tracks. But she was soon distracted. Without permission, her blank stare had returned to the orange. The orange. Probably the best one. It was still there, lolling around like an egg. She liked oranges. She liked oranges a lot. Had to have one every day.

The train went through another tunnel and the lights went out.

When the lights came back on, the orange was gone from its display. One by one, the passengers on the train whispered, "She did it; she got the orange." And there were guffaws and smirks and elbows in the ribs of strangers. And the older woman said loudly, "Good for you, darling, good for you! Nice orange like that, you don't find an orange like THAT every day!" And she laughed at herself, a loud, crazed infectious laugh like "Ahhhhhhhh, hahahaha! Ahhhhhhhhhhhh, hahahaha!" with little punctuating snorts in between. Everyone on the train was caught up in it. Mandy just smiled.

And when she looked over at where the orange had been, the man had covered his mouth with his hand to stifle his laughter and his eyes were merry and bright with tears and he was staring straight at her.

Then the train stopped, the doors opened, and people began to leave. She stayed seated. As he crossed in front of her to leave she said, "So, you weren't asleep at all, were you?"

He replied. "I never sleep on trains. I'm too worried someone might grab something of mine, if you know what I mean."

Their eyes darted sideways at each other and there was a sentence of silence and then she said, "I know. I almost lost my oranges."

And he said, "Yes. And you do have such awfully nice oranges."

Her cheeks burst, she sprayed out through her lips and spilled the oranges to the floor again. More people pushed on, she lost her seat and someone kicked the oranges and the doors closed and he laughed. They held onto the same pole when the train started up again and there weren't any empty seats. She missed her stop and he missed his stop and three oranges were left behind when they got off together.

MANDY AND BOBBY AND SWEETNESS
AND WHAT COULD NEVER BE

In those days, it just wasn't right if white people hung out with colored people. People would talk. But then there are exceptions to every rule, they say. And everyone knows that artists, theater people, and musicians are a different sort altogether. It was easy to excuse a white girl if she was in show biz and the colored boy was a musician.

It had been a while since Mandy had truly had a lover. She had slept with the station manager, Mr. Murphy–big deal. In this instance, she secured a small raise from her job, a job which paid the rent and the necessities of life and which could still be considered show business but certainly off to the side a little bit from her Broadway aspirations.

Even though the match was wrong (Mandy had never even spoken to a colored person before), dark as he was, Bobby had an appeal that few women could resist: he was a musician. So when Bobby invited Mandy to his club saying, "It might be presuming of me, but maybe we could get together at my, ah, club, where I play, I mean. You know I play horn and all. Say on Saturday?"

She did not hesitate to say, "That might be nice–if I'm not busy." Because after all, what could be the harm in that? It was a night out; it was something to do.

So on Saturday, Mandy went to Harlem to meet Bobby. She stood outside the club, across the street for nearly an hour in the October dampness. She felt conspicuous but needed to be sure, just to be on the safe side. The people going down the stairs were mostly colored, but there were a few white people, too. She had to be sure she wasn't alone. She just wasn't that brave.

The doorman said to her, "You in the right place, Miss?"

Mandy replied, "Yes, I believe I am. I came to hear the music."

"Well then, you just walk right in."

And so she did. Down the steps to the cellar she found a chair at the only available table in the very back of the smoky room, near the coat rack and bathrooms. But it was an ideal spot, for she hoped to sit unnoticed, at least for a while. It was very dark; faces glowed from the small candles on each table. The ceiling was low, the music sultry. A magical night. Every table was filled with enraptured people smiling, nodding, listening, talking. Each felt that they were on display in a room filled with coy admirers who recognized their cleverness, beauty, obvious superiority, and good taste for companions. All except Mandy.

She was sure that there were only a handful of white people in the entire place and a sudden panic had seized her. What if Bobby was just toying with her and pretended not to know her? What if he had forgotten all about her? What if the colored people didn't want her there; would the white people protect her if something happened? Then she saw him. Yes, it was him. Bobby with his trumpet by his side, standing on the stage. He was off to the left, leaning against the brick wall. He wasn't playing in that number, she guessed. He didn't see her.

Bobby was a big, handsome man, with chestnut brown skin, short-cropped hair with a part on the side, a broad forehead, arched eyebrows, and the high cheek bones and determined jaw of a Jamaican. His nostrils flared when he was contemplating something and he often stuck out his fat bottom lip. But his droopy eyelids and deep, slow talking gave way to his true calm, contemplative disposition which might be observed as simple shyness, especially around women. Then again, it might be the cool, practiced air of a jazz musician. Hard to say.

There was a clarinet, a bass, a drummer, a piano player, a trombone, and a horn player, and then there was Sweetness, the songbird. She was a tall, big-boned woman who possessed a straight deliberation as a decidedly assertive alto that meant "you better listen to me" business. It wasn't so much her voice as it was her delivery that everyone came to see. Wearing a red dress, she did a howling, moaning, eyes-closed type of singing with an emotional nakedness that caused tendrils of perspiration to roll down her face and down her opulent breasts. At the end of each song, her eyes fluttered open, a weak smile crossed her face and she bowed her head graciously to the applause, as though she was embarrassed at what she had just revealed to a roomful of strangers. Once in a while, she winked or pointed to someone in the audience. They loved it.

The waitress wore a yellow dress with a low cut front that emphasized the boniness of her frame instead of a jiggling bosom as the dress was designed to show off. "Whacha have, hon?"

"Oh, how about a sloe gin fizz."

And then she was gone without a word.

When she returned, Mandy asked, "How much do I owe you?"

"That'll be a dollar."

Mandy gave her a dollar and ten cents and said, "Keep the change." Again the waitress was gone without a word. Not even a thank you. Was she being played for a sucker? A dollar was a lot for a drink. But there was music.

The band took a break and Bobby sauntered off the stage turning slowly to say, "How ya doin?" and "Glad you could make it" and "Good to see you" to people at various tables. But then he headed straight to Mandy's table and sat down. She felt that everyone in the club was staring at her as Bobby took her by the hand and introduced her to the band at the front table. "This is my friend Mandy." There were polite nods and half smiles but a distant response all around until he followed with, "She's in radio," which seemed to lighten things up considerably and made all the difference in their expressions. "Oh, radio, huh? What kinda music do you play? What station?"

He bought her a drink, but the next set was starting so they never sat together and talked. Instead he said, "Isn't Sweetness great? Next break I have to practice for my number, so I can't visit you. I'm sorry. I'll come by after the show, promise. I hope you can stay. I'm really glad you came." Then he walked away.

He didn't play in the next set but again stood off to the left. At the break, he seemed to be practicing, moving his fingers but not blowing the horn. Mandy was dreamy and drunk. She grinned at everyone but still sat alone. She wanted to talk to him, but he said he had to practice. It might not be wise.

In the last set, during the last two songs, Sweetness beckoned to Bobby with her index finger that he could play. The band seemed to be practicing the songs. Most of the people had left and the lights were on. They were clearing the tables.

The first song was a blues number that began with just a walking bass line. Bobby raised his horn to follow and it squeaked. He backed off, but it had resonated like a four-letter word from a baby. He eased in with a low note, but it was late on the refrain. He kept on, but his tone stood out from the band. They plodded on with the bass player rolling his eyes at Sweetness. Bobby stopped playing in the middle of the song, removed the mouthpiece, and tapped it against his thigh with an expression of annoyance that the horn was again not playing right. But the clarinet pulled the band back and they readied as Sweetness leaned into the microphone, taking a swallow from the glass in her hand, then speaking the words like confession, "My man left and that's all I got to say." Then she took her drink and left the stage. She sat down at Mandy's table. The band kept on. Sweetness whispered to Mandy, "It's a massacre." Mandy nodded, but she didn't know what Sweetness meant.

The band tried another song, an original started by piano skipping up seven notes with the clarinet answering. Bobby came in before the notes were out and they had to start again. "Bobby wait to the bridge, wait to the bridge," said the clarinet player. Bobby waited till the bridge then let loose with a voluminous sound that wiped out hearing the bass and the piano. They played it through to the end just the same. "Another one guys?" asked Bobby.

"No, tired," mumbled the clarinet. No one else bothered to answer. Bobby looked around; they were already breaking down. Then he remembered Mandy. He shouted down to her, "You still here?"

Later Bobby and Mandy stood together on the sidewalk outside the club. It was 3:30 in the morning and no one was around when he asked, "Did you have a nice time?"

"Sure. It was a lot of fun."

She smiled. He smiled.

"Well, ah, can I kiss you?"

"Sure." She closed her eyes.

He leaned over and gently, quickly brushed her lips in a dry chapped-lip kiss that barely landed. She opened her eyes.

"How was that?" he asked.

"Fun, a lot of fun."

"Want to come to my place?"

"No, not tonight."

"It would be a lot of fun–"

"No, no, I can't"

"Will you come back to the club?"

"Sure."

"Next week?"

"Okay, next week."

"Can I walk you somewhere? It's late."

"No, that's okay. The subway's only on the next corner." She took a few steps then stopped to say over her shoulder, "Well, bye. I had a nice time."

"Thanks for coming, Mandy. Hey, promise you'll come back?"

"I promise."

"Soon!" he shouted as she disappeared around the corner.

She was nearly asleep when the train arrived a few minutes later. She didn't know that Bobby had followed her, sitting nearby, watching to be sure she was safe.

In time, she learned that Bobby wasn't a member of the band, he just hung out with them waiting offstage for a nod from Sweetness. Late at night, when most of the patrons were gone, they'd let him sit in. He wasn't very good. There were plenty of missed notes and wavers and Sweetness rolled her eyes. But no one ever said anything to him. And when Bobby said, "*We're* rehearsing a new number," Mandy was silent. She was also eight years older than Bobby.

The following week at the club, just before closing, Sweetness leaned over the table toward Mandy and said, "Honey, you *got* to be a friend of my horn player or crazy to come in here by yourself. And crazy we got plenty of– you fit right in." Bobby grinned, elated that Sweetness called him "my horn player" and had accepted Mandy, too. She felt a little more relaxed after Sweetness' words and thus had several drinks during the performance which made her even more relaxed.

At every performance, Sweetness backed away from the mic to sit at the piano while one of the guys sang. This was intriguing. Mandy had never seen a woman play an instrument in a band before; they were only singers. The first time she saw Sweetness play, she was awestruck at her talent, playing right along with the guys, and no one minded. Sweetness could hold her own. It set her to thinking about how much fun it would be to play in a band. So powerful was this thought that it stayed around Mandy's head and was never very far from her consciousness (although it did lay low for a few years). From then on, she listened to music with a self-satisfied smile on her face, imagining that she was the musician, the performer, she was the one bending the note, she was the one laughing with the guys, she was the one bowing to the applause.

Bobby never knew.

From the outside, she looked just like everyone else in the audience. She didn't know that many people enjoyed music this way, as though they were in the band.

That same night, Bobby again asked her back to his apartment and she again said no. But the next Saturday, after a decent two weeks, she agreed that yes, she would go back to Bobby's apartment. Yes, it was risky. And Bobby was so different from Henry. Was that it? Was that why?

Perhaps it was the gin. But as she said the word "yes," an arctic breeze swept up under her dress, and she felt the hairs rise in bumps on her arms. What followed was an intense feeling of desire and anticipation, one that she would recall in her memories of Bobby for years to come. A feeling she had never felt before from just talking, from just saying "yes." It was like the burn of dry ice, a hot, incessant urge she felt *down there*, an emptiness she had to fill that had only one remedy.

And Bobby must have felt something, too. For he stared at her evenly, stuck out in his bottom lip and rocked on his heels. "Well, alright then. Let's go."

His apartment faced the alley and was just two rooms: the kitchen–living room and his bedroom with a shared bathroom down the hall. His brass bed was small and unmade: no sheets, just a ratty blue blanket over the mattress and a pillow without a cover. It wasn't dirty, but it had a man's smell, not unlike Henry.

White sheets covered the sofa and a side chair. Later she learned that the furniture underneath was new. The lamp on the table gave a soft golden glow to the pictures on the wall of colored men in derby hats and stern buxom women. Mandy had never seen colored people in photos like that. They were dressed just like white people. Their unsmiling faces reminded her of the photographs that hung over her parents' piano.

That first night, they sat timidly side by side on the couch and drank whiskey. Mandy had expected him to start right in necking, but he didn't; he was too polite. After an hour she stood up, exhausted by the small talk. "Well, I have to be going."

"Going? You just got here!" And with those words he pulled her back to the couch and toward him with purpose and put his hand under her chin to turn her face and then pressed his lips gently to hers for several long seconds. Then he kissed her a second time, but longer and wetter than the first, and then they embraced and he stroked her hair. When she faced him again she touched his lips with her fingers.

At first, Bobby was very slow and very gentle with Mandy. He had never touched a white woman and he didn't know what to expect. But she kept at him. "It's all right, don't worry. Just do like you usually do."

Problem was, Bobby didn't usually do *it* at all. He wasn't nearly as experienced a lover as she was. Mandy had it in her head that colored people had better sex than white people, particularly a big, strong man like Bobby. But no, he was polite, worried, and hesitant. Even Henry had been more aggressive.

"Come on. You can get started. Don't worry."

They sat on the couch. His large hands deliberated at each button on her blouse until it was undone. He peeled it off and placed it neatly on the rocking chair. When he turned back, he started seeing her breasts, for she had removed her bra and was reaching to place it on top of the blouse. She sat on the couch facing him. He smiled and she was reminded of the oranges and that he was a mischievous man. Bobby sat for a long time staring without speaking, at her breasts then at her eyes. Finally, she turned, leaned against him, and placed his hands over her breasts.

And still he didn't move. He held her breasts tenderly, barely touching her nipples. "Are you sure it's okay with you?"

"Yes, it's okay."

With that, he pulled her to her feet. His hands touched her from the top of her head to her feet, as though he were blind. He removed her heeled shoes, unzipped and dropped her skirt to the floor, then unhooked her stockings which cascaded to her knees. She rolled each one to her feet, stepped out. He watched as her garter belt fell to the floor and she stepped out of her underwear. He placed them on the chair.

She stood naked before him.

Again he asked, "Are you sure it's okay with you? I mean, we could stop, if you want. I won't hold it against you. We can still be friends."

"Do you want to stop?"

"Do you?"

"No."

"Me neither."

"Well, all right then," she mimicked.

She lounged on the couch. He fumbled a bit trying to find a starting place and then he eased in, filling up her whole insides. He placed his hands on either side of her and barely touched her skin as he lowered himself up and down, pivoting on his knees. After a while, she grew worried that he would not come. But he did, stiffening for only a moment without a word or a whimper of elation, silent, no groans of ecstasy, nothing. He was a polite, quiet lover, and she was disappointed. She was used to Henry yelling, "Oh yeah! Oh boy! Oh lady, oh lady, oh lady!"

Over time, they got better together. Much better.

He sought the advice of his friends. They were eager to provide him with a description of their own exaggerated exploits in exchange for details about his trysts with the "crazy white girl."

But it was always Mandy who led the way. She didn't want to disappoint him any more than he wanted to disappoint her. She fought her "not supposed to" thoughts early on in their relationship by daring herself to date a colored man and then later by letting go of her inhibitions.

Their lovemaking was naughty. With Henry it had only been face-to-face with the exception of some playful feather dusting. Perhaps it was so good because it was wrong to be with a colored man. Or perhaps she was simply lonely.

Mandy invented games that lasted all night. One of Bobby's favorites was "bellhop." Mandy would be a famous movie star and Bobby would adjust her hairpiece in an elevator and beg a kiss. At first she would "escape" off the elevator only to return and say, "Oh, all right. If you really must." Then Bobby would beg a touch of her leg and so on, until their game escalated in daring requests on the 100th floor that were never turned down. When he asked her how she came up with the bell hop story, she replied, "Just my crazy imagination."

Bobby had to admit that outside of music, it was the best fun he'd ever had. They met every Friday at the club. After the show, they would sneak into his building at three in the morning. But his neighbors knew about Mandy. Sometimes he stayed awake all night worrying about the danger of their liaison.

She never offered to meet him on any other night or any other place and he never asked. Once a week, only Friday nights. She slept on the couch, never in his bed, and left at six on Saturday morning.

Six months later, Mandy missed her period.

Of course she was scared; it could not be, just could not be. A baby, a colored baby, could not be. She thought about her father. She couldn't tell him, she couldn't go home. A single woman giving birth was shame enough. But this—no this just could not be.

And while falling asleep, she doubted the truth and looked to tomorrow to awaken from the dream. She often found herself staring at her stomach with her hands placed flat against her abdomen. She wore clothes that hid her stomach even though early as it was, there was simply nothing to see. But it was clear. She was pregnant. She didn't dare go to a doctor. After a month passed, she accepted it.

At first, she planned to go away, have the baby, and then put it up for adoption. But then she worried that no one would adopt a child of mixed heritage. She also worried that she would not be able to give the baby up. Maybe the baby would look more white than colored, maybe it could pass; she should wait and see. But no, no, no, she couldn't see it.

As it was, she couldn't take off seven months from work; they wouldn't hold the job for her. She couldn't tell them anyway. So she planned to have an abortion; she knew that several girls from the chorus line went to a certain address. Everyone knew about it. Someone did it on the lower East Side for $25, no questions asked.

But one lunch hour, she found herself standing in front of a store that displayed children's clothes. So tiny. So cute. What would it be? She wanted a girl. Would she be big like Bobby? Or look like her mother? Maybe a musician? Yes, that would be fun.

The window displayed a crib with a white blanket and a teddy bear mobile. She would have a rocker to hold the baby, a just right bundle of softness and warmth. She remembered holding her baby sister. It was her sweet baby breath, the smell of her hair, her yawning, and her clenched fists.

She went in and bought a pair of pink baby socks. Somehow it would work out.

Bobby never knew. She sent him a letter saying she couldn't come to the club anymore, because she found someone new. Anyway, she was sure that Bobby didn't love her. It was obvious from his long looks at Sweetness, drinking her up, and his clumsy attempts to get close to her. He wanted to be near her more than he wanted to be in her band.

Mandy knew Bobby was infatuated with Sweetness and she knew that Sweetness was in love with Monte, the piano player, and that Monte was married to Jasmine.

Bands are like that.

There was never a thought of marriage to Bobby. Her sense of self and her place in the world censored it before it ever reached her consciousness. Oddly, each had remarkably similar aspirations.

Bobby longed to be a great musician and composer, but he never practiced enough to learn the foundations of his instrument. He couldn't read music and had never written a song.

Mandy called herself a performer and had dreams of being a Broadway star, but she could not dance or act. Instead she sang on the radio, on commercials, without recognition, anonymous to the listeners.

A marriage between Bobby and Mandy was doomed for another reason. Regardless of color, there was a more fundamental problem—that of the natural, competitive ambition of the stage performer. Which one—the imagined musician or the wannabe show girl—would play the lead in such a marriage? It interfered with any notion of a wholesome relationship between them. They were both dreaming their lives away.

Sadly, she did love Bobby. But she was wise enough to know that just because you love someone doesn't mean you can live with them.

He wrote back and begged to see her one more time at the club, after the first set. Three weeks had passed. She saw Sweetness glance her way and smile. Did she know?

Bobby stuck out his lower lip and pulled on his nose as he listened to her talk about meeting a "wonderful guy right down the hall." He didn't believe her.

His reply was slow and deliberate. "I'm happy for you. But now you listen to me. If ever you need anything honey, I'm here. I'm here for you. I care about you, I always will, no matter what happens, I'll be there. I take care of my obligations and it's no trouble at all."

She left the club in a hurry as if running away from him could reverse the past. On the subway ride home she replayed his words. Maybe he knew.

In the third month, she miscarried. It began as a small pink stain on a Friday night. Then it was red and dripping out in webs of pain, like a bad monthly. By Saturday afternoon it was over.

The radio was loud and she liked it that way, sitting in the big armchair, drinking full glasses of whiskey, punching and sobbing into a pillow. No one knew, so there was no one she could talk to now. No one would ever know. Maybe she would tell Lorna sometime.

Did she feel relieved at this turn? No. Instead, she felt lonelier than she had ever felt and unprepared for the uncontrollable depth of her despair, not just from the loss, but that there was no one who could comfort her, certainly not Bobby. Why? Why was this?

She wondered whether there would be other babies and why her body had gone wrong. Or had it gone right? She would replay this favorite sorrow–that her body knew she just hadn't wanted it enough, had wished it to go away. And after her tears were gone, it sat in the backroom of her thoughts, waiting for an invitation to roll over her laughter, roll over her smile.

Yet, still, still, she had grown used to the idea. Still, still, she was growing fond of the baby, fond of the secret little thoughts of little hands, little fingers, and little toes. Still, still.

GOOD LUCK AND A BENEVOLENT GOD

"**D**o you mind if I join you?" he asked with a Germanic accent.

"Go right ahead," Mandy replied.

"Do you come to this park often?" he asked.

Mandy began to wonder if the man in the black suit would be a bother. But she took another bite of her chicken sandwich and dismissing that thought, replied lightly, "Every lunch hour when it's nice out."

"Oh, so you are a *working* girl, then?" he asked.

He had gone too far in his inquiry and she decided to sting him. "No, no, not that. I have a job if that's what you mean. And you *do* ask a lot of questions, don't you?"

"Oh, I am so sorry. This is a very bad habit of mine, a very bad habit. Please, Miss, please ignore my rudeness. I meant no offense." And he turned away.

She softened. "That's okay. I don't mind a little company."

"You don't? That's wonderful news! Then perhaps you can forgive my bad manners."

"You're forgiven and it's forgotten. But now it's time for me to get back to work." She stood up and gathered her things. "Well, goodbye. It was nice meeting you."

"Thank you for your company, Miss. Do have a pleasant afternoon."

Mandy crossed the street and walked the three blocks back to the station.

The next day she was sitting at the same park bench when the same man in black came by and again sat down beside her.

"And so we meet again!" he exclaimed.

"Yes. The day is so warm; maybe spring is finally here."

"Another beautiful day."

"Yes, another beautiful day."

The pleasant but very polite conversation between them continued for a few days at her lunch hour at the same park bench. Gradually, Mandy learned his story. His name was Moshe Lipschitz and he lived in Crown Heights. Although Moshe was always excessively polite, he did like to ask her pointed questions that most people would only muse about. So one day Mandy asked him quite boldly why it was that he was always dressed in black and had such a curious beard. Moshe explained that he was a Jew studying to become a rabbi. He also told her that he was engaged to be married. Although this was a surprise, it was not a disappointment. For she did not consider for a moment that Moshe might be a suitable suitor. He was a nice man but plain appearing, and she thought him somewhat odd. But in fairness, she wondered if it was just his religion that made him seem so peculiar.

His skin was very pale, as if he had remained indoors without a sun to touch his cheek his entire life and his hair was ebony black and very curly. But she did find Moshe's thighs fascinating, especially when he was seated beside her on the bench. In this one attribute, he seemed manly and mysterious and she would nearly blush at her distracted thoughts of his pale thighs with the dark curly hair leading to more dark curly hair. Was his underwear black, too?

Of course, Moshe had no idea of the content of these private thoughts. She worried, though, that Moshe might make advances that she would have to awkwardly refuse. But she worried needlessly. For Moshe confessed one day that although he did find Mandy "most attractive," he would never, never dare to act against the laws of God, for he was a Jew and he was nearly married. Moshe said this with such certain conviction that her worries never reappeared and they became good friends.

She soon learned that Moshe was not a happy man. For even though he had lived in America six years, his fiancée Noni was still in their native Poland and refused to leave. He wrote to her faithfully, a letter a week, with money always enclosed. Noni wrote him a letter a week back. But she would not come.

"But why won't she come to America?"

"Because she is *afraid*–that is why. She says that she does not want to leave her mother and I tell her, bring your mother! I pray that my Noni will come one day, but year after year goes by and *still* she does not come. That is why I am a very lonely man, Miss Mandy. And now with this crazy man Hitler, I am very afraid for her safety, very afraid. She should have come with me. She should have *come*."

"We can be friends if you like," said Mandy to console him.

"You are most kind. That would please me, yes. That would please me very much."

When the weather began to turn cold in the fall, they agreed to meet Tuesdays at noon at a small coffee shop Moshe chose. Sometimes he would bring her chocolate. In time, Mandy confided in him like she had confided in no other person in her life. She told him about Henry and was pleased when he remarked, "He was a fool to leave you. I would never do such a thing."

But Mandy blurted out without thinking, "Oh, but you did leave Noni."

"But Miss Mandy, I have told you. She would not come! I had an opportunity–such an opportunity only happens once in a man's life. God made the arrangements; it was a gift. I

145

had to leave Poland without her. It was *God's* decision. This troubles me that you, my good friend, should think that I, Moshe Lipschitz, had any choice whatsoever in this matter."

"I understand now, Moshe. It must have been very difficult for you." But Mandy really didn't understand, because he never explained what arrangements God had made for him. She simply did not want to upset him for Moshe was a passionate man.

Even though Moshe confessed that he did feel "desires" for her, he explained that even their friendship must remain a secret and that if they passed in the street he was sorry but he could not even tip his hat. His people would frown on an acquaintance from outside the congregation, especially an acquaintance with a woman. Mandy never did learn exactly where Moshe lived or what congregation he belonged to and he never asked Mandy for her address either. She wondered why he dared to speak with her at all when he knew it was wrong.

They were both lonely and having no one else to console them, they became confidants through their meetings at the park bench or the coffee shop. She learned about his congregation and their intimate troubles. Their woes were not very different from her own and her family back in Boston. Moshe said that he had no one to tell his secrets to. Another Jew just wouldn't do. In turn, she spoke of her family, her job, and what it was like to be Catholic.

They had interesting discussions. Moshe liked to talk about God. He believed that his every word and every deed was witnessed and judged by God and that his God was not necessarily a benevolent God. Mandy had never met anyone quite like the disciplined and curious Moshe, perhaps that is why their friendship flourished. She found it strange that he would never attribute anything to simple good fortune or to being lucky enough to be "in the right place at the right time."

As for Mandy, she was sure that God was much too busy to see and plan her every action. She thought that God might look in on her now and again and that if there was some great event in her life, maybe God would attend. But for the most part, God did not sit on her shoulder whispering in her ear. She was glad that God seemed to have his back turned when she did something wrong (like the bellhop thing). And yet Mandy's God could be "all knowing" if he had the time. Mandy figured that God just trusted some people to their own instincts and generally left them alone unless they needed help and called his name.

Moshe remarked that Mandy seemed to have a "God of convenience." He thought that God always watched and judged and that there was a reason for everything. He even thought that Mandy had some purpose in his life but he wasn't quite sure what it might be yet. They talked about this often. Mandy would say, "Oh come on, Moshe. We met at a park bench and we're just friends, that's all." And Moshe would reply, "Ah yes, but why?"

She liked to shop at Macy's in Herald Square at Christmas time. After her divorce, she returned home to Boston to visit her parents and her sister Barbara in Somerville on the holidays. One day after work, a week before Christmas, she was looking at tree ornaments and holiday candy. Mandy felt that someone was staring at her, but when she looked around behind her, no one was there. She was so conscious of this thought that she asked a clerk if there was someone watching her from a secret place in the store. The clerk looked at Mandy quizzically. "Why, no. No one's watching you, honey. This is Macy's. Macy's Herald Square. Are you all right?" Embarrassed, she left the store.

The next day after work, she returned to the same department to finish her shopping and again felt that someone was looking at her. She asked a clerk again and this time, the clerk replied, "Lady, you're imagining things. No one's watching you. There's just me and little ole Santa in this department." It was true there was no one around.

Nearby, Santa sat on his throne at the North Pole. There was a long line of anxious parents and children waiting to see him and holiday music played "Silent Night" and "Hark the Herald Angels Sing" over and over. Mandy turned around and looked in Santa's direction to see him staring straight at her. It was *Santa*! She turned back to the clerk. "It's Santa! I'm not crazy! See? Who is he, anyway?"

"Oh, I think that's Charlie. Yeah, Charlie. Don't worry, he's harmless."

"Charlie?" she puzzled. She didn't know a Charlie. When Mandy looked back at Santa, he was staring again but quickly turned toward the sobbing three-year-old girl on his lap. Mandy marched to the aisle with the crowd waiting to see Santa, slipped under the ribbon, climbed up the three steps to his chair, bent over, and demanded in Santa's face, "Why are you staring at me?" The child on Santa's lap began to wail even more and the parents in line strained to see why there was such a commotion. Santa blinked a few times but said nothing. Mandy was agitated now. "I said, *Why* are you... Moshe!" she cried. "What are you–"

"The name is Santa, young lady. Mister Santa Claus."

"It is you! But why–"

"Santa is very busy right now. He'll be happy to see you on Tuesday."

Mandy was so surprised that she could only mutter, "Oh, well, ah, yes. Bye... Santa... Claus."

And Moshe Santa shouted after her, "Have a Merry Christmas! Mer-ry Christmas! Ho! Ho! Ho!"

On Tuesday, Moshe explained that he had been Santa at Macy's for over five years. At first, he did it for the money. "I have to earn a living. A rabbinical student earns nothing. And there is my Noni to think of. How else can I pay for her safe transport? I must do this for her."

Even though Moshe was terrified that he might be discovered, he relished the danger and drama that would follow.

"They will be ashamed Yes. They will be ashamed to learn the terrible truth And I will say to them, you knew about Noni, why didn't you help me bring her?"

"Why don't they help you?"

"That, I don't know, Mandy. There must be something. They have helped others. Why are they not helping me bring Noni to America? Perhaps it is her family, they refuse to listen. They believe they are not like other Jews. Noni's brother married a gentile. But they are in danger. We must convince her family to come. It is very discouraging."

She always had to interrupt him because Moshe enjoyed his own words so much that he would repeat them two or three times, each time louder, and the people in the cafe where they met would turn to stare.

When Mandy learned how much Moshe earned as a rabbinical scholar teaching children, she was incredulous. "Are you crazy? You make twice, no, three times as much as I do! You are paid quite well, Moshe. They are very generous. I can't believe you feel that you have not been paid fairly."

"Others, even younger than myself, in my same employment, are making a better wage than I."

"There must be *some* reason why you're not paid the same. Come on, Moshe. Are you telling me everything?"

"No, I am not. There is something. But it is not honorable for me to disclose this to you. I should not have begun this conversation. And my friend, much as I enjoy your company, you are a woman and not a Jew—there are some things you cannot understand."

Although she was rebuked, she accepted his explanation and they never discussed it again.

A year later, she was still working at the radio station and continued to meet Moshe every other Tuesday at the coffee shop. The country was at war and at each meeting he seemed to grow angrier. He decried that Hitler's atrocities weren't being reported in the newspapers.

One day, she enraged him. "Now Moshe, how could that be? If there was anything going on like you said, don't you think the newspapers would print it? Don't you think we would know about it?" She added, "Maybe your fiancée Noni is exaggerating things a little."

At times like these (and there were quite a few) he would stare in disbelief. Then, he would excuse himself. "Forgive me, I must take a walk."

She remained at the table, shaking her head, wondering what she had said this time to offend him. Mandy honestly didn't know. Once her words were out, she didn't hear them anymore, didn't look inside, didn't regret. It wasn't that she was an insensitive person, no. Talking was just conversation, banter, not be taken too seriously.

One day, he disclosed that the congregation had provided him with a nice raise but that he had decided to continue to be Santa anyway. He explained, "You see, I like to have a little extra do-re-me for personal incidentals. And I love the children. I have none. And I like to wear red. Yes, I do."

She nodded. He was just lonely and often spoke about the seven children he would have once Noni left Poland to join him in America. He never mentioned any friends. She understood why he enjoyed the red suit and sitting children on his knee. They were confidants since there was no chance either could know the other's world. Mandy was the only one who knew his secret.

Moshe knew some of Mandy's secrets, too. He knew about Bobby and the miscarriage. "What a mystery!" he said, smiling.

"What do you mean?"

"We'll never know what pretty color he would be."

She loved him for that.

One Tuesday, he arrived hurried, gasping. "Mandy, Mandy, I have such news! My Noni is finally coming to America."

"Really? Are you sure?"

"Oh, yes. This time she *will* come. Her mother has finally died." He looked at the ceiling. "Oh God, forgive me. That is not at all what I wanted to say." He paused and looked at her sullenly. "And we will still be friends, won't we Mandy? You will still be my dear friend, won't you?"

"Of course I will, Moshe."

But they both knew better.

A week later, she received a sealed envelope at work from Moshe. Inside was a note.

My Dear Miss Mandy,

Noni is coming soon and so I must write to you. With regret, my schedule is such that I will not be able to meet with you for coffee in the near future. I will miss your friendship.
Moshe

Of course their meetings had to stop with Noni's arrival but she had hoped for a better ending than such a brief note. Maybe flowers. Something more.

She returned to the coffee shop one last time. But instead of coffee, she ordered a hot fudge sundae with strawberry ice cream.

Several months passed and then a year went by when a long letter arrived from Moshe that explained his circumstances. As it turned out, Noni had come to America and they were married. But around the Christmas holiday, Noni became suspicious of his daily absence, suspecting another woman. After all, Moshe was a man and many years had passed.

Noni followed Moshe to the employee entrance at Macy's but could not find him in the store. That is until she heard his distinctive voice: "And what is it that you should want, such a fine boy?" Noni rushed up to Santa, pulled down his beard to the horror of all the waiting mothers, cried "Moshe!" and "For shame!" in Polish and generally made such a fuss that all the children began to cry and Moshe was forced by his hysterical Noni to leave his chair at the North Pole, saying, "No, Noni! Let me explain, let me explain."

She did not listen. "I come here and see you, a Jew, like this! After all we have suffered. How? How is this Moshe?"

Disgraced, Noni fiercely disrobed his red suit, snatched off his beard and hat, and pulled at his boots beginning in the Toy Department and continuing on through Women's Better Clothing until finally, when Moshe was clad only in underwear (oddly in the Lingerie Department), she was joined by shrieking patrons who slapped and chased poor Moshe from the store and into the cold December night of Herald Square.

Well, it didn't end there. After confronting Moshe, Noni felt obligated to turn him in to the congregation. Poor Moshe was hurriedly dismissed and he never did have the opportunity to repeat the words of retribution that Mandy had heard so often. In protest and indignation, Moshe then joined a reformed congregation and was paid considerably less for a salary. Noni refused to follow him. Just one year after Noni's arrival in America, they were separated again. Moshe wrote that he believed "his lot in life" was to be a "poor man without a wife." He said that "God must be testing him" and told her that he felt like "her Jesus Christ on the cross." Moshe closed the letter by saying that he wished to see her again but was "too forlorn" to arrange for their meeting. Mandy was distressed, but there was nothing she could do; she didn't know where he lived.

The following Christmas, Mandy looked for Moshe Santa in Macy's. But none of the Santas stared back at her with any recognition. She asked one of the store clerks who replied with sarcasm that she didn't know any "Jewish Charlie Santa Claus." There was no such thing.

Mandy knew there was such a thing. And many years later, when she read the newspaper accounts and understood the horrors, she changed her mind. She understood why Noni was so crazed that Moshe played Santa. Noni had escaped, come all the way to America to be with him, expected to live unashamed as a proud Jew, only to discover that he was a buffoon, dressed, inexplicably, in Christian costume.

This was too much.

Because she could not understand how he could do such a thing, she could not forgive him.

Four years later, Mandy was surprised to receive a letter from Moshe.

My Dear Miss Mandy,

I do hope this letter finds you well. Your old friend wishes you to know that he is married to a lovely

*young woman and we are blessed with two won-
derful, bright children: a girl and boy. I teach at a
university and the money is very adequate to raise
a family. My old friend, I wanted you to know that
there is a benevolent God smiling on me now. I
should hope the same is true for you. Though I
would enjoy seeing you again, the arrangements
have become complicated with the passage of time
and my change in circumstances. I do hope you
understand. Please know that I am forever grateful for your friendship and wise counsel during
the trial of my faith. I wish you good luck and a
benevolent God.*

*Sincerely,
Moshe*

MIDDLE AGE

In 1950, Mandy was forty and fourteen years had passed at the radio station. One Saturday, she woke up realizing with regret that she had forgotten to get herself married. It happened that suddenly.

While lying in bed, the thought came into her head that she was not married and might never be married and it hung around all day long so that she was obliged to face it and try to understand why it still mattered. And she thought thoughts about herself that she had never dared to think for fear that they might tarnish her luck or foretell her future or interfere with her enjoyment of life as she still imagined herself to be young and pretty.

Nonetheless, she did not panic.

Maybe I won't get married.

This could be it. This could be all there is–this life, my job, and nothing more.

Maybe I will be an old maid.

I might be alone the rest of my life.

I might be alone.

That Saturday morning, she rubbed at the spokes around her eyes with mineral oil. She tried to smile the gap-toothed smile of a young girl in the bathroom mirror but saw half-moon creases appear from her nose to her chin. Her hair was shoulder length, longer than she had worn it in her twenties, and dark brown not chestnut. Her bangs now seemed cut too short above her highly-arched, drawn eyebrows. When she pulled her hair back and rolled it into the popular French twist that she often wore to the station, she looked like someone else, someone old.

After that, she tried on every lipstick she owned, all the pinks and reds. She tried on every eye shadow: green, blue, and taupe. But she could not make her face look young and small. And the more makeup she wore, the older she looked. Gone was the sweetness of youth and those delicate, pouty lips that enamored Henry.

She wondered when it left. Did it slip away like a winking stranger getting off a train?

Sure, now and again a man still looked her way, but it wasn't that often anymore. And if a man did look, it wasn't the quality of man she had enjoyed in her twenties. Back then, unbeknown to her, she had developed the habit of glancing away from any man who might become a possible suitor. If a man admired her before she admired him, he was dismissed.

It was Henry's fault.

Mandy always believed that she would meet another man just like him and that this time around she would be more attentive. But that didn't happen and it might never happen. She was forty. Would someone like Henry notice her now, at forty?

Perhaps she really didn't favor sharing her life with a man. Maybe that was it.

Her routine was a collection of habits that filled the week and made her a busy person. She went to work five days a week and sometimes on Saturday mornings. She bought flowers every other Thursday. On Saturdays, she went to matinees alone. She wrote letters to her sister Barbara, her mother, and Lorna once a month. She did the laundry on Tuesdays, went to the bookstore on Friday nights after supper, attended travel lectures at the library every other Wednesday, and on Saturday night there was mass and the next day she lazed about with Marmalade and Larry, her cats, and the Sunday paper before taking an afternoon walk.

She still worked at the station, had to, what else could a woman alone in New York do? Rudy was good to her. She worked through the Depression and the War and sent money home to her mother in Boston and even her sister Barbara when her husband was out of work.

At Rudy's radio station, she sang commercials in a trio with her pal Rachel-Jean, a soprano, and Joe, a tenor. They went to parties, they laughed. She didn't miss Henry at all. But one day, Rachel-Jean eloped without a word of goodbye.

Just two weeks before, at a movie together, Rachel-Jean said, "Forget it, we're not serious. He loads trucks. Good for a laugh, that's all."

"You can do better, Rae-Jean. Lots better," Mandy had said.

But in the middle of a love scene, Rachel-Jean whispered, "I hope it's not too late for kids. I really want kids." That was the only clue.

On Monday, there was a new girl in the recording booth. "Hi, I'm Evelyn. Rachel-Jean's replacement. I'm so happy to meet you."

"What, is she *sick* again?" Mandy smirked at Joe.

Evelyn said, "Oh, no, Mandy, I'm so sorry. I thought you knew. She was married on Saturday and they moved to his father's farm on Long Island. Were you friends?"

"Oh, yes, yes. I knew all about it. She told me. She told me she was thinking about it but I, I didn't think she'd go through with it, you know? Wow. Well, I hope it works out for her."

Joe looked at his shoes. He knew Mandy was bluffing. Rachel-Jean had given notice last week because she was eloping with George and it was supposed to be kept secret from Mandy. She was afraid Mandy would try to change her mind, say that George wasn't good enough.

When they began to rehearse, Joe stood beside her as he usually did. She stared out beyond the music stand as if she was trying to see something far away. He rested his hand on her shoulder for just a moment, almost a hug. She nodded, smiled a bit, but didn't turn.

That day she left work early. She'd thought that Rachel-Jean was her friend. That day she began to pull back a little, became a little quieter, and began to think about her life the way it was, not how she hoped it would be. She wasn't a star and would never be a star. She might not even catch a husband, because she was no longer brave enough to flirt.

WEINSTEIN'S PIANO PALACE

Some women become more content with age. They become less concerned with their outward appearance and instead discover a new freedom, even revelry, in intellectual and artistic endeavors. There may be a chug of consciousness, fresh observations and thoughts never noticed or explored. Once a pretty woman is released from her prettiness, she may find herself soaring above the men around her. This happened to Mandy. She was fortunate to have the kind of youthful pretty that glows in the cheeks and glints in the eye. It was the kind of pretty that gives off a beckoning scent to men and even to little boys. Mandy was lucky; she didn't even have to try.

So when that prettiness fades in a woman like Mandy and when she has not done the expected marrying thing, either a quiet confidence grows or she becomes embittered that heads no longer turn. Fortunately, after some difficult lonely years, Mandy had a second wind at forty-five. It happened quite by accident without any thought or planning, as these things often do.

One day, on her lunch hour, Mandy walked by a piano store. Something made her turn back and she found herself looking through the window. She regretted that she had been such a stubborn child, shunning her mother's piano lessons. Ordinarily, she would walk right past. But this particular day, she went in. Perhaps it was the visit the previous weekend to her mother's grave that set her remembering Friday nights around the piano when the neighbors would crowd into their parlor to sing, dance jigs, and drink pails of froth.

Mary Flanagan was crazed, boisterously unladylike, and not apt to pay attention to her embarrassed children while she was wailing Irish ballads and slamming the keys of their old upright. She put on a show, downed pints like a street-walker, and wiped the suds from her lips onto her sleeve. Mandy hated to see her mother act so lowly. Sometimes her mother would open the back of the piano so that the sound was clear and high, sort of a plinkety-plink, honky-tonk sound. Sometimes her dad would sing, "The Maid Who Sold Her Barley" or "The Sign of the Bonny Blue Bell."

But now that they had passed on, her memories softened. She developed a certain humored admiration and fondness for her mother's temperament as her mother and as an en-tertainer in their tiny parlor. And with this understanding she saw that her own need for attention and a career on the stage had probably come from her mother. Why wasn't she more inquisitive about her mother? Why didn't she ask whether she wanted to be a performer, too?

Like most children, Mandy thought of her *only* as a mother, nothing more. And in the many years since her di-vorce from Henry, she visited at Christmas for a day or two when the apartment was so busy with family and friends that they were rarely alone. Why hadn't she chosen to visit at a quieter time? Because Mandy had wanted it that way: she didn't want to be cornered by her mother asking about boyfriends and why she *still* wasn't married. "What is to be-come of you, unmarried and alone in New York? You need a husband, that's all there is to that. You're still good looking. You should try a little harder to accommodate a man."

"Ma, I have a good job and a nice apartment."

"At least you have that. It must be fun on the radio. I wish we could hear you. But you should have more than that, don't you think?"

"I will, Ma. I just haven't found anyone."

"You're too picky, that's what it is, isn't it? Too picky? Worried that they'll walk out on you like–"

"Please, Ma. I don't want to talk about it."

"Yes, you're right, of course. You've done well by yourself and I'm proud of that. Maybe you don't need a man. You're doing swell all by yourself. And I certainly did appreciate your assistance when Pa was let go. We would have been out on the street if not for you wiring us money. Don't think I'm not grateful, Mandy. We are lucky you have a decent job. It's just that, well, I want you to be happy with a family. To have what–"

"I know. That's all you ever talk about. Nothing else."

"I suppose I do. I'm sorry for that. Truly I am."

Weinstein's Piano Palace was just a storefront with a long, cavernous warehouse for every kind of piano. There were rows and rows and rows of black uprights, grands and baby grands, player pianos and a strange, two-keyboard piano with mirrors.

A young orange-haired salesclerk came up to her. " 'Elp you Ma'am?"

"I just decided to look around is all. Sorry to disappoint you. I'm not really going to buy a piano. I just wanted to look, curious really. That's all. I pass this store every day."

"Oh," he said, looking dejected. "Well, this is all we got, just pianos."

"I'll just look around if you don't mind."

"Suit yourself. I'll be in the back if you need me."

"Okay."

Then he shouted from the back, "I don't think you're going to walk off with one!"

"Don't think I will," she replied.

Mandy walked in and out of the rows of pianos. She sat on their benches. She spun their stools. She rested her hands on the keys. She looked inside at the hammers. Inside, the pianos all smelled the same, like musty velvet.

As she was opening a piano bench, someone began to yell from the other end of the huge room. "Honey, go ahead. You can play it. It's all right. These are instruments. You can't tell much by how they look. It's how they sound. Go ahead. Go ahead!"

He was a short, bent-over old man in suspenders, wearing a yarmulke, giving her an order. She was intimidated, so she obeyed and began to play. But she quickly realized that (like her mother) she had to sing and play or she just couldn't play at all. She began timidly, quietly singing in just a whisper an old song.

"I'll be down to get you in a taxi honey. Better be ready 'bout half past eight. Now dearie… " But it just didn't feel right, so she stopped. The keys felt fat and stiff.

"Try another one. Go ahead. Try another one. They don't bite."

She walked down the row of uprights, then sat down quickly as though it were the last seat on a crowded train and started to play again. "I'll be down to get you in a taxi…"

But it just didn't feel right either.

She walked to the end of the row and up the next. She tried another piano. And then another. And then another. And then another. All the while the old man yelled from the back, "That one's got a stuck B flat."

"That one came out of the club down on Broadway, Tuesday it was. The strip joint, remember?"

"That's it. That's it. That one's a nice piano. Yes siree! But it didn't get played much, looks brand new. A pretty piano, collected dust. Not a show-tune piano. Good for church songs. Yeah. Try another. You don't seem like the churchy type, to me. No offense. That's a compliment in my book."

"That piano we found in an 'pahtment in Harlem. I don't know who owned it. They called us to come take it out. Nice springy sound though, don't you think? No bad keys, either. Someone played this a lot. Funny, they left it behind. Nice piano like that. But pianos aren't too portable–that's why we're in business here. Ha, ha! But we don't pick up just *any* piano. We... nice touch you have there, lady, nice touch. Pretty voice, too."

It did sound nice, clear and easy; it moved along, strolling, jazzy-like, tripping and nimble. She sang louder, couldn't help herself. "Tomorrow night at the downtown strutters BA double L-*Ball!*" She surprised herself and slammed the last chord hard with the pedal down just to hear it resonate in waves throughout the big hall.

What a sound! She grinned at the piano. Really nice. Uh-huh. It also had white polka dots all over. She loved it even though it cost $175.

"It's a good buy, a really good buy. I'll give it to you for $150, how's that? By the way, I'm Lenny. This is my place. Ten dollars'll hold it."

"I only have five."

"Five dollars'll hold it."

The next day as Mandy counted out the cash into Lenny's palm, he said, "You know, I may be out of line, honey, but I bet you was in show business in your younger days, am I right?" He caught himself quickly. "Sheesh. Not that you're old now, no, you're just a youngster. Look great. So, am I right?"

She was momentarily taken aback by his observation that she was no longer young but understood his clumsy attempt at flattery. She replied in a silky, coquettish voice, "Why yes, yes, I was in the thee-a-ter."

Lenny's words rushed out as he lovingly folded the bills one-by-one into his wallet. "Ya never lose it. Never do. Maybe your family played? Huh? That it? You ought to put your talent to good work. They're looking for someone to entertain the old people down at the Jewish home. You'd be just right. No pay though. But they'd love ya. Boy, they'd love ya. Show tunes. They like that. All them old songs. I'm just telling ya this but you'd be perfect. Perfect. I do it once in a while myself. We have a reg'lar band down there. Some talented guys join me. They have a nice stage, piano's nice too, you'd like it. People come in from off the street just to hear us. It's all just for fun. Think I play piano? Naw! I play saxophone. Ha! The old folks love it. You oughta come down. You got a good voice, nice and clear. God, we need a singer bad. None of us has any voice at all. You better come down. We need a piano player too, now that Mort died. In fact, I'm not gonna sell you this here piano unless you promise me you'll come down. Now what da ya say, honey? Okay? Okay?"

"I need to practice."

"Okay, practice. Then come."

The piano came on a Saturday through the window. It was quite a time. All the neighbors hung out their windows and children gathered on the fire escapes and the sidewalk below. Lenny waved at her. "See, now I know where you live. So, you gotta practice and then come play." Then he directed, "A little more, a little more. Not so fast, not so fast. This way, this way. Jimmy, wake up, will ya? Okay, bring her in, slow, slow, slow. Down, down, down. Okay, okay! So, where do you want it, lady? Mandy, right?"

She wanted it right there, right there in the middle of the living room. Polka dots and all. As soon as they left, she began to play. And she played it all night. And she played it all the next night and the next night and the next. Pretty soon the neighbors pounded on the walls and poked a broom handle at the ceiling shouting, "It's 11:30 lady! All-right-all-ready. Will ya shut up! Some people gotta work you know! Come on! Give us a break!" But she ignored them. And in time, the downstairs neighbors got used to it, especially when she played "Happy Birthday" for their little boy.

There was just something about music and there was just something about Mandy. Yes, she was one of those people. Music didn't simply resound in her ears and float away. Music became her companion, her buddy. It sat right down in her heart like a good cry taking over all the empty space that a husband and a family were supposed to fill. She hadn't noticed the music in her pretty days. Not really. And so now she was like a passionate mistress, gladly giving in to the piano, longing for each time her hands would set down on the keys. She bought sheet music to all the popular songs and practiced, practiced, practiced.

Two months later, she set out for the Jewish home, worried that Lenny had forgotten his invitation or that she was too amateur and would embarrass herself. But Lenny hadn't forgotten. When he saw her walk in, he stopped right in the middle of a song so that all the old people in the hall turned to stare at her while he yelled, "Oh, my God, my God, you're here, you're here! You had me so worried, lady! I told all the guys about ya–they thought I was making you up! Ha! Geez, you come right up here and sit right down. We were just learning a new tune. Everybody, this is Mandy."

And with that they started right into "Five foot two, eyes of blue" before she had time to be scared. And they did love her, the audience and the band. It was fun. And the best thing about it? She was the youngster, the spark, the glamour.

She fit in because she had a good ear and could harmonize and improvise with ease, just like her mother. Although she was quiet, she wasn't timid and soon grew more confident of her ability. It wasn't long before she developed her own style, one that colored the music, certain chords, certain rhythms. She had a certain *way* that she played. It was not a sophisticated style, not a learned style, but it was delivered, received, easily understood by everyone she played with and those that listened.

Unlike the young Mandy, the middle-aged Mandy avoided the spotlight and declined every opportunity to leave her piano and become the lead vocalist. As a woman, someone was always trying to get her to stand alone at the microphone. But she declined. She was very happy to simply play in the band with her hands busy on the piano keys, singing to herself. Sometimes she sang at the piano. Soon, she met other musicians who invited her to play with them at clubs, Bar Mitzvahs, and parties. And even though there was no one special in Mandy's life, she was having a great time.

It is a fact that musicians, even old musicians, know how to throw a good party. And some might say that it is a fact that sometimes musicians imbibe a little too much.

No matter. She was having fun again.

After a year of playing at the Jewish Home, she began sitting in at a club on Sunday afternoons down in the village where all the young beatniks would go. She wore polka-dot clothes and big earrings. Mandy became known around town as the "woman in red" because she usually wore an exotic feathered red hat and red lace gloves with the fingers cut out (similar to her old *Extravaganza* costume). She was particularly flattered when other women musicians followed her to clubs to ask advice.

She knew that her popularity wasn't due to her musical talent but because she charmed a sympathetic audience. The more-talented musicians were humored by her, never threatened, so she received many invitations but declined most. She was quite a spectacle, often just what a gig needed for appeal, for color and distraction to offset mediocre talent.

And yet there weren't any men that were of romantic interest to her. She was older now, forty-five, and it had been years since she had dated. She was cautious. At gigs, she soon learned that only the elderly men (or the married ones) were flirtatious; no one approached with serious intent. But this suited her just fine. For Mandy was at last content with her life; she had finally succeeded in show business and she was managing just fine. Sure, she wasn't on Broadway. But she had gained respectability and notoriety at the clubs. Even the neighbors inquired where she was playing and whether "her band" was available for a wedding.

No longer was she the "old maid" in 23B.

She was a musician.

Deep down, she had a child-like longing for recognition from friends, family, and even from Henry, yes Henry. She still thought about him. Wondered where he was and whether he was happy.

To her consternation, Lorna and her sister Barbara never visited her in New York. They were always too busy with their families. Once in a while the bellhop she had met years ago wandered in with his wife, bought her drinks, and embarrassed her with his adulation and standing ovations. And even though some years had passed, she fantasized that Bobby would someday stroll in and see her at the piano and exclaim, "Mandy! Where you been hidin'? Why didn't you tell me you were so good?"

But Bobby never did stroll in. New York is a big place.

WHEN IT'S TIME TO GO YOU KNOW

Mandy worked at the radio station singing commercials, acting in skits, and typing. In 1949, Glen their songwriter announced that he was moving to Hollywood to try to make it writing movie music. The problem was, he left the very next day. Although his sudden departure was inconvenient for the station, in show business it was not unusual. People seemed to be yanked out west by a giant golden hook. California was like that. Sudden. And what is show business except taking advantage of an opportunity? On hearing of Glen's departure, Mandy's words were: "Oh that's wonderful for him. I hope he makes it. By the way, has anyone replaced him yet?"

Writing commercials paid a lot more than just singing them. Besides, she was the old lady of the group (an uncomfortable position at that) and her voice just didn't have the same sweet range of her youth. Now that she had gained some notoriety as a musician playing around the city, singing commercials seemed rather silly. Luckily, the station manager had no one ready to take Glen's place so he was inclined to give Mandy a try, even though the songwriters had always been men.

It was "The golden age of radio." Everyone in America listened. Sometimes the commercials Mandy wrote were played on stations in Boston and heard by her old friend Lorna and Barbara, her sister.

One of her most popular commercials was sung on radio stations all over the country for Easy Rise Yeast. It went this way:

My cakes used to be so flat.
My husband was so sad.
But now we use Easy Rise and now they're fluffy and high.
Yes, high, high, high! Oh, now they're fluffy and high!
We use Easy Rise and now they're fluffy and high!
La-ba, dee-dee, dah. La-ba, dee-dee, dah.

Another catchy one she wrote for Suds-a-Plenty laundry detergent boosted sales and became a very popular tune that was parodied in jokes:

Oh, look at that awful stain!
How will you ever get it out?
Why, just use Suds-a-Plenty
and watch the dirt wash out!
Oh, watch the dirt wash out!
Oh, watch that dirt wash out!
Why not save a penny with Suds-a-Plenty
and watch the dirt wash out!

She enjoyed her job and the money was good, especially for a woman. She also had a natural talent for a jingle. She wrote all the station commercials and helped with the scripts for the announcers and their guests.

Over the years, she saved most of her salary from the radio station and had a nice cash income as a performer. But things were changing. The station was changing their format. Again. Writing commercials was out. So in 1956, after two and half decades at the station, they let her know that she needed to move on. No one came right out and said to her, "Mandy you're too old," but they said it very clearly and deliberately just the same.

She had always had the desk by the window with the view of the intersection. There were six desks in the office. One Tuesday, she arrived at work to find that someone had moved her things to the desk in the farthest corner of the room, behind the duplicating machine. Although everyone (except her) knew her things were moved, no one looked up when she walked in. No one cared enough to warn her. They were snickering, eyes darting sideways to each other. So she understood.

They wanted to get rid of good ole Mandy.

Taking off her wet raincoat she demanded, "Who did this? Who moved my things? I've been at the same desk by that window for twenty-five years. Twenty-five years! John. John, who did this?"

John, the only nice one, replied candidly, "Well, I think they wanted to let the new girl have it, Mandy. That's what I heard."

"But why? I earned it. I've been here for over..."

"Twenty-five years. Yes, we know. We *all* know," John said not so nicely.

And there were knowing grins all around.

She was outnumbered and alone. All the good old people were long gone. Joe died three years earlier. That new girl Evelyn that replaced Rachel-Jean had lasted one year.

When she thought about it, she hadn't felt comfortable for a while. She didn't belong anymore. These were kids. They were indifferent. They didn't care. She had no allies left. Things had changed. There was rock and roll and there was television.

People watched the *Tennessee Ernie Ford Show, Queen for a Day,* and *The Milton Berle Show.* Radio programs that featured skits were gone. The radio station was having financial problems; the ratings had slipped badly. Now people listened to radio for popular songs, not stories and talk. Most of the commercials were written by ad agencies. When Rudy died leaving the station to his nephew, the fate of the station was uncertain.

They had an older audience and there were fewer listeners overall, and many were blind. The station manager was nervous. At a meeting, he accused Mandy of having dated and old-fashioned material right in front of the staff. A coworker even dared to call her commercials "frumpy." Was it true? Perhaps. She still wrote songs in a forties style even though it was the fifties.

There was rock and roll with Elvis and Buddy Holly (she liked them both). The world had changed. Now, she wrote scripts only for visiting guests and hardly any commercials. Sometimes there wasn't enough to do. Rather than cut her hours, she convinced the station manager to let her do bookkeeping (which she hated). There was talk of changing the format to rock and roll and sports.

The Friday they moved her desk, she began to think for the first time about leaving her job. It wasn't show business anymore, it was a job, just a job. Why stay? Why stay at all?

And lately, playing in the clubs wasn't much fun either. They made her wait, pushed her aside, made her play alone between sets, not with the band. She felt denigrated. Some nights, she gave up waiting to be invited and just went home. It was discouraging.

The New York music scene was changing to jazz and rock formats and she was stuck in the forties. She had fewer invitations to play. In September, Lenny retired to Florida and the band broke up at the old folks' home.

Two weeks after her desk was moved she was walking home to her apartment at six o'clock on a dreary December evening. It was a Tuesday and it was snowing globs of weighty flakes. An inch of new snow had fallen and there were patches of ice on the sidewalk. She walked between the piles of dirty crystalline snow, along a narrow slippery path carrying groceries, a Christmas present for Jan, her little niece, and on her wrist, her black patent leather pocketbook. (She loved the shape of it). Just as she rounded the corner two blocks from her apartment, she heard him–a man in a plaid jacket. He rushed from behind, yanked hard at her pocketbook, and pulled her down.

She fell hard, hands out front, palms scrapping the ice, chin and right knee banging the sidewalk. She looked up to see him scoop up Jan's present and dash away. Blood trickled from her nose and cut lip. Her stockings were torn. The groceries were spread across the sidewalk and into the street. "Help me! Someone help! I've been robbed!"

But there was no one to hear, no one around to help. She was alone with the steady flakes whirling down, hearing the quiet tingling that icy snow makes as it lands.

How did she let it happen? She heard him but didn't see him–he was too fast.

She worried. Maybe he'll come back. Could be right around the corner of the building looking through her purse right now; he could be in the alley watching. She lay there on the sidewalk, seeing people hurry by at the end of the block, minding their own business, not seeing her because it was a short side street with warehouses, closed stores, and no apartments. That's why she always walked this route, to avoid the crowds. No one would walk by for quite a while; maybe a truck would drive by, see her and stop. Maybe. She imagined her coworkers might be amused if they knew. She wouldn't tell them.

With deliberation, she pushed herself up to her hands and knees, crawled to the street, and heaved up to a stand by embracing a fire hydrant. She left the groceries behind and shuffled with a stiff gait, arms wrapped in front, panting little clouds into the December air. She stared ahead zombie-eyed and thought, "Only two blocks, only two blocks away."

When she rounded the corner to Amsterdam Avenue with her apartment in sight, people slowed to stare and one man shook his head in pity. No one stopped to ask if she was all right. They let her stagger by.

What a mean world. Who do they think I am? Damn them! Damn them!

Finally, she was home. Holding tight to the rod-iron banister, she pulled herself up the front stairs of her brownstone. At the door, she found the spare keys in the iced crack of the stoop and let herself in. She nearly tripped over the cats on her way to the sofa.

They leapt up, crouched around her, waiting for her to reach out.

She told them, "I'm alright. Just shaken up. I'm alright. I just need to rest."

Hours later, she took a very long, very hot bath while staring at the ceiling swirls, listening to the faucet drip and thought about how very quiet her apartment was, how she had no one nearby to call, and about how solitary her life had become.

She went to bed and fell asleep making plans to leave the city.

THREE

WALLINGFORD, CONNECTICUT

Mandy sat at the kitchen table listening to the house after the slam of the front door. The movers had just left and at last she was alone in her own house. She told her brother Ned, "Find me a nice little house in a nice little neighborhood, then call me." The real estate agents had to be patient as his words were delivered one by one. "Well, is it... in good... shape? Toilet... flush and... all? She can't be bothered... with a fixer-upper. My sister was... an entertainer... you know. She'll be... paying cash." The last part caught their attention.

Ned was delighted with his assignment. His favorite sister would live nearby. Almost a year had passed since his retirement and he was very lonely. He missed working. Missed the machines, the smells, his place on the factory floor and knowing they needed him and respected his skill, that everyone had a job to do, his lunch buddies, and even the Christmas party. The company was sold and the new owners contracted out the machine shop. The labor department said he could learn something new, but he didn't want to work anywhere else or learn anything new. That was it. He took his lunch box and went home. He didn't belong to any clubs, kept to himself pretty much. So when Mandy called he could hardly contain himself.

He bought a map and put a red dot on every street where there was a house for sale and then drove by. If it looked like a "nice little house," he made an appointment to go inside. Ned didn't smile at the realtors, scrutinized everything, raised an eyebrow, and pointed a bony blaming finger at them if something seemed amiss. He flushed the toilets, ran the faucets, turned on the lights, opened and closed the cabinets, inspected the furnaces, and commented in his painfully slow voice in every basement he visited, "Must've... flooded... here... couple a... times...eh?"

After two weeks, there were three finalists for Mandy to see. She chose the three-bedroom ranch-style house with a one-third acre lot located near the center of town in Wallingford. "I can walk to the library." She still had her cats, her piano, the box of old letters that Henry had written, and her scrapbook of performances.

She settled in. On Sundays, Ned took her to the Episcopal church. He waited in the car reading the paper. "No need... to go... in. Got nothing... to feel... guilty... about. You do... I guess," he joked. She joined the choir but never played the piano in public again. "My hands just don't move that well anymore," she told Ned. "Arthritis, I think." She made dinner for Ned on Tuesdays and afterward he insisted that she play something. "Just a... little... tune... to help... everything... go down." He was never happier.

On Thursdays, Ned took her grocery shopping. Within a few weeks, everyone knew Mandy at the grocery store. It was her stage. She pretended to be a cranky old lady. She still enjoyed the stage (age hadn't changed that) and they never caught on to her. No one suspected that it was an act.

Ned enjoyed the game. She smirked and passed conspiring glances at him, her accomplice as he pushed the cart through the store and spoke only once to correct a misconception. "I'm not... her husband. I'm... her... brother."

Her intention was just to create a little scene, something to laugh about later, nothing serious. "Young man, young man, now why would I buy such a *green* banana? It'll take weeks to ripen. Ned, look at this zucchini, it's mushy, see? And this cantaloupe has white fuzz on it. Young man, don't you have anything better in the back that's fresh? We followed a big truck in here. I wonder if you could go look through some of those boxes for me? Find me a nice bunch of bananas, will you? The produce at every little market in the City is better than this. Go look. The customer is always right. Right? This coupon was good yesterday, why can't it be good today? What difference does it make? This is a gigantic store. Is one little, itsy-bitsy coupon going to upset the apple cart?"

"Tsk! Give that poor woman a break. Who cares if she has twelve items? She's already placed them on the counter. We don't mind waiting for her to check out all fifty of her items. I don't have anywhere to go. Do you? Well, then, let her check out. See, no one cares."

"Here, I've got an extra five. Take it, take it. They'll never let you out of here if you don't pay up. Don't be embarrassed. When someone offers you something you need, take it. I wouldn't offer it to you if I didn't want to do it. Besides, this place gets all my money every week. So, what's another few dollars? Someday you help someone. That's the way it works."

"She's not an animal! She's my little *chat*, Miss Purrfect. See? She's quite content to rest on this pillow like the queen of Sheba. You didn't mean to walk on the chicken, did you? Isn't she something? Found her in a bag on the sidewalk on Park Avenue. She'll be good now. Won't you honey? Sorry, she's very fussy. Next week I'll bring my other little sweetheart."

Soon, they inquired politely, "How are you doing today, Miss Flanagan?" but snickered behind her back. The cashiers rolled their eyes when she insisted on getting her change counted the old way or paid using a hundred pennies.

But Mandy brought them together. The store employ-ees enjoyed telling stories about her. She was just what they needed–made the place lively. Everyone else was a docile shopper. It became a tradition to send her a Christmas card signed by all the employees. "We value your service. You are one of our very *special* customers," it read.

Sometimes Mandy took a bus to New Haven for the day. Ned always offered to drive but she wanted to go by herself. When he knew that she was going to New Haven, he fol-lowed the bus, and parked nearby wherever she went. Why did he follow her? He had nothing better to do. Maybe she might need him. The bus might break down.

It surprised her that after almost forty years the New Haven Green had hardly changed at all. Maybe it wouldn't change in the next fifty years or even one hundred years. Maybe it looked the same as it had one hundred years ago.

She liked to walk around downtown. Sometimes she went to Horowitz's, the fabric store, to touch the bolts of fabric and imagine the costume it would make or to Goldie Libro music store to buy sheet music or records. Sometimes she went to Liggetts, the drug store for silly little things, band aids, and aspirin.

And yet she always ended the day sitting on one particu-lar park bench. That's really why she moved to Connecticut. It was the bench, the same bench where she sat waiting for Henry to show after their divorce decades ago. And even though she was an old lady now, she still liked to pretend that he was there, rounding the corner out of sight, hurry-ing across the green toward her, coming back.

SUMMERS WITH AUNT MANDY

To escape the hot pavement summers of Somerville, Jan visited her Aunt Mandy in Connecticut for the month of July. She went every summer from the time she was six years old until her early teens for a few weeks of suburban sunshine.

Years later, Jan's parents wondered if the visits to Aunt Mandy had somehow influenced Jan to become "different," but then again, maybe it was Uncle Mike's genes that were to blame. He was the priest, and before that he was something else.

Aunt Mandy and Jan shared secrets and had a lot of fun making Coke floats. Jan made friends with the neighborhood kids and Aunt Mandy bought her a blue bike with red streamers that she rode in the town parade on July 4th. They put baseball cards held by clothespins on the spokes and it made a cool "flap, flap, flap" noise. Jan frayed her cutoffs like the other kids and wore a Huck Finn straw hat and she ran through the sprinkler to cool off. Aunt Mandy played the piano and she sang. They played war and gin rummy, watched television until they fell asleep on the couch.

Aunt Mandy took her to the movies on the weekend. They rode the city bus to New Haven, had ice cream sundaes at Kresge's and pizza in Wooster Square. Uncle Ned bought a blow-up pool and made newspaper hats. Jan was always impressed that her aunt knew the bus driver, the ticket sellers, and the waitresses by name. She told Jan it never hurt to be friendly. It just might help. Might just get you an extra scoop of ice cream or a ride right to your door on a rainy day.

Jan always arrived from Somerville by train. The New Haven train station was very busy and had the highest ceiling Jan had ever seen with long wooden benches always filled so that many people had to sit on their suitcases while the announcer said words like "Holyyoke" and "Grandah Centrahl New Yawk" and "Greensfahm" and "Leavvinga on-a tracka fivva" and "Onatima from Baston" and everyone looked up at the big long board that flipped around and said where to go and what was "On Time" and what was "Delayed." when she had to leave Aunt Mandy always bought her *Archie* and *Little Lotta* and *Dot* and *Richie Rich* and a Coke and potato chips and a tuna fish sandwich and told the conductor to watch out for her and told Jan, "Now don't you forget to write me, young lady," and Jan sat by the window and waved and waved until she couldn't see Aunt Mandy crying and waving anymore.

One summer, a man came visiting Aunt Mandy. Jan wrote home and said the man was very nice and took them to the zoo. He was a nice, big, colored man named "Bobby," she wrote, and he was very good at checkers.

Bobby showed up one day out of the blue. He was older and dressed in a suit; Mandy hardly recognized the young musician from years ago. But she had read about him, his success owning a chain of drug stores. She kept the article and when she moved to Connecticut, sent a card to him at the main store, giving her new address and nothing more.

"Hi, Mandy. Can I come in?"

"Bobby?"

"Yes, it's me. I just want to talk."

And talk they did. He was unhappily separated from his wife and needed advice and a few days to think things over. Jan was visiting and very curious. She had never spoken to a Negro before. Mandy worried about what Jan would think and she knew that her sister wouldn't approve.

Oddly, Jan and Bobby hit it off. Yes, it started with checkers, but it went beyond that. Just something about the both of them at that particular time in their lives. No explanation was needed. He knew who Jan was at twelve before she knew herself and she saw right through him, that he felt defeated in the eyes of his wife.

Mandy listened to them. She played piano, they stopped playing checkers and sang. Mandy made spaghetti and meatballs. They had ice cream sundaes.

Meanwhile, a neighbor had called the police to report that a Negro was seen entering Mandy Flanagan's house. Two policemen knocked on her door to check things out.

"Hello, Miss Flanagan. We had a report from a neighbor that you have an unusual visitor. Is everything okay here?"

"You mean my niece Jan? Or do you mean my friend Bobby?"

"You understand I'm just following up on the concern of a neighbor, that's all."

Bobby stepped up. "I can go, Mandy. I don't want to imperil your reputation."

"Nonsense! You tell that busybody down the street that I am perfectly fine. My visitor is a wealthy business owner from New York and he will be staying here a few days."

"That's all I need to know. If you need any assistance, any at all, just call us. We patrol this neighborhood every day. It's just that he is, you know, unusual for this neighborhood."

"Tell her he's not moving into the neighborhood. He's just visiting."

"We just wanted to be sure that–"

"I understand, Officer. Thank you and goodbye."

After the policemen left, Jan asked, "Why were they here? Are they afraid of Bobby? Is it 'cause he's a Negro?

That stinks." She turned to Bobby, "How do you deal with that?"

"I play checkers."

Two days later, Angeline, Bobby's wife, appeared at the door.

"He's here, isn't he?"

"Yes. Playing checkers. You want to talk to him?"

"No, actually, I want to talk to you."

"Me?"

"Yes."

"Okay."

Jan appeared behind Mandy.

"Who's that?"

"My niece, Jan. She's visiting."

"Hello, Jan."

Bobby came from the bathroom. "Angeline? How'd you find me?"

"Wasn't too hard. Said you were visiting a friend in Connecticut. She's the only one we get a Christmas card from in Connecticut."

"Angeline, I just need to take a little break. I don't mean nothing by it. Just a—"

"Never mind with that. I want to speak with Mandy. Alone."

"Well, she's not to blame. We didn't do anything for you to worry about. "

"I know that."

"Jan, why don't you play a game or two of checkers with Bobby so we can have a private talk, okay?"

"What about?"

"Now, Jan, be a good girl and play checkers."

"Okay."

Angeline and Mandy sat outside on the new double swing in the backyard while Jan and Bobby played checkers at the kitchen table.

"What do you think they're talking about?" asked Jan.

"I don't know. Really, I don't. Sure wish I did."

"Do you have any kids?"

"No. Why do you ask?"

"Just wondered, that's all."

"Oh."

"Let's get started."

Outside, the fireflies were beginning to wink in the night when Angeline got right into it.

"We can't have children. We've tried for years, but now I'm too old. He told me about you. Did you have a baby with Bobby?"

"Why are you asking?"

"Well, that answers my question," Angeline said. "You did get pregnant by him, didn't you? It would have been a brown baby, so I'm not gonna ask what happened back then. So that's my answer."

"It wasn't meant to be."

"I was thinking it's me that's the problem, not getting pregnant. He always says he doesn't care."

"But you still want children."

"I'm too old," said Angeline.

"Too old for what?" Mandy asked. "Do you want to be a parent, or do you need to be pregnant? Which is it?"

"Well, I know what you're getting at but there's more to it than that."

"Is there? Why not adopt or be a foster parent?"

"He won't do it."

Mandy looked off into the distance. "Then you do it. Just get started. He'll come around."

"I don't know, really? I'm not too old?"

"You're a lot younger than me. Forty-five, maybe?"

"Forty-six," Angeline replied.

"Well, just do it. What do you have to lose?"

"I don't know, I always—"

"Why wait? Have a few. He'll come around."

"Really? Think so?"

"Yes."

"Bobby never knew, did he?"

"Me? No, I don't think so. It was a long time ago. I wanted to keep it but ..."

"You couldn't keep it. Wrong color."

"No, I lost the baby anyway. Never told anyone."

"I understand."

"How did you guess?" Mandy asked.

"He said you broke up and he never knew why. Seemed likely to me. "

"Is that when he met you?"

"No, that was when he started the pharmacy. The girls were all over him."

"How'd you meet?"

"Waited it out. Had a toothache one night. Went to the store. He was very nice."

"I bet."

They laughed, then listened to the shouts of children playing hide-and-seek down the block until Mandy said, "We better go in, bugs are coming out."

Bobby and Angeline were just driving away when Barbara and Anthony showed up at the door. "Mandy, I'm taking Jan home. I don't approve of the company you're keeping."

Jan was twelve. She never forgave her mother.

HOW JAN BECAME HERSELF

One of the first signs was that Jan wasn't inclined to play with dolls the way other little girls played with dolls. One day, she gave all her dolls crew cuts. Her mother Barbara told her, "Jan, honey. You shouldn't have done that to your dollies. Now you can't put pretty little ribbons or barrettes in their hair. Now you can't comb their hair."

Jan replied, "Oh, it's too much work. The dollies don't like to wear barrettes or ribbons. They like it short."

Barbara expected that in time Jan would realize what she'd done to her dolls, but she never did. After all, it wasn't unusual for a little girl to cut her dolls' hair expecting that it would grow back. But Jan was unconcerned. Whenever she received a new doll, it got a haircut, too. To her mother's consternation, Jan's father referred to her dolls as "The Marines" and then gave her some miniature army trucks and guns. Jan loved them. Her father played war with her while her mother seethed. He'd say to Barbara, "Hey, it doesn't matter! She's just playing. Leave her alone." But Barbara was worried and was quite annoyed that her husband seemed to be encouraging Jan away from frilly things.

For a time, Jan played with the other little girls in the neighborhood. But she grew bored and began to follow the boys around. They let her join their baseball games but only because they were short a player or needed someone in the outfield. Jan had a good arm and a good eye. Her father practiced with her and it was soon apparent that she was a better ball player than her brother Tommy would ever be. And she could hit. Now the boys invited her to play because whoever was on her team usually won.

In time, the boys disappeared into Little League where girls weren't allowed. Jan joined the Girl Scouts but dropped out because all they did was sew, not camp. She read a lot. She was a good student. In high school she excelled in sports, particularly field hockey. She went to the Junior Prom and the Senior Prom with the same shy boy. She liked him. Her mother loved him. Jan kissed him and he felt her up. They didn't do it but almost. He was drafted, went to Vietnam and came home an amputee. Years later, she visited him in the veterans hospital. She told him everything before she knew it herself. He was a good listener. He understood. They stayed friends.

She went to college, dated, but remained a virgin long after all the other girls had done it many, many times. She and her roommate became really close, especially during thunderstorms. Her roommate was a virgin, too. Jan still didn't think of herself as anything but a normal college student who liked boys.

But if she liked boys, why hadn't she had intercourse with one? At first, Jan didn't like the idea of a penis inside her. This thought hadn't changed much since she had attended the health movie on menstruation and discussed the facts of life with her mother in sixth grade. A penis might be dirty. Was it her Catholic upbringing? No. Most of the good Catholic girls she knew were really good at being bad. So that wasn't it.

A few years later in college, after hearing her friends talk about their exploits, Jan decided it might not feel so awful if she got used to it. Maybe she'd try it, just once. He'd have to wear a condom, though, that's for sure. But somehow, although she'd agreed to it in principle, in reality, she was never attracted to any guy long enough to make it happen.

There was Jeremy with the soft brown eyes. He lived in the dorm and they became friends staying up all night talking, drinking. One night she asked him to sleep with her to "you know, just get it over it." But he confessed that he was gay and had always figured that she was, too. He wasn't interested in sex, not with her anyway. Maybe later. You know, just to see what it was like.

In her junior year in college, she realized with certainty that thinking about sex with a man just didn't thrill her. Maybe it never would. Why bother having sex with a man just to have sex with a man when she really didn't want to? Maybe she wanted to stay a virgin, stay pure forever. She thought about being a nun for about five minutes.

By her senior year in college, she realized that it wasn't so much the purity issue or that she didn't want to have sex with a man.

They got up so damn early; it was always drizzling and cold and they had to beat the boys to the river. But once inside the shell with the feel of the wood, the oar in her hands, the smell of the oily water with all the girls pulling together, the rhythm took over. She didn't think. They pulled the water, they moved out. Sometimes she just listened to the delicate tinkling sound of the droplets falling from their oars as they skimmed the surface. She pulled back to dip down again and lean back into the smooth, luscious water. Pull, raise, pull, raise. "You're quiet today," said Karen with the glasses and dimples. Karen who hung out in her room, who borrowed her sweatshirt, who gave her a long hug at 3:00 last night. Karen with the big calves and the small breasts. Karen. Jan smiled and nearly broke rhythm. She knew. Knew that she wanted to kiss her, hold her, lie beside her, touch her. She knew. She knew.

And she was glad.

THE BAD KID AND THE SAD YEAR

The stuff in the yard and the excessive makeup began after Jan's last summer visit to her aunt when she was fourteen. It was Halloween. No one quite knew for sure how it started, but the rumor began that Mandy was a witch. A neighborhood kid told his mother that Mandy had put a razor blade in an apple she had given him. Of course it wasn't true. Mandy didn't give out apples; she always gave out Good & Plenty, year after year, Good & Plenty. Two men in two police cars came. They parked in front of the house and left the lights flashing for all the neighbors to see and wonder.

"We need to ask you a few questions. There's been a complaint."

"Complaint?"

"Where do you keep your razor blades?"

She was taken aback. "Why would you me ask that? What's wrong? What's happened?"

"We just need to know."

They continued with their questions for one hour. Finally, they said it. "Mrs. Summers says you gave her son an apple with a razor blade in it."

Mandy was horrified. The tears rolled. She sat motionless. She couldn't talk. One cop spoke, "We're sorry. We have to investigate these things. That woman complains about everything. Her son is out of school more than he's in. Look, we're not going to charge you with anything."

They tried but could not comfort her and they were still talking as they backed out the door, apologizing and leaving her still sitting on the couch crying.

She was so deeply hurt that such a thing could be suspected of her that it colored all of her daily moments. Nothing cheered her. Ned told her, "Cops... shouldn't have... scared you... like that... they know... those... kids... are lyin.'"

Many nights her pillow was wet with the anguish of the night and the bright loneliness of the day was too much for her. She even stopped playing the polka dot piano.

The neighborhood kids began to ring the doorbell and run away. They'd phone and say, "Witch, witch, come scratch my itch!" and hang up. They would stare through the windows and throw tomatoes and eggs at the front door. She was afraid to go to the mailbox. When she went outside, even the silly parents would yank their kids indoors.

That year, Mandy went to visit her sister Barbara in Somerville for Thanksgiving and stayed until long after Christmas. Barbara told the family that they needed to be "extra nice" to Aunt Mandy because she was so sad. In January, after Barbara's husband Anthony had to fish Mandy's teeth from the toilet piping for the second time, he sternly told Mandy that she had to go home to Connecticut and "face the music."

In a now famous family story, Barbara was so angered by Anthony's insensitivity to her sister that she threw the full sugar bowl at him that broke on the wall behind him, sugar everywhere. She marched out of the house, staying out all night long. To this day, no one knows for sure where she went. Her son Tommy, just seven years old, ran bawling to the neighbors and asked to be adopted. Jan ran to her room and sat in the closet.

When Mandy finally did return to her house in Connecticut, it was strangely quiet. Something had happened. She learned that the boy who had accused her of the razor blade apple had accidentally killed himself with his father's gun while playing soldiers with another neighborhood boy in their basement rec room.

The following spring, the lawn ornaments began to appear. Mandy figured that if she put cute little animals in the yard, the neighborhood children might like her again. But for some reason, she kept adding more. Ned helped. He wanted to cheer her. Bag ducks. Peeing boys. Windmills. A glass pond. Baskets with plastic flowers. Wind chimes. Santa on the house and a giant blue star on the garage. Within a year, her yard had become a menagerie. The neighbors no longer thought that she was a witch. They thought she was crazy.

WHERE BARBARA WENT
THE NIGHT SHE RAN AWAY

After she threw the sugar bowl at her husband for being so mean to her sister Mandy, Barbara was so crazy angry that she had no plan whatsoever but grabbed her pocketbook and her coat from the hall closet and off she went. She was captive to the thoughts in her head that ran round and round. *That man! Why did I marry that man? Why, why, why? It was the stupidest thing I ever did. Insensitive boob! Why did I marry that man? Why, why, why?*

She got to Davis Square, saw a poster and boarded the subway for downtown Boston, changed trains and headed to the Boston Garden arena. It was a Saturday night.

Barbara was a tall woman. She was somewhat gawky in her movement. She leaned forward at the waist and marched with bent elbows and clenched fists—a determined sight. Her red hair flipped up on her shoulders. Long bangs hung over her black frame glasses. She fumbled in her bag for her red lipstick, a necessity whenever she went out anywhere.

There was a crowd ahead and the sign on the marquee of the arena read, "Circus Tonight!" She bought a ticket and went in.

Even though the show had just started, she had the best seat imaginable. There was a single seat in the first row, right smack in front of the center ring, not twenty feet from the ringmaster. He was grand and there was so much to see.

She bought popcorn and began to forget her troubles. The band played Sousa songs and the spotlights swirled around the arena in anticipation.

Elephants ran out in a line ridden by women in scant glittering leotards and feather plume hats. One by one they stood and placed their front feet on the backside of the elephant in front of them to form an impressive pachyderm circle around the ring. She wondered if the elephants tired of running in circles. Were they always circus animals or did they remember the open savanna? There was the lion tamer. He poked a chair at the lions while they sat on pedestals. There were trapeze artists and the famous high wire aerialists "The Flying Wallendas." And there were the clowns.

Toward the end of the show, two clowns rounded the center ring on a tiny fire engine. They threw buckets of confetti at the crowd and then stopped in front of Barbara and sprayed seltzer at each other. One of the clowns ducked so that the fizzy water hit Barbara straight on in the face with a long hard spray, drenching her face and blouse. The crowd pointed and laughed at her. The clown cupped his hand over his mouth with an exaggerated expression of concern then disappeared behind a curtain near the orchestra.

She found a handkerchief in her bag and wiped herself off, but it wasn't much help. People in the audience still pointed at her in amusement. Hearing the crowd murmur she stood up and turned to the bleachers behind her and then bowed to the crowd. People applauded. It was as if Barbara were someone else and not just "Anthony's wife," not just a mother. Normally, she would have maintained her stern composure. Normally, she wouldn't run away to a circus. But tonight it was okay to be funny.

The announcer said, "Thank you ladies and gentleman. You've been a great audience! We invite you to come back and see us again next time we're in town. Good night." As

Barbara was putting on her coat to leave, a tall, thin man with droopy eyes approached her.

"We're just so sorry, ma'am, that we seemed to get you straight on! It wasn't part of the act, believe me. I sure hope we didn't do any damage."

It took Barbara a moment to understand his meaning. "You mean the water? Oh, it's okay, no harm done really. I mean, I really enjoyed myself. It was very entertaining. Well, maybe not the shower but the other stuff. Which one were you: the one on the fire engine or the one that got me wet?"

"I'm afraid I'm guilty as charged! Look, why don't you come back behind the stage and my wife will dry you off. Good coffee, you know."

Although she knew she should say a polite, "No thank you," and leave, she just didn't want to go home yet. He seemed nice enough, why not? Anyway, Barbara had always been curious about the circus people. Yes, it would be an adventure.

He led her to the women's dressing room where there were a dozen women changing from costumes to street clothes. Barbara was introduced to the clown's wife, Sheila, who sat before the long mirror removing makeup. She was also a clown.

Glittering costumes, false eyelashes, wigs, and make-up were everywhere. Barbara removed her blouse and was given a blue satin robe with silver glitter writing that said, "The Greatest Show on Earth." The clown wife Sheila spoke of moving and crowds and good Italian restaurants and how the ring master was a jerk and the third one in a year and how they don't buy much because it wouldn't fit in the trailer but they ship it all home to Florida where they have a real house with a pool and how her nose was sore because the fake nose bothered her real nose and did she have any kids and why was she here alone.

So, Barbara told her how she had run away because her husband was an insensitive boob. The clown's wife Sheila said that her clown husband was lots of laughs but that he was an insensitive boob, too, and that it was hard to run away from a circus when most people run away *to* a circus. This was a familiar laugh among them.

After a while, there were just five women left talking in a cinder block dressing room in the arena. There were a couple of clowns, an elephant rider, a trapeze artist, and another one she didn't recognize. Of course, they sat around and talked about men.

Barbara couldn't get over how they just accepted her right off. They asked how many children she had and what they looked like, what her house looked like, what her husband did and on and on—not just to be polite, but because they really wanted to know. Barbara was surprised that they wanted to know about her ordinary life.

And they spoke about men in the most intimate way. They talked about how kissing was important and it made all the difference as you got older. How sometimes men have this smell that is not sweat and hair and semen but something else more basic and characteristic, sort of like lions or tigers, but not animal, no, not animal, but earthen and testicles and cracks and the way they walk because of it and does your man put it on the left or the right and how must that feel and they really should wear skirts, it doesn't make sense it's so delicate, did you ever accidentally hit him there and what does that feel like, not so good probably, ha-ha, and there's really no comparison, aren't we lucky, and women's' bodies are more beautiful anyway, don't you agree?

But it grew late.

Finally, the clown wife Sheila asked Barbara when she was going to go home. Barbara replied, "I really don't want to go home."

So the clown wife Sheila said she could stay in their trailer. But Barbara dared to ask a silly thing: "Can I sleep with the elephants?"

"You want to do what?"

"Sleep with the elephants. You know, outside, near them."

"Well, you can't sleep real near them, they might mess all over you or back into you by mistake. But you can probably sleep outside nearby. I can ask George."

George didn't seem to mind, said "sure" very nonchalantly, as though it were a perfectly reasonable request that everyone makes. And the clown wife Sheila didn't ask why either.

So Barbara slept on her coat on the straw wrapped in a blanket between the elephants and the trailers parked in the driveway behind the arena. It was a warm night in May.

Barbara was very happy with herself. It was a clear sky. The elephants wrapped their wrinkled trunks around the straw and stuffed it into their mouths, flapping their ears as they eyed her warily with their little tiny eyes. Except for some snorting and the rustling in the hay, it was quiet and still and she soon fell into a deep sleep.

She dreamt of hanging towels and underwear and shirts on the clothesline in the backyard on a windy day. But the wind was blowing sugar all over the clothes. She flew up over the house and over the neighborhood with arms outstretched. And when she looked down, she saw her daughter Jan hanging a rabbit by its ears on the clothesline.

In the morning she had coffee with the clown family. She braided the hair of the trapeze artist. They talked about men some more and about shaving, beards, full beards, goatees, handle bar mustaches, and Hitler. That ended the conversation and she decided to go home.

Barbara's poor, insensitive boob of a husband walked the streets of the neighborhood until dawn. Anthony fell asleep on the front steps for all the neighbors to see, waiting for her to come home.

Barbara arrived at noon with eclairs from the bakery downtown. As she walked down the street, she was happily singing over and over, "It ain't gonna rain no more, no more. It ain't gonna rain no more. How in the heck can I wash my neck if it ain't gonna rain no more." She had some straw stuck to her coat and smelled a little peculiar but was otherwise still quite normal.

THE DAY TERRI MET AUNT MANDY

They had been seeing each other for about month. Their relationship was still fragile and uncertain when Jan invited Terri to go to church with her on Palm Sunday. They were starting to exchange polite friendly kisses, ones that brushed the lips and demonstrated that neither had yet built up the confidence to linger longer in passion. After the church service, they planned to have dinner with Aunt Mandy in Wallingford.

Terri was twenty-eight, recently divorced, and determined to be "more fun"—the words her ex-hubby said as he left her a few months before their divorce. She lived alone in a small, cluttered condominium in Branford. Sometimes she could smell the salty breeze and the wet sand from the town beach down the street. One day, standing before the bathroom mirror, she gathered her tangled mass of frizzy black curls hair into a ponytail and cut it off. Now she had a short bob. She was bored with her life, bored with herself.

Jan was twenty-three and lived in a funky apartment in a house on a busy street in Worcester Square in New Haven, the Italian neighborhood. Her house was identical to the sad looking funeral home next door and it was a block from the Italian bakery, the corner calzone restaurant, and the mom-and-pop grocery store. The apartment wiring was so outdated that she couldn't use her hair dryer and the toaster oven at the same time or it would blow out half the power in the house, including the other two apartments. The land-lord had wired it himself.

Jan's thin brown hair was usually tucked under a red baseball cap or it fell straight to her shoulders, parted plainly in the middle, bangs hanging in her eyes, ears pro-truding. She had freckles everywhere, a space in the mid-dle of her front teeth, and sideways eyeteeth. Not pretty in the conventional sense, yet she had an endearing smile that beamed like a disarming weapon of sweetness and sincerity on everyone from the mechanic to the ticketing cop. She seemed to be such a *nice* girl, everyone's sister but no one's girlfriend. Perhaps it was because she was a little chunky, a little square, a little short, and always wore a watch with a brown leather band and a belt. Her collared shirts were always neatly tucked into khaki pants. She wore loafers or jogging sneakers. She had big hands.

"My family is pretty close," Jan announced to Terri as the car door slammed.

"Do they know—I mean, are you out?" asked Terri indelicately.

"Oh, yeah. That's not a big deal anymore. My mother said that out of all the kids, cousins and all, they expected that one of us had to be different. Even when I was kid, my par-ents said that I probably had Uncle Mike's genes."

"Uncle Mike?"

"He's a priest."

"Oh."

On most Sundays, Jan came to Wallingford to drive Aunt Mandy to church and then she'd stay for afternoon dinner. They'd discuss the sermon and politics and enjoyed reciting all the oddities that made their family a family. When the Sunday crossword was done, usually around dusk, Jan went home to her New Haven apartment.

"Aunt Mandy's a pip. I don't know why she bothers to go to church. She doesn't believe in any of it. She's always so critical of the service. But sometimes that guy in front hits you with a zinger, and we look at each other and say, 'oh wow, we gotta talk about that.' You know, why are we here, what is our purpose, how did it all begin, who was Jesus. You know, the really big stuff. But she tries to avoid the minister's handshake going out the door, where he cups your hand and says, 'And how are you getting along, Miss Flanagan?' She hates that, makes her feel old."

"Why do you go then?"

"Oh, he's a good guy and little dorky and we really like the ceremony. You know, the robes, the songs, the pageantry of it all. It's really cool, don't you think?"

Terri didn't know what to say. She never thought about whether she liked church or not. You had to go, that was all there was to it. Church was just something you did every Sunday, a habit. When she didn't go, she felt as though she'd skipped school. "No. I like a simple service. No finger pointing, no incense, and no doctrine."

"No, da-da-da-doctrine, huh? What are you, a useless *Unitarian*? Ha! I heard about them. Me? I like it when he slaps the pulpit; well, that just *really* turns me on."

"It does?"

Of course Jan was just teasing Terri. She did that quite a bit. Terri was gullible.

On this particular Sunday, Aunt Mandy decided to stay home to cook a nice dinner since Jan was bringing Terri to dinner. It was a special day. But Jan was supposed to stay alert at church so she could update Aunt Mandy about the sermon and all the goings-on.

They arrived five minutes late and so they had to sit in the folding chairs way in the back, near the lobby. "They're Catholic outcasts. Had a falling out centuries ago. The

203

Episcopal Church pretends to be Protestant, but they're really just Catholics that are too poor for incense."

"What?"

"Never mind. Just fooling with you."

Terri agreed that the stained glass windows were awesome. When the service was over, they waited until the minister was surrounded by elderly parishioners so they could slip out the door and avoid the handshake that Aunt Mandy dreaded so much. But somehow Reverend Shuttan noticed them dashing away and waved his hand in the air in a jolly gesture as though they were twenty rows up at Fenway.

"Geez, how did he see us?" asked Jan unlocking the car door. "I lost ten points on that."

"What difference does it make whether he sees you or not? You didn't have to shake hands, right?"

"Oh, I don't know. It's just something my aunt and me try to avoid, that's all. We like to feel like we got away. That religion and Christ didn't get us and that we still need to be saved."

"Saved from the minister?"

"No, actually he's all right. It's all the *stuff* that goes along with the Jesus and God thing."

"Jan, I still don't get it. Why do you go to church if you don't like it?"

"Told you. We do like it. We don't like some parts of it. We're trying to get it. I wish I did get it. Really. If I believed in that stuff my life would be so simple, so easy. But I think too much, so life is a challenge. I always have to make the decisions, be in charge, and that's too much work. "

"Okay. Well then, why not just believe in God and Jesus? Why not just—"

"Terri, just let it go. I can't explain it to you so easily 'cause I can't explain it to myself and I'm not going to try now."

"Okay."

"And you didn't say what you believe."

"Me? I don't know. Haven't thought about it."

"Haven't thought about it? I take this stuff very seriously, you know?"

"Okay."

"Hey, maybe I'll be a nun someday."

"You?"

"Never know. I like hanging out with women."

"I noticed. But there's a bit more to it than that."

It was April and as they left the church parking lot, it was clear and windy. Everything seemed vibrant and full of cartoon colors. The sun was a yellow against a chrome-blue sky, the clouds formed animal shapes, faces, and heavenly puffery that stretched and smeared.

Jan drove an old turquoise Oldsmobile with fins and whitewalls, a classic. The steering wheel was made of clear plastic with little blue specs floating in it. Those silly foam, dingle-ball dice hung from the mirror over the dash. With an all-white interior, it was a fun car for frolicking. They were intoxicated with the day, each other, and that boat-of-a-car sailed.

Soon after they left the church, they were driving down the highway and Jan shouted to a blue Chevy going very slowly, "Fucking asshole! Stay on your side! What a jerk! Get off the fuckin' road, pervert!" She palmed the horn, "Ehhhh! Ehhhh!"

As they drove alongside the car, Terri saw that it was being driven by a little old man who gripped the steering wheel with both hands. He turned to glare at Terri.

She was mortified. "What did you do that for? It was just an old man!"

"He shouldn't be on the road, gonna kill someone."

Terri stewed.

To change her mood, Jan drove faster and moved from lane to lane, looking over her shoulder each time to be sure the car would fit. When there was no traffic, for a laugh, she hung her left foot out the window and made the car swerve back and forth across the lanes all the while grinning and glancing from the road to Terri to see if she could rile her. And finally, Terri had to relent, yelling, "All right, all right, all right!"

Jan slowed the car and moved into the right lane.

"Jan. Now bring the foot in, *please*."

Jan had won Terri over and the old man was forgotten.

It was such a spectacular car that people pointed, smiled, and waved.

Terri enjoyed the ride. The window was down, she rested her hand on the butterfly window so that her elbow could hang outside the car, her hair fluttered in the wind, and she wore sunglasses.

Everything was just right, the essence of cool.

A half-hour later Jan pulled off the highway to Wallingford. Soon there were white, pink, and blue split-level houses. Some had garages. Some had little nameplates hanging from the mailbox like "The Swensens." Some yards had weeds and patches of dandelions already sprouted, some yards had people sitting in lawn chairs wearing plaid pants and holding blue plastic tumblers of something who stared at them as they drove by.

A stop sign. Turn left. A stop sign. Turn right. The houses became Cape Cods. Some had dormers, some had breezeways, some had gingerbread trim, some with fat old beagle-like dogs whose tails unwound when they woofed from the driveway at kids and cars. But then a different house appeared. Terri chuckled, "Hey, will you look at *that* house! Who lives there?"

Of course, it was Aunt Mandy's house.

They turned into the concrete driveway. "We're here?"
Jan shut the engine off. "Yup. This is it."

They got out and Terri looked around.

On the left side of the yard was a bent-over, cutesy, red-polka-dot-bloomers-showing lawn lady. She faced a cute little lawn boy taking a pee. Two bag geese stood on each side of the flagstone walk that went from the garage to the front door.

In the center of the yard, three wooly lambs surrounded a cute Bo Peep. Behind her, there were three pink flamingos each standing on one leg around a mirror pond that was edged with white-painted rocks. One was drinking from the glass pond. Near the driveway was a wheelbarrow filled with blue, yellow, and pink plastic flowers.

On the roof, near the chimney, was a giant, flat, wooden Santa that held a big, real-looking pipe in his teeth, with reindeer, sled, and waving hand. He chuckled, "Ho-ho-ho" into a bubble over his head.

A six-foot metallic, sequined blue star sat on the garage roof, shimmering in waves of light blue and deep blue in the wind, stunning the eyes, reflecting the sunshine. Terri found it difficult to ignore the star; something about it made her want to keep looking up.

There was a tree, a twenty-foot maple, between the walk and the driveway that held several wind chimes of brass, glass, wood, iron, and ceramic. When the wind blew, they sounded, "Bing, bong, bam. Ting. Tinkle-tinkle-tinkle, tinkle-tinkle-tinkle. Bing, bong, bam. Ting. Tinkle-tinkle-tinkle, Tinkle-tinkle-tinkle."

Terri heard something, a mysterious, ghostly sound like the wind across a field of tall, waving autumn grass. "Where's that sound coming from?"

"What? The quiet sound, you mean?"

"Yeah, that."

"Look up."

At first, Terri looked toward the wind chimes hanging on the maple tree. But that wasn't it. On the roof was the giant star made of ruffling blue sequins, reflecting the sun, gracefully tapping in the breeze. "Oh," she marveled.

The neighbors seemed to like their privacy. The property was divided by a stockade fence on one side and a tall redwood fence on the other.

The front door opened and there was Aunt Mandy puffing on a long gold cigarette holder like a movie star. She threw her head back to exhale into the air and said in a husky voice, "You're here! It's so good to see you. An old lady gets lonely, you know. Come on in girls, come in. Dinner's almost ready."

Aunt Mandy was thin and petite. She wore dark fifties-style glasses that turned up catlike with a gold chain that draped in wide arcs. Her hair was a bluish tint that was pinned up in a neat French twist and she wore powder-blue eye shadow, black eyeliner, and pink lipstick that matched her pink turtleneck, pink stretch pants, and pink toe nails sticking out from gold sandals.

When she spoke, it was a little loud, in a throaty voice that carried with it a touch of Boston *Pahk the cah*, theater, and tobacco. She smiled at Terri in the most sincere, indulging way. "Sit down girls. We have so much to talk about."

The television was turned on to some religious program, but the sound was off. Red curtains framed the picture window. An upright piano with stool, black with white polka dots, filled the side wall.

They sat on a nubby couch and Aunt Mandy faced them in a matching armchair.

"Celery?" she offered, handing Terri a silver platter of cream cheese-stuffed celery sticks and olives.

"Sure." Terri took one.

"Okay." Jan grabbed two.

"So. How's your mother? I owe her a call. We usually talk on Tuesdays and this week just slipped by. She's probably mad at me."

"She's fine, just fine. Had some dental work done to cap a tooth that always bothered her. Didn't want any Novocain, but the dentist insisted."

"No Novocain? Ow. I'd never do that," said Terri.

"Oh, I can see my sister doing that. Barbara has always been such a martyr. She's always trying to show off how much stronger she is than the rest of us. And she is. I shouldn't talk that way about your mother. But it's true, isn't it?"

"Not really. I don't think not using Novocain means my mom is taking the higher ground. She just doesn't like losing control of her tongue for a few hours."

"Ha! You might be right about that."

Jan and Aunt Mandy discussed relatives and neighbors and how some teenagers put a peeing boy and a bloomer lady together in an embarrassing pose, about a problem with her ornaments and the town, and about putting down her dear old dog with the bad breath.

All the while, Terri felt that she was nodding and smiling too much and wished she could jump in with something witty to say. Instead, she sipped her ginger ale and tried not to look at her watch.

"How long have you been best friends with Jan?" she asked Terri.

"Oh, just a few weeks."

Aunt Mandy glanced at Jan. "That's nice."

Jan took a big bite of celery and mumbled, "It is nice."

Terri suspected that she wasn't the first "best friend" to visit Aunt Mandy.

"Do you play piano?"

"Not so much anymore. I used to. Quite a bit."

Jan added, "Oh, she's being modest. She sings, too. Hey, remember that summer you learned all the Beatles songs and we'd sing them together?"

"Yes, I do. That was a fun summer, wasn't it?"

Their conversation was interrupted by a chattering, blooping noise from the kitchen. Three cat clocks with swaying tails and pop-out eyes turned around to announce that it was one o'clock.

Jan and Aunt Mandy sang together, "There-they-go -again!"

"Oh. Those are cute," said Terri.

Dinner was lamb chops, peas, and whipped potatoes with glasses of milk. For dessert they had Rice Krispie treats, Jan's favorite.

Jan took some home, wrapped in wax paper, tied with rubber bands.

At the front door Aunt Mandy said, "I hope we'll be seeing you again, Terri."

"Thank you for dinner. It was delicious. And I loved the cat clocks."

Back in the car, Jan said that Aunt Mandy never turned off the television. It kept her company.

PINK FLAMINGOS

On the Monday after Mandy met Jan's new girlfriend Terri, she found an important looking letter from the town in her mailbox. It said that she was: "Hereby requested to appear at a town meeting" at a date and time to be determined regarding a complaint from her neighbors about her yard display. It seems that the same neighbor who had accused her of the razor blade apple and whose son had died in the gun accident had begun a petition which said that she had adversely affected the market value of their houses by her lawn display. All of her neighbors had signed the petition because they felt sorry for their neighbor's loss from the gun accident and were also a little annoyed with the spectacle of Mandy's yard. Sadly, some neighbors still believed that Mandy had given out razor blade apples.

Mandy was very upset about the whole thing, but she also did not believe her yard really looked that bad and she was afraid to battle her neighbors all alone. She liked her yard. Everything belonged there. The bag ducks and peeing boys *had* to be in the yard, they just had to. So, when she got a call from the civil liberties lawyers inquiring whether she would like representation, she was overjoyed and eagerly consented. The issue soon became a front-page story for the local paper and UPI, AP, and the television news stations picked it up, too. For three weeks, the letters to the editor filled two whole pages in the *Wallingford Post*. The news programs loved it, too. "Just what would you do if THIS..." (the camera would pan Mandy's yard), "was in your neighborhood?"

As for Mandy, she rather enjoyed the attention. She was a celebrity. She was asked to pose again and again beside the lambs in the yard, beside the flowered carts, and beside the peeing boys.

Her case was a fun one for the lawyers, too, because it was sure to be a landmark case. There were six civil liberties lawyers defending Mandy and more called every day. They came to her house for hours planning their strategy and she made them Rice Krispie treats and Kool-Aid.

Finally, the hearing date was set. When her lawyers faced the town lawyer at the zoning board hearing, the hall was so packed that Mandy's neighbors couldn't find seats and complained. So the hearing was rescheduled a week later at the high school auditorium. This time, the front rows were reserved for her neighbors.

The hearing began with lawyers from each side giving speeches for the record and for the camera and for their careers and they strutted up and down wagging their fingers and flapping their jaws in a great display of passionate oratory wearing their most expensive dark suits.

Mandy's lawyers argued that art was art and should not be judged by morality or be misjudged just because it was displayed in a suburban neighborhood.

The town lawyers said her yard display did not qualify as art because she had not intended it as art. So then they all argued about the definition of art and then they argued about the definition of intention. Then Mandy's lawyers called witnesses that paint pink flamingos and bloomer ladies who gave testament to their artistic integrity. Her lawyers argued that it was her First Amendment right, her patriotic right, gosh darn it, as an American citizen to freely display anything she wished in her front yard. They argued that instead of going down, property values would probably go up because the neighbors would get more traffic from people driving by Mandy's house. Then they called appraisers to comment. But the appraisers had conflicting ideas about whether an ornamental display should be considered an adverse condition or ignored in their valuations. The lawyers went on and on.

But as it turned out, according to the town ordinance, the town could only politely request (not order) Mandy to remove the things from her lawn. When this was revealed, the Mayor turned and asked outright to a hushed auditorium, "Miss Flanagan, would you consider doing all of us a big favor on this hot night? I'm not going to ask you to remove *everything* from your yard. No. I only would like you to consider removing *some* things to sort of, tone it down, as you will. For instance, take down the Santa and the star until Christmas–those things drive me crazy. Or the donkey carts, whatever. Now, what do you say to that? That's fair, isn't it? Miss Flanagan? Miss Flanagan?"

Everyone stared at Mandy as she pursed her lips trying to decide which ornaments should go. But it broke her heart to consider removing even one bloomer lady or just one pink flamingo. She had grown so fond of each one and where they belonged in the yard. And she believed that the ornaments had become accustomed to each other, too. To see a friend disappear would cause sadness for them all and for her. And Santa—well, Santa spread joy year round. So Mandy whispered to her lawyers that she just couldn't do it.

Then the lawyers started up again. They had both exhausted their arguments and now seemed to think that their best strategy was to "wear-down" their opponent by pointing their fingers, getting all riled up, and quoting boring cases word-for-word from legal texts. The auditorium was hot and it was getting late so that many people began to leave in disgust. Finally, when it was almost midnight, the Mayor looked at his watch and realized that he had missed the basketball finals on TV. He was not happy. He hushed the crowd, silenced the lawyers, and turned to Mandy. "Now, we are willing to listen to reason. Just what do you suggest we do, Miss Flanagan?"

The crowd grew silent. Even the lawyers stopped jabbering. Mandy cherished this rare theatrical opportunity. She stood up slowly and turned to face the expectant crowd as though she were receiving an honorary degree, hesitating just long enough to be assured of their attention. Quite passionately, as though she was the Queen of England herself donating a teacup for display, she stated, "I will agree NOT to place additional ornaments on my lawn." Then she turned to the Mayor and quietly asked if she could please "go home now" and sat down.

The town lawyers smiled broadly, jumped off the stage, shook some of the neighbors' hands, and made a big deal of Aunt Mandy's statement as though they had won a really big concession and deserved a really big fee. And the civil liberties lawyers also slapped each other on the back and shook hands in hearty congratulations as though they, too, had won. And then the town lawyers congratulated each other on their fine arguments. It was confusing to watch. The townspeople did not know that successful lawyers often did this so that it appeared as though they had won, were always right and could later boast about it, inflating both their reputations and their fees.

That night, Mandy's neighbors went home sweaty and tired but nonetheless satisfied. However, in the morning they awoke restless, with a vague uneasiness that they had given away something important to someone a bit more clever the night before and they didn't much want to talk about it anymore.

NOTHING STAYS THE SAME

O ver the years, Mandy's Wallingford neighborhood changed as people moved out and new people moved in. A year after the petition, the father of the boy who had died was arrested for battering his wife. Soon, their yard became overgrown with weeds. A year later, the property was foreclosed, auctioned off, and bought by a nice Italian couple from New Haven, Alphonso and Louisa Rossetti.

One summer day, Alphonso rang Mandy's doorbell and invited her to their house for a party saying, "It will be nice. Maybe we find you a husband, eh?" Mandy was worried that the neighbors might still harbor a grudge about her lawn display but she decided to go anyway.

As she walked across the front yard toward the party, Louisa ran out and grabbed Mandy's hand shouting, "Looka who's here! Our neighbor Mandy with da beau-ti-ful yard!" All the neighbors laughed at this but it was good-hearted laughing and they turned to her one by one and said, "Hi, Mandy, how are you?"

The Rossettis were originally from the Italian city of Amalfi, so they gave great parties. Mandy was so relieved that no one had made a fuss about her yard that she played bocce and checkers, ate spaghetti, drank wine in the garage with the women, and danced with all the old Italian men in the driveway until late at night. She was one of the last ones to leave the party.

The next summer, a Guatemalan family moved next door to her. Aside from four children of their own, the Chacon family also had foster children staying with them. Sometimes Mandy counted ten children playing next door.

Marilyn Chacon had been a corporate accountant in California but now did tax work at home and cared for all the kids. Her husband, John, was a math professor at the local college. When they drove around looking at houses, John was humored but not offended by Mandy's yard, because it reminded him of his father who made colorful, painted donkey carts (full-size and miniature) for the tourists back in Guatemala. Mandy's yard looked familiar. Marilyn especially liked the design of the house with the master bedroom and bath over the garage, away from the kids. They both thought that the price seemed unusually low. So they bought it and quickly erected a swing set in the backyard.

The Chacon household was always loud and chaotic. A kid was always laughing, a kid was always teasing, a kid was always crying, and they ran around and around the yard and rode their bikes up and down the short driveway. Although Marilyn tried to shoo the kids from Mandy's yard, they delighted in playing in her front yard "wonderland." Mandy didn't mind a bit. When one of the little boys rang her doorbell clutching his crotch and asked to use her bathroom, she realized they weren't afraid of her.

Seeing that the children had taken to Mandy, Marilyn asked if she would watch them while she attended class to finish her MBA. It wasn't long before Mandy became a member of the Chacon family and spent many of the holidays with them. They called Mandy "Grandmama." To the neighborhood, Mandy was now considered a kindly eccentric. But just the same, she always went away to a spa at Halloween.

WINDOWS AND DOORS

One morning Tonio, one of the Chacon children, stood on his toes and rang Mandy's doorbell.

"Hello, Tonio. What can I do for you?"

"Grandmama, know what Sara did?"

"No, Tonio, what did Sara do?" Mandy asked.

"She sat on the sheep's back and then she broke the sheep's neck. Do you know what? Do you know what Josh did?"

"No, Tonio, what did Josh do?"

"Um, he, um, he, um he broke the pond. The glass, I mean."

"Oh, dear. How did he do that, Tonio?"

"He was pretending like he was ice skating with the bird."

"You mean the flamingo?"

"Yeah. The pink bird. En, en, then he just broke it trying to slide. He broke it into pieces."

"Oh. Well, thank you, Tonio. I'll have to get someone to fix it, I guess."

"No, you don't. My dad says he's going to fix everything. This week he said."

"Oh, really? Well, that's very nice of him. Now, since you were so brave telling me about all the broken things, how would you like a nice, big Toll House cookie?" Mandy asked.

"I never had a Toll House before."

Several days later, on Saturday morning, Mandy noticed a man in her front yard and she thought, "Oh, oh, the town again." But he seemed to be examining the lawn ornaments one by one. She opened the front door and shouted with authority, "Can I help you with something?"

He spoke slowly, in a deep voice with a Spanish accent. "I am Carlos Chacon."

"Oh, you must be John's father, is that right?"

"Yes, yes. I am John's father."

"And you're fixing my ornaments?"

"Yes, yes." He picked up the broken sheep and put the head and neck together to demonstrate. "Is no problem, no problem, Miss Mandy."

"Oh, good. Thank you, Mr. Chacon."

"Call me Carlos, please."

"Okay, Carlos."

He worked in the yard all morning. Mandy parted the curtains from time to time and Carlos would look her way and smile.

After a few hours, he took off his shirt and draped it over a bloomer lady. Mandy could not help but watch and smile to herself at his industry. He was good. She pulled a chair up to the window to watch, flipped through magazines, smoked, and sipped coffee. She admired his strong shoulders and barrel chest with white curly hair. He was shorter than her by a good three or four inches. Guessing from the lines around his eyes, he was probably in his early seventies. Like me, she thought. He looked like a short, Mayan Hemingway with his round Santa face and white beard. Same beer belly. Can probably drink like Hemingway, too. Yes, for his age, he was quite striking. He sat in the full sun, working with his hands. First, he cut a piece of round glass to replace the mirror. After that, he moved around the yard patiently carving new features on some wooden figurines while patching broken pieces on others. And in a box, there was an assortment of brushes with small cans and jars of paint in a dozen colors. He dabbed at the weatherworn details with a long fine brush.

Carlos was an artist.

He sat on a milk crate as he worked. In addition to the paint box, he brought two toolboxes, a bubble level, a white paint bucket, hammers, two screwdrivers, and a drill which were spread around him in an ordered circle. He also wore a leather tool belt that sagged to his hips showing the elastic band of his underwear. Were they boxers or jockey shorts? "I'm such a bad girl," she said aloud. His smooth brown back glistened with sweat in the sun.

Carlos was no dummy. He knew that Mandy was sitting by the window watching him. Twice, he purposely held the hammer in one hand and the legs of an upside-down flamingo awkwardly in the other, striking an odd pose that popped the muscles of his arm like Alps. He enjoyed her attention.

At noon, she stood at the front door and sang, "Car-los! Come in for lunch! Car-los! Come on, it's lunchtime."

He said, "Okay," and immediately dropped his hammer to the ground and unbuckled his tool belt, letting it slide to the ground, and put on his white t-shirt. He followed her into the kitchen.

"Would you like a baloney or a ham and cheese sandwich?"

"Ah?"

"I see. Do you want this? Or this?" she said, pointing to the lunch meats.

"Ah, that one."

"Coffee? Coke?"

"Coffee, please."

They sat at the kitchen table in silence. Soon it was 12:30. The cat clocks rang out, "Brrranng! Brrranng!"

"Ha! I like that, I like that," he said. She noticed that when he smiled, deep canals framed his eyes, and his lips parted to show a wide space between his front teeth.

"Are you just visiting or on vacation, Carlos?"

"No. Not a vacation, I will be a cit-zen. Ah, um... Sep-tem-ber."

"You're staying and becoming a citizen of the United States?"

"Yes. Yes."

"Oh, that's very nice. John and Marilyn are wonderful neighbors. And those children! What a handful."

"Yes, yes."

"Is your wife staying here, too?"

"Wife?"

"Ah hah. John and Marilyn, Carlos and?"

"No, no wife. Em, morte, she died, long time. Miss Mandy, wife?"

"No. No, husband now, he's gone. It's just me," she said, looking at the wall.

He pushed away from the table and stood up sticking his broad chest out in a macho pose, ready to return to work. "Thank you, Miss Mandy." But when he opened the front door to return to work, he was surprised to see that the sky was dark and it had begun to rain.

Mandy stood behind him in the living room. "Oh, oh. Carlos you'd better get your tools from the yard. Can you work inside?" She pointed to the basement. "Inside? Can you work inside?"

"There better," he said, pointing to the garage before dashing out.

He had to make three trips to the garage with his tools and the sheep with the broken foot and the flamingo with the broken neck. He started to arrange his tools to begin work but the rain accelerated and began creeping along the floor into the garage.

Mandy was still watching from the back door when he pulled on the rope, closing the garage door with a thud.

She was disappointed. With the garage door closed, she couldn't watch him anymore. Oh, well.

At the same time, next door at the Chacon's kitchen, an animated conversation between Marilyn and John was going on. Fortunately, two of the kids were at church school and the other two were playing with friends down the street.

"I saw him go into her house, John. You know how your father is. She's a woman alone, she's no match for him."

"He's my father, for Christ's sake. I know how he is, but what am I going to say to her—watch out, my father's a gigolo?"

"Yes! You can call her up and tell her. If *you* don't, I will. Mandy's like family, she has a right to know. I'd feel awful if something happened."

"You're blowing it all out of proportion, Marilyn. What could happen? She's too old for him. He likes the young ones. Besides, Mandy can take care of herself. She was a showgirl, you know. She's probably had a lot of experience with men."

"And what's *that* supposed to mean?"

"Nothing, nothing. Why you getting so upset about—"

"And I suppose because my *sister* is an actress, you think she's been around the block and deserves what she gets? Is that it? Is that what you think?"

"No, no, no! I was *not* talking about your sister. But your sister... your sister ain't no angel either, babe. You've got to admit that."

"*What* are you *talking* about?" she shouted.

"What I meant was..." and the discussion continued on for some time until John yelled, "End of discussion!" while waving his arms like an umpire saying "safe!" over home plate. She said, "Hmpf!" as John tramped downstairs to the rec room, turned the television to the Red Sox game, and then kicked back in his plaid easy chair to watch. But there was a rain delay.

Waving his arms like an umpire was John's tactic to end disagreements in the Chacon household and it infuriated Marilyn. She stomped upstairs to make a phone call.

Of course John knew that Marilyn was right (she was right most of the time). His father *was* a gigolo and now that the game was delayed, he was preoccupied with worry about what his father might be doing next door with Mandy.

What if something bad happened over there? Marilyn would never forgive him. He went to the small window in the laundry room, parted the curtains, and peered at the side of Mandy's garage. He couldn't see anything. The rain was pelting in sheets and the garage door was still closed. He really wanted to know what was going on but didn't dare go upstairs to have a better look from the picture window in the living room. Marilyn might catch him and know that he had doubts about his father, too.

So he went back to his easy chair and idly pressed the TV remote, flipping by program after blurred program. Marilyn hated that he controlled the remote, but she was upstairs anyway, probably at the picture window, he figured. The lights dimmed, the power almost went out, and thunder boomed. No game today.

Maybe I should turn off the TV and go upstairs, check to make sure the kids are okay, he thought. And look out the picture window.

Next door Mandy smiled to herself, thinking of a man she met in an elevator long ago. She went to the bedroom to spray Secret Passion perfume on her neck and her wrists, touch up her makeup, and unbutton the top button of her blouse. Couldn't hurt, she thought. She returned to the kitchen to put Oreos and Vienna Fingers on a plate covered with foil.

It continued to rain in sideways torrents and the lightening quickened. She dashed from the back door through the yard and to the side door of the garage wearing a plastic bonnet, carrying the plate before her.

Carlos was busy using an electric saw. His shirt was off.

"Cook-ies, Car-los, cook-ies," she sang.

As he looked up to see Mandy with the tray of cookies, her wet bonnet and fresh lipstick, there was a loud ripping "CRACK!" The saw stopped and the lights in the garage went out.

"Oh, my God. Look! Everything's out! It must be a power outage."

"Yes, yes. Miss Mandy okay?"

"Yes, I think so."

Instinctively, they both went to look out the small windows in the garage door that faced the front yard. "My tree! Oh, no, look! It split the branch right off! My chimes are on the ground. Good Lord it's so dark!"

"Oh, Miss Mandy. This is not good, not good."

The storm was on top of them. Lightening, sudden shimmering bolts of it, illuminated the yard in a surreal yellow light accompanied by astounding cracks of thunder, while the wind stroked the bushes, tussled the treetops, and pushed the rain dancing in chorus lines across the driveway and up the street.

Thrilled with the danger, they repeated together, "Oooo" and "Ah" with each flash and boom. Mandy hadn't noticed that Carlos had put his arm around her, resting his callused hand gently but purposefully on her shoulder.

At the next crack of thunder she gasped, "Oh my," and Carlos deftly turned her toward him and pulled her close. She played along, whimpered a little, acting fragile, saying, "Oh, no, oh, no. Carlos, my tree, my tree!"

Carlos whispered, "Is okay, Mandy, is okay," while patting and rubbing her back. She rested her head on his shoulder, allowing herself to brush her lips across his smooth, salty skin. They rocked in a gentle sway, the rain furious on the roof. She said, "Oh, Carlos. I'm so glad you're here." It was then that he boldly led her by the hand to a stack of fertilizer and seed bags sitting on the floor along the back wall of the garage. There they sat.

He kissed her face and lips with short brushes of his lips and she kissed him back, letting him cup her breasts through her dress even long after the storm had blown over, until they were caught by John and Marilyn Chacon rudely rolling up the garage door to a brilliant sunny day yelling together, "Papa!"

THE DOCTOR'S DANCE

Her chest X-ray was displayed on a lit panel. The doctor's index finger made circles around a large black spot that he described as the "troubling area of concern." Mandy became somewhat distracted listening to the doctor, because she recalled that those exact words had appeared on the front page of the *New Haven Register* the previous Sunday. But that "troubling area of concern" referred to a low-income housing project displayed in the newspaper photos. She also recognized the words "festered" and "source of irritation" among the doctor's words. Those words, too, sounded familiar. Meanwhile, he continued in a hushed but droning tone, one intended to sound sensitive and concerned for this was a serious moment.

Perhaps she just didn't want to hear what he had to say, sitting composed and trim in her navy blue pantsuit. The blue pocketbook with the gold snap sat on her lap. She nodded at his pauses to act as if she were attentive. She heard only the very last of his lecture: "I'm so sorry, Mrs. Flanagan, but you need to put your affairs in order."

This she understood. These words meant: *You're going to die and there's nothing we can do about it.* She anticipated that it might be bad news today. Why else did they call her twice at home, insisting she come in as soon as possible? But now that his words were out, now that she understood what he was saying, she needed a moment to think it through.

Maybe this young doctor was wrong. Maybe it was all a terrible, terrible mistake. The tests were wrong. A demented lab technician sabotaged her X-ray because he had a grudge against the hospital. He would be found out. They would apologize and redo it. But no. There was no mistake. It was true. Of course it was. She was going to die. Soon. She already knew that.

"Mrs. Flanagan? Mrs. Flanagan? Is there someone we should call? A friend? A relative maybe? Do you have somebody we can call? Mrs. Flanagan?"

She thought of many people, most of them long gone from her life, and she wondered why she would think of them now when it would do her little good. They weren't here. A nurse patted her shoulder, her back. She forgot the nurse was there in the room, had been there the whole time. That was the first hint something was wrong.

She focused back to the polished floor office. A few moments passed as the doctor and the nurse looked down at her, waiting for a reply. "It's *Miss* Flanagan. No. No. I'm all right. I'm okay. You are *sure* of what you're telling me, aren't you, Doctor?"

"Yes, quite sure, I'm afraid. But if you like, we can go over the X-ray again."

"No, that won't be necessary." She looked up. "How long do I have?"

"Ah. A good question to ask." He smiled. "Wish I knew the answer to that one. I'd win a big prize. But I'm afraid, well, only God knows that." He winked, trying to charm her.

Wrong thing to do. Mandy erupted. "What? Are you sure God is the *only* one who knows? You're a doctor, aren't you? Can't *you* tell me? Or is it that you just don't want to *upset* me. I *need* to know! You must understand, this is very inconvenient. Very, *very* inconvenient!"

"Yes, I quite understand, Mrs., Miss Flanagan, believe me, I do understand!" He looked to the nurse standing silently in the corner. She shrugged.

"Tell me what you know, Doctor. Don't hold back."

"Well, it could be *weeks*, or, or, if you're lucky, it could be *months*. We just don't know. That's the best I can do. Really. I'm sorry, there's just no predicting when it will happen."

"What if I quit smoking, will that give me more time?"

"I'm afraid that won't change things now. You should have..." but he caught himself as the nurse gave a piercing glance. She smoked, too.

Mandy reflected on his words and his faux pas before she cleared her throat and spoke. Her voice was small. "Well, what should I do now?"

Relieved that her outburst was over he said, "I suggest that you obtain a lawyer and settle your estate. You might consider the new facility in Branford. It's one of a kind. Very comfortable, right on the ocean. They'll take good care of you. I'll make a referral, if you like."

"Yes, please do."

And now Mandy was embarrassed and ashamed. She hated the way the nurse and the doctor conspired. It was condescending. But worse, she wasn't ready with any smart words of her own, something she could throw back at them to show she had the upper hand. Here was the most dramatic scene of her life, and she forgot her lines. It was awkward. But maybe the worst was over: learning that she was going to die. Death itself might not be so bad. She believed that.

Now, she needed to go home. She stood and said, "Thank you, Doctor," and walked out.

She heard the nurse say indiscreetly, "Poor dear."

That made Mandy regret her words, the last ones she said to the doctor. Why did she thank him? He should have told her. She wasn't thankful. No, she wasn't thankful at all.

As she strode to the elevator, she said aloud, "He knows, he just wouldn't say. He knows all right. It must be soon. It must be really soon."

WHAT TO WEAR TO YOUR FUNERAL

It was a Saturday but because of the rain, it felt like a Sunday. Raining and raining, raining and raining, an early October rain. The broad oak leaves were falling to the lawn and sailing down the driveway to the street, down the gutters, and out to the sea. Either the summer had been too long and hot or maybe there had been too much rain, for the leaves were falling early in muted, muddy colors. It would not be a pretty Connecticut fall this year.

Mandy undid her robe and laid it across the pillow. Her breasts hung low like socks. She made an effort to stand straight but her shoulders bent forward, rounding her upper back, pushing her head forward. Her pale skin seemed to barely cover the bumpy vertebrae of her backbone and the wings of her shoulder blades, the blue of the veins in her arms, the age spots on her hands and arms she hated. She wore her white hair with a faint blue tint, carefully styled in a French twist.

She took her bra and wrapped it around her stomach with the fastening in front. She hooked it together and turned it to the back. She pulled the straps on over each shoulder, pulling each breast up high on her chest. "Way up high where they belong. Stand up and say hi," she said aloud.

She lit a cigarette with the snap of her initialed gold lighter, inhaled deeply, and raised her open-palm hand to remove the cigarette from her lips, bent her head back and exhaled, her lower lip jutting out to channel the stream of

smoke toward the ceiling. She had little pink triangles of lipstick under each nostril and her cheekbones were streaked
with red rouge. Her eyeliner swept up catlike against her
black false eyelashes and electric-blue eye shadow painted
her lids. It was eight in the morning.

"What can I possibly wear? What to wear, what to wear?"
She spoke to herself in a raspy singsong voice while peering
into the tidy closet.

Pushing the hangers roughly apart, Mandy pulled a red
velvet dress toward her. "Beautiful dress. Can't fill out the
top anymore. Tch. Tch. Ha! What would people think? Red
for a funeral! Ha! I should wear it. I really should."

Next she viewed a pale green suit. "Noooo–makes me
look like an old lady. Ha!"

She took a blue satin dress from the closet, then a lacy
pink dress, and laid them at the foot of the bed. "One of
these," she spat out, voice hoarse and cracking. Then it
began once again. The coughing reached deep down into
the center of her body, her face turned red, she shuddered
and grew light-headed. She sat down on the bed clasp-
ing her chest, coughing and wheezing, and then fell over,
face-first into the dresses, silent and still.

A minute passed, maybe more. She seemed to be dead
all right. But then, she sprang upright and shouted out
with a clenched fist, "There! You didn't get me this time,
mister! Ha! And double ha!"

She stood up and resumed her task, this time happily
humming a bit while cigarette after cigarette burned in
the ashtray on the bureau.

The sound of the rain and the sideways pelting against
the window grew louder. She stopped a moment to look
out to the front yard. One of her bag ducks had fallen
over. Who would tend to them when she was gone? Why
hadn't she made plans to give them away? She was more

disturbed by her forgetfulness than in the subject of her worrying. But what did it matter now? "Who would want those old things anyway? Shouldn't grow too attached to things," she said to the window.

She stepped into the blue satin dress, pulled it up, put her arms through the belled-sleeves, and began closing the front snaps. She tied the white satin bow at her neck.

The dress was above her knees and below her thighs, not a conservative length for an old lady. But if you looked at her legs with a little imagination you just might think she was thirty, well, perhaps forty.

She stepped into the blue spike-heeled shoes with the sequined bows, walked to the closet, closed the door, and stood before the mirror. She reached for the yellow feather boa on the top of the closet saying, "Feathers always help" and then, "Comfortable. Still looks ok, too. Mandy, you're not so bad for an old broad."

She smiled, parted her lips. Rows of wrinkle lines stretched across her forehead and spoked out from her eyes. Folds and lines gathered around her lips like a draw-string bag; her skin had begun to sag at her jaw. Oddly, another consequence of aging was that she now enjoyed the sculpted look of high cheek bones and with a little lipstick, sometimes the pretty Mandy still showed through.

She resumed looking at her clothes and thought of the casket.

"Open or closed, open or closed. What should I do? What should I do? Uh oh. A spot. Needs dry cleaning. Tch. Must have been the... the what? When was the last time I wore this old thing? Well, at least I won't get anything on it the next time I wear it. Ha!"

BREAKING THE NEWS

On a sunny day in August, Mandy phoned her sister Barbara in Somerville. "Barbara. It's Man-dy," she said in a little Shirley Temple voice.

"Mandy! I'm so glad you called. We've got to start planning the holidays. Right around the corner, you know."

Mandy was impatient. "You mean Christmas? Oh, come on, Barbara, it's too early! Anyway, listen, I don't expect to be around for Christmas... I'm sorry to tell you this... but I'm dying."

"What? What did you say? I can barely hear you; you're speaking in a whisper. Mandy, what did you say?"

"I said, I'm dying! Look, I can't talk any louder. My voice is going. Listen, will you?"

Barbara always spoke loudly, but now she began to shout. "Are you serious? Dying? The smoking! It's the smoking, isn't it? Mandy, I told you to quit! I—"

"Look I'm not deaf! Stop bellowing!"

There was a pause. Then she was wheezing and coughing again. Barbara could hear her long struggling breaths, gasps, and a sharp throaty hacking that was quickly muffled. The phone crashed to the floor. Then she heard nothing.

Barbara screamed, "Mandy! Mandy! What's happening? Are you all right? Mandy!"

Mandy now had a whispery, throaty voice so she spoke slowly and deliberately like a priest at a confessional. "I'm okay. I'm okay. I just dropped the phone, that's all. Barbara? Are you there?"

Barbara was scared; this just wasn't Mandy's confident, husky voice. "Of course, of course, I'm here!" Barbara yelled.

"Stop shouting, will you! Yes, it was the smoking. It's cancer and it's too late now, so don't sermonize. And don't you go crying on me. There's nothing that can be done. Nothing. So forget it."

When Mandy heard her sister's sobs she became more consoling. "Look, I'm old, Barbara. Everyone has to go sometime. I'm plenty old. I lost my looks long ago. And God knows I'm too vain to want to live much longer without a man's wink. I'll be seventy-three next week. Seventy-three! I shouldn't be so old!"

Barbara was crying even louder now as Mandy continued. "I should have died young, like Marilyn Monroe! Yes! With a real dramatic ending... I just hope it's fast... Stop crying will you! You're crying for yourself 'cause I don't mind dying... I really don't," she said sternly. Barbara quieted her sobbing. "But Barbie, it's so frustrating! You know there's so much to be done all at once. The house and all."

"Oh, I knew there was something wrong at Easter! I knew it. I knew it! When you went to the bathroom that time, you were coughing up blood Mandy, weren't you? That cough! Remember I told you to see a doctor? Remember? Did you go? Well, did you?"

"Barbara, it doesn't matter, anymore... do you know what that doctor said? He said he doesn't know when I'm going to die. He's got to be lying. Can you imagine? At my age, they're afraid to give me bad news."

They were silent a moment until Barbara delicately offered, "Mandy, the doctors don't know everything. They aren't God, for heaven's sake. They may *think* they are but they're not. Jesus, I still can't believe what you're saying to me. Go get a second opinion. Maybe there's something you can take. Some kind of operation?"

"No, there isn't. Too late. Listen, you'll be getting a little letter in the mail."

"A *lit-tle letter*? In the mail?"

"Yes. About the preparations for my funeral, silly."

"What?"

"Don't worry, I've paid for everything. All the details have been worked out."

"You're serious, aren't you?"

"Yes, I'm serious. I'm ready. My bags are packed. It's time to kick the bucket."

"I can't *believe* what you're telling me, I can't believe it. Mandy, what am I going to do without you? I've got to sit down. I've got to think things over. I've got to—"

"You do that," said Mandy. Then she hung up on poor Barbara.

It was Barbara's habit to go to the mailbox every day at noon. On the third day, the letter from Mandy arrived. She opened the envelope to find another envelope inside that said, "To be opened when I'm dead" in an even-lettered loopy script. It was followed by Mandy's usual, smiling daisy. She held the envelope in her hands and stared at it hoping to learn its contents. Although tempted, she dared not open it for it would contain only sorrow. Sorrow could wait until tomorrow. She put the envelope inside the cupboard in the old napkin holder, the place where wedding announcements and invitations to baby showers go. She made herself a cup of tea and then relined all the kitchen shelves with paper.

THEN SHE DIED

Three months passed. It was a Tuesday morning around 9:30, and a nurse had just come by. She was lying on her side with her hands in a praying position under her pillow. Her nose and mouth were covered by a clear plastic oxygen mask. There was a red quilt that Barbara had made on top of the other two white blankets. Her legs were drawn up and she looked small under the weight of the blankets. Her white hair was tied back loosely in a yellow ribbon and she wore Chinese silk turquoise pajamas with pink flowers. Her chest heaved and fell awkwardly with each breath. Her skin looked grayish; she wore no makeup.

Mandy had a smile that turned up slightly at the corner of her mouth, which seemed to brighten her half-closed eyes. It was a look of conspiring amusement, of a private joke just told but there was no one near. The bed curtain was open a few inches. She stared at the four people surrounding the bed of the new patient across the aisle. She did not know that she was staring at all. For Mandy floated on a morphine high, drifting in and out of heavy-headed visions as though she were happily looking out the window of a train puffing through the green Swiss countryside on the way to her summer home.

The bed was soft. The pillow was soft. She felt cozy-warm and lovely. Occasionally, she had an ordinary thought that lingered a moment like the smoke stream of a cigarette just exhaled. But when her mind turned to pause, to grasp, to understand, the thought simply vanished from her consciousness and she was gently returned once more to her sweet narcotic journey. Because Mandy could not think anymore, she did not worry anymore. But best of all, she had no more pain.

Just before the end, her breathing became awkward. Even though we would like to believe that in the end there are flashing pictures and brilliant insights, the last thought Mandy had before she let go of the rope swing of life—the very, very last thought that she had—was to wonder whether she had ordered enough scotch.

She inhaled and her chest rose but then it dropped out of rhythm like a dropped drumstick from a stiff arthritic hand. She inhaled a second time and her chest rose, but not fully, and again fell defeated just as before. She did not inhale again, her chest did not rise. This time, there was only a long, low sweet sigh that whispered from somewhere inside her that could only be heard if your ear was close to her lips, ready to hear a breathy secret. That was all there was.

In the unmeasured time and absolute quiet of another world, her transparent soul was already striding away in the deliberate gait of someone anxious to be somewhere. But death made an honorable pause and gazed back at the bed with a smug smile before striding forward again into a silver-mercury sea.

When the sound returned, a nurse said to a volunteer, "It's time to check Mandy's meds. Want to come?" The clanging curtain was yanked open.

"Oh, dear, I think she's..."

"Good for her. Such a nice passing," said the nurse.

THE LETTER

Just after ten o'clock, they called from the hospice to tell Barbara. It was time to open the letter. Barbara sat at the kitchen table and cried onto the typewritten pages.

Dear Barbie,

Yippee! I've gone to that great chorus line in the sky! Don't you grieve too much, Barbie, I know you. Sometimes you're a little too pensive. You can grieve for me, dear. But not now. There's too much to do.

First, as you know, I want to be cremated. But you can still have a church service with the casket on the altar (closed) with me in it, of course! Do me a favor and make sure that Reverend Shuttan does the service, not that new guy. I bought the casket, talk to Benedicts, they know which one and the cremation details. I want Jan to spread my ashes. I already sent her a letter about how to do it. My will is with Attorney Bowman on Main street in Meriden (I gave the house to Jan).

After the service, I want to have a big party, probably at Ned's house makes sense. I've paid for the catering and booze, talk to Beth at Elm Foods on the Boulevard. I've paid for the obituary. Make sure it has my picture from The Extravaganza.

Now one last thing. You need to call everybody listed below so they know I'm dead. I really want everyone to come to my party, it's important. Tell them that my last wish was that they should have a drink on me, it's my dying wish you might say. You've been a great sister. Tell me to "Break a leg!" I'm hoping for a second audition upstairs!
Your loving sister,
Mandy

Barbara folded the letter, said, "Break a leg!" slamming her fist on the kitchen table, bouncing the sugar bowl to the floor.

She stared at the mess. Got the broom, swept the sugar and ceramic pieces into the dustpan, and dumped it into the trash under the sink. Maybe a plastic sugar bowl would be better, she thought.

She sat down, had a cup of tea with her tears, and eleven sugar cookies.

Then she found the old bottle in the garage, carefully retrieved the ceramic pieces from the trash, and glued them back together.

FOUR

EIGHT YEARS LATER THEY MEET AGAIN

Terri squeezed through the crowd by the door, exited the sanctuary, and raced across the parking lot toward her car, happy to be outside, glad to be leaving the service. If she hurried, she wouldn't have to wait behind the slow-driving mourners leaving the parking lot. But just as she unlocked her car door, she saw Jan at the far end of the parking lot, waving, trying to get her attention, jogging toward her.

Terri leaned against her car, arms folded. "I came. So where were you? Missed the whole thing."

Jan gave her a quick hug. "There you are. Hello, stranger."

"What happened?"

"Whoa, give me some slack. I had to clean up Uncle Ned's house for the wake. Thought I'd make it but guess not. How was it?"

"Fine, I guess. You know, like a funeral service."

"Looked like a good turnout. Well, I feel bad that I missed it. There was nothing I could do. Aunt Mandy was special."

Jan had crinkles at the corners of her eyes. Her freckles were nearly gone and she was rounder, older, looked different. "My God, you're wearing pink lipstick and a skirt. Geez. Almost feminine," said Terri.

Jan smirked and stepped toward her. "Hey, lady. You're not afraid to give your old lezzie girlfriend a hug now, are ya?" Terri smiled and they embraced in a rocking bear-hug that ended when Jan had to wave as her mother drove by. "You're still looking good, lady."

"You too, Jan. I just noticed your hair–it's long. Looks good."

"Whoa, give me some credit. I try. Hey but don't tell my mother I missed the service, okay? You saw me at the back of the church, right? You promise?"

"Okay. Only thing is that she saw me sitting there by myself."

"Huh?"

"Your mother. And she smiled at me. That was a surprise. She never liked me before."

"Oh, well, today is different. Nice that she remembered you, I guess. Let's get going, okay?"

"Get going? You mean to the wake?"

"Yeah. I mean, that was the plan...go to my Uncle Ned's house. It's not done yet. Not exactly a wake in the old-fashioned sense but lots of alcohol and... you're still coming, right? 'member I said—"

"I just thought that maybe the plan had changed when you didn't show up."

"Oh, no, no. I still need you girl, don't desert me now. Besides, we just met. We need to catch up. We *have* to go. Follow me, okay? It's not that far. I have Uncle Ned's car. See? Over there. Classy, huh? A Rambler. He has my rental. I'm staying at his house."

"Not with Barbara? I mean, your mother?"

"Too complicated."

"I loved that old Chevy you used to have. Remember the day we came to this church and then went to dinner at her house?"

"Completely forgot." Jan saluted. "Let's go. Just follow me. See ya in a bit."

Terri was relieved. Everything would be fine; there was no flame, no feelings at all. Jan seemed okay, just older, and something else seemed different that she couldn't figure out. There would be other people around. Maybe they could be friends again. And maybe they could finally talk about it.

THE POSTCARD

Terri started the car and turned on the radio. Then she heard what was playing. Oh, the cosmic irony of it! Why was *it* on the radio? Why *that* song now?

It was that old song by Al Anderson, "No Good to Cry," from when he was with the Wildweeds, the one that always hijacked her soul, made her sing, and become melancholy remembering the postcard from Jan.

Terri still had it somewhere, probably in the shoebox of letters, the one in the trunk or maybe in the attic or in the basement. But it was still somewhere in the house.

A married woman shouldn't keep stuff like that around. Should have thrown it away long ago; should have, but didn't.

She remembered walking back from the mailbox and seeing the San Francisco address, recognizing the boxy writing in green ink. "*Sorry. Good Luck. Good Bye. Write! Love ya, Jan.*"

That was it—no warning. One day, Jan just moved away.

A few months later Terri met Sam.

And now here she was, eight years later, married with three kids. And here was Jan waving her arm in circles, motioning for her to park in the driveway behind the Rambler.

Life was funny.

THE LONG WAKE

Jan held the back door open for Terri. "You go first. I'm right behind you."

"Okay."

As they stepped into the kitchen, Jan continued, "See, this way we can ease in slowly through the kitchen, unnoticed, get a beverage and maybe avoid—"

"Avoid what?" Terri nearly bumped into Barbara. The kitchen was crowded and so was the living room.

"Jan, where have you been? Did you miss the service? It was beautiful. You should have been there."

"Got there late. I was in the back, Mom. Way back. Hey! Look who's here."

She shoved Terri forward.

"Terri! How sweet of you to come! I saw you by yourself. It means so much to us. Jan must have told you that we—" Barbara stopped, squinted.

A short, buxom woman grinned and came forward, holding out her arms.

"Lor-na, Lor-na! My God! You just come right over here and give me a hug."

Lorna's hair was raven-colored and elegantly coifed in a French twist. She wore red lipstick and a flowered dress. "Hello, Barbara."

As they embraced, Jan guided Terri to the living room with the liquor table and trays of canapés.

"Lorna, how long? Twenty? Thirty years?"

Lorna chuckled. "Longer. Oh, boy, don't even try. We'll be here all day. God. It has been a long time. Very long. And here we are–two old ladies." Her face fell into a sad mask. "I still can't believe she's gone."

"Neither can I, honey. But it's all right...just as long as I keep busy... I, I just need to get through this. Today, I mean. Then I'll be okay. Well, maybe not okay, but you know what I mean."

"Look, let me help you in the kitchen. I'm no good just standing around. Give me something to do."

"No, no. There's a caterer, so we're all set." She paused. "Lorna?"

"What? What is it? You can ask me anything."

Barbara leaned closer to whisper, "Do you know they're *all* coming?"

Lorna straightened up. "What do you mean, *all*? Who's coming?"

"Men. All those *friends* of Mandy's. Didn't you notice at church? Remember I told you she sent me this letter to open after she died?"

"Oh, yeah. What was in it?"

"She wrote it all out: names, addresses, phone numbers of all these men to invite. I had to call them. Me. Men I didn't even know and invite them here. She wanted that."

"God! She never told me about that."

"I'm surprised she didn't say something to you. I mean, you've been such great pals all these years. By the way, that's Jan, over there, you remember my daughter? Drinking the beer."

"Jan? Little Jan? I am so very old."

Reverend Wally Shuttan walked into the kitchen. "Good afternoon, ladies."

Barbara smiled tightly. "Oh, hello, Reverend. You did a very nice job. Everything. Except for that little boy and

Henry's outburst. See? There's my daughter Jan and her friend, Terri."

The Reverend waved and Jan waved back. "Was Jan there? I mean at the service? When I acknowledge someone from the pulpit, I like to nod to them. I looked but didn't see her. Her friend, I did see her."

"She was in the back. Way back."

"Oh. Could be, but I know my church and I didn't see her."

"Way back."

"Oh. So, she's from San Francisco, right? I can tell. I mean, too bad she didn't sit up front with the family." Barbara frowned, but he continued. "Really, a very nice turnout, don't you think? Lovely flower arrangements, just lovely."

"Reverend, I'm being rude. Let me introduce you to Lorna, Mandy's best friend from childhood. I've known Lorna for many years."

"Really? It's a pleasure to meet you today. I mean it's not a pleasure just *today* but it is a pleasure." He nodded and grinned at Lorna, thinking: nice dress, big flowers.

Barbara noticed him noticing. "Yes, everything went okay at the service, don't you think? I mean, you do a lot of these, don't you?"

He finished chewing the cracker before replying. "Well, yes, I do. Unfortunately, people die all the time. We had a nice turnout today and that's not always the case when our elderly members pass." He paused, looking somber. "But that other thing that happened this morning." He shook his head. "Now that *was* strange. Never happened before. Not in *my* chapel."

Barbara was concerned. "What? What strange thing happened this morning?"

"Well, since you asked, I'll tell you." He cleared his throat. "This morning, I discovered a *man* in the sanctuary. He had the coffin open taking pictures of your sister. Naturally, I didn't think that was appropriate...that is, unless you gave him permission?"

"Me? No. I don't know what you're talking about."

"I didn't think so. Don't worry. I chased him away."

Barbara raised her voice. "*What* are you telling me? A *man* opened her coffin and took *photos*? What did he look like?"

Terri, Jan, and just about everyone in the house glanced toward the kitchen. The pleasant banter seemed to hush.

A woman in a white apron appeared with a tray beside the Reverend. He picked a shrimp, dipped it into the little bowl of cocktail sauce, gobbled it down, and dabbed at his mouth with a cocktail napkin.

"Reverend Shuttan?"

"Hmm? Oh, yes, yes. He wore a gray sweatshirt." He had another shrimp.

"Did he look like anyone here?" Barbara pointed toward the group of men in the living room.

Barbara, Lorna, and the Reverend eyed the men in the living room. The men looked up, smiled.

The Reverend glanced toward Lorna, hoping for an ally. "I really can't tell you what he looked like, Barbara. All the kids wear those sweatshirts these days. I couldn't see his face clearly, too far away. Need my glasses to see distance or close up, for that matter."

"Reverend. Please. Tell-me-what-you-saw."

Was she questioning his integrity? That was preposterous. After all, he was preacher, a man of God. "Barbara, I told you what that I saw. He opened the lid of the casket and he was taking pictures of her when I walked into the sanctuary. I told him to stop, he closed it, and then ran off. Some people like keepsakes of the departed. That must have been what he was doing."

"Taking pictures of my sister in her coffin?"

"Well, of course it was your sister, Barbara. I mean, I certainly hope so! Who else do you think would be in the coffin?"

"Who was he and why was he doing it? That's what I want to know. Did you ask him what he was doing?" Lorna touched Barbara's arm, trying to calm her.

"Yes, of course I asked him."

"And?"

"He mumbled something I couldn't hear... then I chased him outside to the parking lot."

"So you saw him in the parking lot?"

"No, no. I wasn't quick enough. I don't know how but he got clean away."

"Did you close it?"

"Close what? Oh, no, no. No need. The fellow did that before he left."

"Did you open it up to look inside—just to be sure she was okay?"

The Reverend found her question so appallingly indelicate that he felt his own voice rising to the shrill tenor he had learned to suppress at divinity school. "Look *in*? Sorry. I did no such thing. It's just not right. Your sister wanted it closed. And I certainly meant to honor that request. Barbara, I know this is not what you wanted to hear, but if you're implying that I was in any way responsible for this incident, you're mistaken."

Lorna jumped in. "Oh, no, no. She doesn't mean that *you're* to blame. She's just upset. This is a terrible shock."

He relented. "Of course, of course. You're right. It is shocking news."

Barbara spoke to Lorna. "Some *weirdo* in a gray sweatshirt took pictures of Mandy."

Lorna nodded, gave a beckoning glance to Jan in the living room.

Barbara continued, "She wanted a closed casket."

Jan joined the discussion. "Don't shoot the messenger. He's just telling you what happened, Mom."

"Yes, I'm so sorry, Barbara. You asked, so I had to tell you."

"Everything was going just fine, just the way Mandy wanted it. Then you tell me *this*." When she began to sob, the Reverend offered his cocktail napkin.

"Mom, come on. Aunt Mandy wouldn't want you to act like this. And you have to mingle with the guests. People are waiting to meet you."

Lorna took Barbara's hand saying, "That's right, kiddo. You're doing a great job. Time to move on. These things happen."

Even the Reverend touched Barbara's shoulder. "I *am* sorry, truly I am. I struggled with whether to tell you. I asked God to give me guidance but it was early in the morning and there was no clear answer, so I asked Polly." To Lorna and Jan he added, "She's my wife, not a parrot, people always ask. Polly said I should tell you if it came up. So that's what I did."

But Barbara wasn't listening so he turned to Lorna and Jan for sympathy. "I do hope I did the right thing. It was the right thing, wasn't it?"

No one answered.

Barbara spoke, "Jan, honey, why don't you rejoin your friend in the living room and show Reverend Shuttan the beverage table. He must be parched."

"Okay, Ma."

Glad to be released from the kitchen, the Reverend found the beverage table without an escort and handily poured himself a plastic tumbler of beer. He took a long drink and moved toward the group of men.

Jan found her drink, leaned toward Terri, and whispered, "My mom just had a total meltdown."

Barbara and Lorna were alone in the kitchen. "Barbara, forget it. Who knows what that was about? Besides, you need to finish the story about how you had to call Mandy's old boyfriends. That's what I want to hear about."

"You're right. But I have my suspicions—you know who I mean."

"You can't be sure of that."

"No, I can't." She brightened. "Okay, I'll tell you. I was mortified calling all those men. But you know Mandy. That's what she wanted, so that's what I had to do. It was her last wish. Know the strangest part?"

"What?"

"They all came."

"The guys? Where are they?"

Barbara pointed a celery stick toward the living room. "Of course there's Henry, Bobby (he's a Negro, you know), someone named Guido, and then this other man named Carlos. Actually, come to think of it, I never did talk with this other one. His name was Mushie or something like that. I just left a message on his machine."

"*Mushie?*" asked Lorna.

"Uh-huh. Funny name. Lives in New York City some-where. Of course I know Henry's still in the Boston area and Bobby probably lives in Harlem since he's col... er I mean, African American."

Lorna studied her. "Barbara, Bobby doesn't live in Harlem. He lives in Westchester. In a very nice neighbor-hood, Mandy said."

"Wait. Wait a friggin' minute. I remember him now. Bobby was the colored man who visited Mandy that summer, years ago. Jan was there. It's coming back to me." Barbara looked down, chewed on her lower lip; something was wrong.

"Barbara?"

"I'm all right."

"So, who's Guido?"

"Him? I don't know. That one has me stumped. Lives in New York, too."

"From work, maybe?" offered Lorna.

"Carlos lives next door with his son and all those kids. Speaks Spanish."

"Huh. Why do you think Mandy wanted them all here?"

"To impress us with how many boyfriends she had? So they could meet each other? I don't know. Just wish it wasn't me doing the calling. I was a little concerned when their wives answered the phone."

"That must have been awkward."

"I only spoke with two women directly. Funny thing is, they didn't seem concerned. Even said they were sorry. Didn't sound suspicious or anything. I thought it was strange. Could be that when you're as old as we are, it doesn't matter anymore. You know your husband as well as you're ever going to. "

"I suppose so. So, these guys were her boyfriends?"

"I'm guessing. She was never real specific about her love life, leastways, not with me. She ever mention them?"

"When we were younger she told me some things. But when I was married and busy with the kids, our relationship wasn't the same. Maybe she was afraid I'd disapprove." Lorna sighed.

"Funny, I always thought she shared everything with you, made me a little jealous if you want to know the truth."

"Barbara, she loved you. I'm sure you know things that I don't know."

"Well, enough of this Lorna. I'm being rude. You've had a long drive. Go fix yourself a drink in the living room, have something to eat, and mingle. I'll catch up with you in a bit."

"Bathroom?"

"Down the hall, to the left."

"Of course."

Barbara wondered whether she ought to warn Lorna about the pile of yellowing girly magazines between the toilet and the tub that she had neglected to remove.

Terri and Jan sat side-by-side on the couch. Terri leaned in. "So, how is she?"

"Oh, I don't know. My mother gets, you know, a little wound up."

"Yeah. But I mean, she should get upset today, she's allowed." Terri looked around. "I was just thinking about your aunt's house. She was such an unusual person."

"She was. One of a kind, all right. Gonna miss her. No one like her." Jan took a long swallow of her beer. "You know she left it to me."

"Left what?"

"The house, her house."

"Really? You going to move back to Connecticut?"

"I don't know. Depends."

"On what?" Terri asked.

"You know, I do have friends back there. And a good job. Can see the Golden Gate Bridge from my office."

"Yes, but you don't have a house and the yard's already decorated."

"That's true."

FRANK SINATRA AT NED'S

A young Frank Sinatra sang out from the speakers of a record player near the window in the living room. The men stood in a circle, drinking, talking, laughing.

Terri and Jan sat on the couch and offered Lorna a seat beside them. "Thanks, girls. But I'd rather stand a while. I've been sitting all morning."

"Lorna? I don't think that you've been properly introduced. This is my old friend Terri."

"Very nice to meet you, Terri, but you don't look so old, especially compared to everyone else in this room."

"How do you know Mandy?" Terri asked.

"She was my best friend from childhood. We lived on the same block in Boston. Grew up together. And Jan, I don't think we've ever met. Mandy had your school pictures on the piano and all over the wall, so I feel like I know you. But only as a little girl."

Barbara entered the living room and stood by Lorna. It seemed crowded due to the waisthigh stacks of magazines and newspapers that lined the walls. Jan had covered the stacks in sheets hoping they might resemble tables. When Lorna leaned against one, it moved and she gasped as Jan grabbed her elbow and cautioned, "I don't think you should lean on that. It's not very sturdy."

Barbara frowned, took a sip of her drink.

Lorna asked, "Barbara. Is Henry here?" she pointed to the four men standing near the front door.

"Not yet. But I expect he'll grace us with his presence soon."

Jan nudged Terri, humored by her mother's disdain for Henry. Terri looked on blankly. She didn't know these people, didn't get it, and didn't care.

But Lorna had noticed.

The Sinatra record ended and it was quiet, but only for a moment. Across the room, there was a commotion from the men. Henry had arrived. He was shaking hands and introducing himself around.

Terri whispered to Jan, "Your aunt was a pretty popular lady in her day."

"She was. And beautiful." Jan squinted, recognizing the African-American man. Had to be him. And Henry she knew from the photo Aunt Mandy kept on her bureau. He looked distinguished, a gentleman.

Barbara thought much less of Henry. Her expression said, *that old fart.* She scowled, set her drink down, went to the stereo, flipped the record over, centered it on the top of the stem, swung the arm across, turned the knob, and heard the record splat as it fell onto the turntable. The arm swung over the record and the stylus settled down into the first groove of "New York, New York."

Barbara retrieved her drink and stood near the couch, unnoticed by Lorna, who was absently swirling her index finger in her gin and tonic. Jan and Terri were busy eating from plates that towered with hors d'oeuvres.

When Sinatra sang, the room became animated. Henry snapped his fingers and closed his hand around an imaginary microphone. Lorna thought, *it's not fair, he still looks good.*

Barbara touched Lorna's arm and blurted to the women, "I discovered this great recipe for pot roast."

Terri pointed with a fork. "Oh, yeah? I'd love to hear it."

"Well, all you do is start with a good cut of—"

"Mom, you know I don't eat meat," said Jan.

Terri and Lorna waited on the sidelines for the volley to begin between mother and daughter. Sure enough, Barbara said, "Well, of course you don't, Jan. I just find it's a comfort to talk about ordinary things right now. If that's all right with you?"

Lorna jumped in. "Well what about veggie lasagna? My son's a vegetarian and a good cook. Claims to make the best spinach lasagna in Boston."

Jan feigned interest. "Oh, yeah? I'd like to hear it. Mine stinks, just layers of tofu, tomatoes, and zucchini."

Barbara took a long swallow of her martini; it had a very nice, relaxing effect.

So the conversation went on to discuss Christmas cookie recipes, butter cookies, almond crescents, little rum balls, chocolate truffles and more until Lorna commented, "You know, I don't think I've ever talked about recipes at a wake before."

"I *like* talking about cooking," said Jan.

"So do I," cooed Barbara.

It was during a lull when Terri felt compelled to jump into the conversation, turning it in another direction as she inquired, "So, Barbara. How did she die anyway? Was it bad?"

Unfortunately, Terri's graceless words jumped right into the air to fit the silence created by the exact ending of "New York New York" so that her words were heard very clearly by everyone in the living room.

Jan looked down, shook her head from side-to-side. She forgot that about Terri.

Lorna looked away, took a swallow of her drink.

As for Terri, she recognized this moment, this gaff, as just one more of her idiotic social blunders. But she reasoned that it didn't matter so much this time–hey, probably never see these people again. Lately, it seemed that her clumsy moments seemed to be multiplying. It happened so often that she began to notice a pattern emerge from bystanders; her poorly chosen words seemed to bond those around her. Even timid people were inspired to speak up, thankful that Terri's gaff was not their own.

Lorna, Jan, and Terri waited uneasily for Barbara's certain eruption. Maybe it was the three martinis or maybe it was Frank Sinatra but to everyone's surprise, Barbara took no offense. Instead, she was invigorated. This was the invitation she needed, what she had been waiting for all day and until now, no one had asked.

Barbara desperately *wanted* to talk about Mandy's death. "If my sister were here today she would say that it was just *thee-a-ter*. Her last performance."

Jan and Lorna nodded, relieved that perhaps things weren't going to go so badly after all.

They were wrong.

As Frankie began to sing, "If you're going to love me, it's no good unless you love me all the way," Barbara heaved, her chest rose like a diva and she let go. "I wasn't there when she died! I *wanted* to be there! I should have *been* there! She was only there two weeks! Only TWO WEEKS! She didn't *need* to die there with all those *strangers*! But she wouldn't let me come down and take care of her! She didn't want to be a bother, told me to leave her alone. She even said that dying would be an adventure! Can you imagine? An adventure!" She looked to Lorna for acquiescence and said quietly, "You know Mandy, once she's made up her mind."

No one was so cruel as to correct the tense of Barbara's words.

Lorna said, "Yes, she can be pretty stubborn all right."

Just as Barbara seemed to be calming down, she started up again, this time with even more exuberance, displaying a bit too much angst, even for her sympathetic audience.

"Oh, I tried. Believe me, I tried. But Mandy wanted it that way, nice and orderly. I don't know, maybe it was better. God. She was so sick. I saw her the Sunday before and I don't know if she even recognized me. Her *own* sister. It was awful. She rolled over and smiled but she didn't say a word, not a word. It was heartbreaking. I held her hand, but you know they had her all drugged up."

"Ma, it's all right. She was on morphine."

"The hospice people were wonderful, just wonderful. She didn't feel a thing. Do you know that Mandy went there to interview the staff? Can you believe that?"

"Yes, I can," said Lorna. "She knew how to take care of herself."

"Packed up the whole house and gave it to charity, everything except the piano. It all went to charity."

"Mrs. Tarnowski, what about the lawn stuff?" asked Terri.

This brought Barbara back down. "Well, yes. I think everything is still there last time I looked."

Jan smirked. "Better be."

Barbara continued, "Oh, yes, she planned every detail. Paid for everything. So, is it all right? Does it look okay? Does everyone have enough to drink? Ned gave me such a headache this morning. If Jan hadn't arrived, I don't know what I would have done."

Lorna touched her elbow. "Everything's fine, Barbara, just fine. You've done a wonderful job. Mandy would be so pleased. It's a really good party."

"To be correct about it Lorna, this is a *wake*–not a party. We're not really celebrating, are we?"

"We're celebrating her *life*. Your sister had a very full, very colorful life. You have to admit that."

"Yes, she did. She sure did. Well, I'd better go check on the caterer." Then Barbara was gone.

Jan pretended to wipe sweat from her brow and turned to Lorna. "She's holding up pretty well, don't you think?"

"I think your mother is doing fine but she exhausts me. Funny thing is, she sounded just like Mandy. I need to sit down with another beverage. Excuse me."

Carlos, Guido, Henry, Bobby, Ned and Reverend Shuttan stood talking near the front door. Ned was just six when Henry was courting Mandy. Otherwise, none of the men knew each other.

Henry asked, "So, Ned, this is difficult to ask, but did Mandy know it was coming?"

Ned thought about this. He didn't socialize much—was the quiet sort—because when he did talk, everyone grew so impatient they'd interrupt to finish his sentences. He didn't stutter; just spoke very slowly. But today was special. He wanted to learn what they knew about his beloved sister Mandy and he knew they would be attentive and patient with him. He needed to talk about her.

"Oh, yeah, oh yeah, of course, she knew... handkerchiefs of blood... it was the smoking, that's what did it... it was the smoking. Couldn't even talk at the end on account a the coughin'... She'd start up and just couldn't stop... made everybody sick... just as well... I guess... But she was my favorite sister. I'm really gonna miss her..."

Henry moved closer. "I'm sorry to be so inquisitive, but when did she find out?"

"Well... had to be... just about three... maybe it was four... no three... months ago... I think. She went quick. Real quick. The doctors... they didn't exactly know... when... she'd go... but I guess... she looked pretty bad."

"They couldn't do anything?" asked Henry.

"In-oper-a-ble, that's what they said. She was... real upset that she didn't know... when it would... happen. She hated surprises, you know, wanted to be... prepared. Those doctors, they don't know everything."

"That's the Lord's job," said the Reverend.

They all nodded.

Ned continued. "She had this little medal made... wore it 'round her neck... and it said what to do... with her... just in case... just in case she died... before she got to... got to... that place in Branford and sometimes Mandy seemed so... dizzy, as a kid but she knew what she was doin' all right... she knew what she was doin' when she died. You know, this party... this party is all on her. Yup. She wrote it all... down... Said who to invite and everything. All paid for. Poor Barbie... had to call you guys.... She's my sister too, ya know. Mandy wanted a good sendoff."

There was a bit of shuffling and respectful nodding. But Guido couldn't help remark in his usual Bronx wise-guy way, "I get that. But if you're dead, you're dead, right? I mean, what difference does it make? The medal and the party and stuff?"

The Reverend was anxious to jump in to testify in defense of God, Jesus, and the Bible about dying so as to set matters right. But he restrained himself from preaching and just listened. This was man talk. No one ever talked this way around him (and it gave him a good idea for a sermon).

Ned dabbed at his mouth with his handkerchief, as he was prone to do from time to time when spittle formed at the corners. It also gave him time to think before answering. "Well... I guess you had to know Mandy... Maybe you just had to know her a little bit better... Um... just how... just how... well... did you know her?"

Guido was a short, wiry man with a big head and large hands. He had a pencil-thin mustache, a broad forehead, and big white teeth like Clark Gable. While the guys watched, Guido raised his beer bottle to his lips and took three swallows to empty the bottle, his Adam's apple bobbing until he placed the empty on the table beside him with deliberate aplomb. Next, he took a handful of pretzels from the table behind him and as he stuffed two pretzels into his mouth, he began to speak. "Well, Ned, I guess I didn't get to know her all that well. Matter of fact, I was kinda surprised that she kept track a me after all these years... cause I didn't know where she went. But I thought about her a lot, I did, yes, I surely did. She was the most glamorous gal I ever saw! You shoulda seen her years ago in that red getup! And then she played piano at the club. She was so glamorous. A real star if there ever was one. So if Mandy wanted me here, then, well, by God, I'd come, I had to come."

Henry listened soberly. Guido had seen Mandy in the red costume.

Guido reached for the peanuts, jiggling them like dice as he continued. "The long and short of it is, guys, I knew her a long time ago for a very a brief time. Nice girl. Very attractive girl. I remember it like yesterday." He hesitated a moment, studying the attentive faces of his audience, then said with sudden animation, "I guess you might say our relationship went *up* as fast as it went *down*, for Christ's sake! It was over so quick, too quick. I wanted more time but Mandy, well, she had other plans, big plans. So she left me. Fellas, that was the Mandy I knew."

The men nodded, clapped Guido on the back, and smiled knowingly. As Guido reached for more peanuts, he remarked, "But boy, oh boy, it sure was fun, if you know what I mean!" Then he winked.

Henry was drinking bourbon. Whenever someone mentioned Mandy's name, he was inclined to take a substantial swallow. Even though Henry was not yet inebriated, he was clearly on his way, bobbing with emotion. The drink skewed his sensibilities from forlorn to machismo. He was emboldened by his new comrades. Henry Russell, retired certified public accountant and ex-husband of Mandy, chimed in distastefully, "You got that right, fella. Could that girl kiss! And she'd try everything. How did it go with you?"

Realizing that the conversation had taken a rather sudden, *intimate* jog in a direction that a brother and a preacher would feel embarrassed hearing, Ned backed away from the group murmuring, "Getting a beer."

"A beer sounds good," said Reverend Wally, following Ned to the kitchen.

Guido raved, "Oh, yeah. We got down, too. Sure did, what a time!"

No one knew that Guido was talking about a ride in an elevator. The women frowned and moved to the kitchen.

Seeing the women exit encouraged the new friends to continue sharing their exploits about intimacies with Mandy. They seemed to enjoy the telling of it as much as they must have enjoyed doing it (if they had actually done *it* at all).

In the circle, Bobby was the silent one. No one could tell if he was offended, ill at ease, or even amused. He didn't smile. Every now and again, he tugged on the cuffs inside his tweed jacket and took a swallow of scotch.

When he first arrived, he hadn't even removed his hat when Barbara approached. "Bob–if I can call you Bob–"

"Call me Bobby. That's what she used to call me."

"Okay, Bobby. It was so good of you to come. Mandy bought this just for you." She held up a bottle of Chivas Regal. "She said that it was your favorite. Is it your favorite?"

"Oh, it used to be. Haven't had this in quite some time. That was sweet of her to remember. But wait a minute. She told you what I *drink*?"

"Oh, yes. She bought all the liquor before she died; she planned ahead. You were on the guest list. She really wanted you here."

"I don't know what to say," said Bobby.

"Don't say anything. Go in the living room and eat something. I'll pour it for you. Take it on the rocks or straight up?"

"Straight up."

Bobby stayed with the men as Barbara removed his empty glass twice and brought it back refilled. She ignored the others. At times, he wondered what he was doing there, whether he'd made a mistake coming to this little house. They did not know that he was a very wealthy man and comfortable at the podium at business events. And he was high up in the national NAACP, too. He remembered Barbara and the ruckus that happened when he visited Mandy so many years ago. Now, as the only person of color, he felt a bit self-conscious and wished his wife had come along. Something always felt unfinished when he thought of Mandy; something nagged at his heart. She was the first white person he trusted and the first woman he loved. But that didn't explain it. He needed to be here with these strangers but didn't know why.

He stuck his tongue on the inside of his cheek and moved it around before leaning forward to speak, in a tone that was both low and conspiring, his eyes moving from Henry to Carlos to Guido.

"Okay, guys. I'll tell you. This is all strictly confidential between us, got that? You wouldn't believe the stuff that we did in my 'partment. See when I was young, I was a musician back then, see? Now I own some drug stores. But back then, before my wife that is, we would go back to my place in the city after the show was over, understand? Friday nights, it was. In my living room. We did it on the rug, on the couch, on my horn case once."

Henry had to interrupt. "Just, just how did you meet Mandy, ah, Bob is it? One of her shows maybe?"

"Call me Bobby. No, nothing like that. She wasn't performing when I met her. She was in radio and wasn't married. We met on the subway. She dropped something... can't remember now...when I saw her again in Connecticut my wife and I were having some problems. Mandy gave us good advice. Her niece was there at the time. Must be that young lady over there," he said, pointing to Jan. "We played checkers. Barbara's her mother, right? She keeps bringing me Chivas. Well, Barbara arrived at Mandy's mad as hell to fetch her daughter. She didn't like me, didn't like me being there."

Henry interrupted. "Oh no, you, too? She *hates* me. Always has." He rocked on his heels, proudly. "Sorry. Go on."

"Mandy was so upset. Barbara had the wrong impression. Patched things up with my wife, and lickety-split we adopted six kids. But... what a girl Mandy was. She was my first girl. She did this thing... this thing with a boa, you know, that feather thing?" he looked from one man to the other.

Henry frowned and felt that he should be indignant, protect Mandy's honor. After all, this was his ex-wife he was discussing. Liberal as Henry tried to be, Bobby was a colored man. He had difficulty imagining Mandy with him. What did it matter anymore? He wanted to learn about her life and what he missed. He had no right to judge. "Yes! I do remember feathers. Ooooo. Yes sir, Bobby, I do remember she liked to play with feathers. Nearly forgot about that. My old bones get goosebumps just thinking about it."

"Feathers?" Guido grinned.

"She'd take one out and then..." Henry shook his hand. "Like dusting."

Carlos Chacon was still learning English and so he didn't understand every detail of what was being said. But he did understand the feathers and demonstrated by fanning one hand while grasping the other hand around an imaginary pole that he slid up and down all the while saying, "Like this, sirs, like this, eh?"

Henry slapped his thigh. "You, too? My God! You knew her as an old lady. How long ago was that?"

But Carlos didn't understand. He said, "Aha," and then began to shake an imaginary feather with his right hand while his left hand walked like the itsy-bitsy spider up-the-waterspout demonstrating another variation.

"Oh, my," chuckled Bobby.

"Yes, yes, like that," said Carlos, pleased that everyone understood.

"Oh, what a girl, what a girl she was," said Henry.

"She learn that from you, man? You were married to her," Bobby asked.

"Me? No. For a young girl, she was pretty forward that way, inventive you might say.

Nothing too naughty–just fun, you know? I'd have to say that Mandy had a gift, a true gift."

"Made me a happy man. Amen to that," said Bobby.

"Amen," they said in unison.

Barbara was sitting at the kitchen table with Lorna and Jan, listening to Terri brag about her talented children when she noticed Ned outside with the reverend, opening the garage door. He must be showing the reverend his old newspapers and magazines, she thought. Seeing the reverend made her recall "the incident" that occurred earlier. As Frankie started to sing, "I've got you under my skin," Barbara stood up and marched into the living room to face the men. "I wish I knew which one of you did it!" she bellowed. Then she returned to the kitchen table.

"Mom! What was all of that about?"

The men looked at each other and shrugged.

Guido said, "I don't know what she's so mad about, do you? But I think we should cool it, fellas. Change the subject. She's getting the wrong idea and we want to be respectful. "

They nodded.

"That Barbara, she's a tough one," said Bobby.

"You got that right," said Henry. "Never liked me one bit."

"The lady's sad, she's just sad," said Carlos, "like me."

They all nodded.

"But other lady with flowers on dress? She's nice."

They all nodded.

OLD FRIENDS

Henry came from the bathroom and headed to the kitchen for a refill. When he returned to the living room, he squinted at the woman on the couch. "Lorna? Lorna? I didn't see you over there. My eyesight is as bad as my manners. Could that really be *you* after all these years?"

The old man moved toward her, stabbing his cane forward with each stride. She wiped her mouth, having just finished three cocktail shrimp and two stuffed mushrooms, to find herself face to face with Henry, an old man with white hair and a long mustache.

He was exuberant. "My dear, you look just wonderful! Simply the picture of health."

Funny about that. He was still charming, still polite, and still alive.

"Henry? It's about time you came over to say hello. You old coot. You should be dead. Whoever thought you'd outlive Mandy?"

"Lorna! How dare you. How *dare* you! Is that any way to greet an old friend? You should be *dead*? Oh, no. I outlived my first wife and my second wife, imagine that? So I'm available, again. Pipes are a little rusty, I admit. But they should work, if I ever get the chance to find out. By the way, where's James? Couldn't make it?"

Lorna's words rushed out as she saw the hors d'oeuvres coming her way. "I'll say he couldn't make it. James has been gone for over five years now. He had arthritis, diabetes, high blood pressure, and then phlebitis, remember?"

"Oh, oh, yes, I guess his health took a turn then... I do remember his problems. How insensitive of me. I was so looking forward to seeing him again." Henry had the talent of changing his face from mirth to ardent sympathy in a flash whenever it was needed. Now he looked somber, his cheery glow gone.

"Henry, it doesn't matter. We all have to go sometime. This was Mandy's time. James was having trouble getting around and when his eyes got so bad that he couldn't read anymore, he gave up. And what good is retirement if you can't read all those books you've set aside and can't travel and enjoy your grandchildren?"

"So true. What good is money without good health?"

"But I can't complain. I'm quite comfortable now. We had *four* children, you know, and seven grandchildren."

Henry looked her over and saw just what the reverend had seen earlier. A short, buxom woman with an olive complexion, a little gray-streaked but mostly wavy, black hair, twisted high except for a white strand that fell over one eye in a youthful way. With her carefully drawn red lips and her tightly-waisted yellow dress, she looked much younger than a woman in her seventh decade. "I simply can't believe you're a grandmother. A beautiful young thing like you."

But he saddened again and spoke in a hushed voice, "Lorna, I can't believe Mandy is gone. I truly hoped to see her again... I *lived* to see her again. And James gone, too. I always wondered what happened to you two. Of course, I read about the bank from time to time and I thought about calling. But Margaret, well, she felt uncomfortable around Mandy's friends. You know how it is. I wondered about you, though. And I wondered about Mandy. I'm ashamed to say that I missed her quite a bit, quite a bit. Margaret knew it, too. We hardly spoke the last few years. When I retired, she moved in with her sister down at the Cape and I hardly saw her at all. That's where she died three months ago, pneumonia. We didn't even live together at the end. Bet you didn't know that, did you?"

"Well, no. I'm sorry to hear about Margaret. We noticed your picture in the paper from time to time. Symphony patrons, was it?"

"That's right." He grasped her elbow and spoke so close to her that she could smell his bourbon breath. "Listen, Lorna. What *did* happen to Mandy? I never knew. It haunted me all my life, *all* my life. You can't imagine how sad this occasion is for me. She was my youth."

He looked sullen, clasped his hands anxiously, begging, "Do you think she ever *cared* about me? Did she ever say anything to you, about me? Did she ever say she *missed* me?"

"Oh, Henry. It was a long time ago. She never really came right out and said it to me but she missed you, in her own way."

"How do you know? Tell me."

"Well, I guess it's what she didn't say. She must have been quite hurt, you know, because she wouldn't talk about it. That's the way she is, ah, was. I worried when she was quiet. She didn't like to talk about it. And of course, it was better to pretend that she had never been married rather than say she was divorced. You know how it is, people imagine all sorts of things."

Henry looked dejected. "Yes, but did she never say anything at all to you, about missing me? You were her best friend?"

"Early on maybe, when we were out for a good time and she had a few drinks. She'd say something like, 'He'll be back, Henry will be back'. She really did believe that someday you'd return to her, Henry. I didn't pay much attention, didn't want to encourage her. But honestly, she really did believe that. She always thought that it was all just a simple misunderstanding. Those were her exact words, 'a simple misunderstanding,' that's what she said."

"Well, Mandy was Mandy. I wouldn't call it a simple misunderstanding. She believed what she wanted to. But I loved that girl. Truly, I did. Never loved Margaret, no. That was my mother's idea. She never gave Mandy a chance, cut me off, you know, when we got married. We had only twenty dollars when we eloped. Twenty dollars in New York. And Mandy couldn't save a dime, not a dime."

He shook his head, took a swallow of his whiskey. They were quiet a moment until Lorna said, "But you had some fun, didn't you Henry?"

"You bet we did. Lorna, looking back now, well, those were the best years of my life, the best." He slipped away, introspective, gazing at nothing, then raised his glass. "Mandy, I swear, the most fun I had was with you. Thank you." He clinked Lorna's wineglass and drank his whiskey straight down.

Lorna turned away, ready to leave, but he caught her arm, "Lorna, I really must apologize for my gaff. I'm so sorry to hear about James. You know I can't quite imagine you without him. How many years were you married?"

"The kids were planning a party for us, our 45th wedding anniversary. James didn't make it."

It was getting dark out, the moon rising, the day gone. There were magazines and newspapers that lay open on the stacks in the living room. The men had moved from standing near the front door to sitting on the couch and the La-Z-Boy chair. The living room was small and it wasn't difficult to overhear conversations. The men spoke about sports, politics, and the places they'd been, but the conversation always returned to Mandy and no one seemed to want to leave.

Jan and Terri leaned against the doorway to the kitchen. Barbara was napping in Ned's bedroom. Henry and Lorna stood near the front door talking as a scratchy "Rhapsody in Blue" played.

Henry leaned toward Lorna. "But she was out of control. You were her best friend. You knew about her lovers, didn't you?"

"Yes, I knew about them. Or at least, I thought I did. But I have no idea who those guys are." She pointed her chin toward the men.

Henry shrugged with ambivalence. "Oh, they're just, they're just, you know, some boys she knew," he mumbled.

From the doorway, Terri interrupted, "Oh, I heard they were more than friends."

Henry ignored her. Jan chimed in, "Hey, don't worry about our delicate ears. It isn't something I haven't heard before a dozen times from my mom."

Lorna was stone-faced.

"I suppose not," said Henry reluctantly.

Lorna said, "Henry, you must have suspected that Mandy was determined to make it in show business. Everything else was secondary. Everything. It was her dream to make it ever since I can remember. And don't forget how young she was. We were just kids then."

"Lorna, Mandy was..."

Jan elbowed Terri. "Quiet, I want to hear this."

"Don't you blame her! At least Mandy had her dreams. What did I do? Nothing. I was a good wife. A good mother. At least she stuck out her neck. No one should have robbed her of that. Not you, not anybody."

"Don't sell yourself short Lorna. You were a good wife and mother, that's what a man wants, so don't blame me for Mandy. I didn't want to rob of her of anything. Give me some credit. I just wanted her to cut out all that... *foolishness.* She didn't need to do it. And a lot of good it did her, didn't it?"

"She was *very* successful."

"Successful? Are we talking about the same person?"

"She was in dozens of shows!"

"Lorna, Lorna, Lorna. I don't know what Mandy told you in her letters but she was in only a handful of shows and they all closed or she was fired. She was cast in only one legitimate show that I remember. I know this is hard to hear, but she was not successful in show business and she fooled around on me." He noticed the men listening, everyone listening.

"Henry, you *knew* what Mandy was like when you married her. Don't pretend you didn't know," said Lorna tartly.

"Lorna, Lorna. I knew, but I didn't know. I loved her. I thought she'd change. I wanted children. Listen, there were many things Mandy said she wanted but they just weren't true. I was never really sure she loved me. I gave her so many second chances but she was always looking over my shoulder. I couldn't take it anymore. Mandy had gone over the edge of common decency. James told me all about it. You know, the time you were staying at the Ritz? That was the last straw. That was the only legitimate show she was in. Now, you can't blame me for being mad about that, can you?"

Lorna looked puzzled.

"You didn't know, did you? James never told you?"

"Tell me what?"

"I think it's that chap over there–the wiry guy in the camel jacket and the pencil bar mustache. He was a bellhop at the hotel. Mandy was smooching him in the elevator at your hotel."

Guido shrugged.

"And then it happened again. I found her with a young man, in our apartment, no less. Said they were rehearsing.

I remember it like yesterday. Left with tears in my eyes. Sat in Central Park for a couple hours just feeding the damn pigeons, didn't know what to do. It got dark and then I drove back to Boston. I didn't know what to do, didn't know whether I was being foolish, and I didn't want to call my parents. So I called James."

"He never told me," said Lorna.

"Well, we thought it best that you..."

"You thought it best that I didn't *know*?"

"Lorna, listen. She was your best friend. I made James swear that he wouldn't tell you and apparently he kept his word."

"Apparently so."

"I didn't want to divorce Mandy, but James convinced me that she wouldn't settle down. He told me about finding her with that guy at your hotel. A bellhop! I still get angry when I think about it. My parents, well, you know they never did like her. It didn't take much to convince them that I'd made a mistake. They were overjoyed when I showed up. My father was gloating that he knew I'd come to my senses. So, that's how it ended."

"But Henry, that's *not* how it ended, is it?" Lorna pressed.

The arm of the stereo was bobbing at the end of the record waiting to be picked up. The room was silent again, everyone straining to hear their conversation.

"Well, no, I mean yes, I mean, well I'm not proud of it. I didn't know she told you about it."

"Oh, she did," said Lorna with satisfaction.

"I guess it doesn't matter anymore. Listen Lorna, I was weak. I loved the girl. You understand that, right? I just couldn't help myself."

"Uh-huh," said Lorna.

"Try to be fair, Lorna. I'm an old man now."

"So what happened? Tell me about New Haven."

Henry sighed. "Well, we'd meet in New Haven. I tell you, things were better than they ever were when we were married. Better. Mandy was so pretty then, so vibrant, turned everyone's head, her eyes... you know it was better when we weren't married. She was a wonderful girlfriend but not a good wife."

"That's no excuse for what you did."

"Maybe not. But..."

"What happened? She called me from the train station that day, crying," said Lorna testily.

"Crying? She did? Well, everything was going along fine until I ran into Margaret's cousin Malcolm on Chapel Street in New Haven. He was at Yale for some reason I can't recall. Well, he insisted we have lunch. And then Malcolm proceeded to say that he thought he'd seen me in New Haven a week ago and inquired about the pretty woman with the red coat. That's just how he said it, 'the pretty woman with the red coat'. Of course it was Mandy he meant. I bought her that coat. But I told him it was my sister. I suspect he didn't believe me. The lunch dragged on and on and I couldn't get away from him. That blowhard! Can't stand the fellow to this day; I hope he rots in hell. Oh, yes, he's dead. Well, I think he knew about Mandy all along and just wanted to see me squirm. It was awful, just awful. She was waiting for me at the Green and he kept going on and on."

"So, you stood her up, didn't you?"

"Lorna. You're not listening. I had no choice. It was the worst day of my life! Believe me, I never wanted to hurt her. I loved her. But then the baby was born and I had to tell my sister Elizabeth everything so she'd provide me with an alibi. And oh, what a mess. Elizabeth was furious. She threatened to tell Margaret and our parents if I didn't break it off immediately. We just couldn't carry on anymore. It was over."

"Uh, huh."

"I honestly thought that Mandy would call me, to ask what happened. But she never did, she never did. She probably thought that we were going to get back together and that I'd divorce Margaret. Almost did. But that was just impossible. All those men. I just couldn't trust her. Can't have a wife like that."

"Really? And Margaret can have a husband that fools around?"

"Lorna, that's not fair! There were other things, private things about Margaret I just can't discuss. We barely consummated our marriage. Thomas isn't even my own son."

"Oh."

"All of it doesn't matter, does it? You see, Margaret was pregnant when we married. I didn't know about it. Her parents and my parents arranged for us to meet at the club. We dated very briefly. Pretty soon I was engaged. The marriage was a rushed affair. I believe my mother was worried that I'd go back to Mandy and Margaret's mother just wanted Margaret legitimately hitched. I was a sucker for Mandy and then I was a sucker for Margaret. I was the victim. When Margaret began to show, I put two and two together. I'm a CPA for heaven's sake, I can count. She told me that it was a sailor. A good family like that and a sailor! Geez. I was bitter. First Mandy and then Margaret. And what could I do? Divorce her? By then, I was working for her father. It was too scandalous to think of. So, I said nothing and Margaret looked the other way when I was gone weekends seeing Mandy. That was our arrangement. Mandy never knew about the birth of Thomas."

"You could have told her. I was the one to tell her you had a baby. You should have said something."

"I should have, but I didn't. And I never saw her again. "

No one noticed that Barbara had entered the living room, her nap over. "Henry, you were *never* going to leave

Margaret. It was always about the money, wasn't it? If you loved Mandy, you should have told her everything."

"Barbara, please, I did love her. But tell me, why did she want me here?"

"I don't know. Why did she want them?" she said, pointing to the men.

"Please know that I am sorry. I have never regretted anything more in my entire life."

IN THEIR CUPS AT THE WAKE

Elvis sang, "Since my baby left me. I found a new place to dwell. It's down at the end of Lonely Street that Heartbreak Hotel. Well, I never been so lonely. I never been so lonely."

Terri was alone on the couch. Her feet were drawn up under her, her arms were folded across her chest, and the dark frizz of curls that had been neatly tied back early in the day were let loose and wild. Her head rested on the sofa back, her mouth gaped open, and she snored in low guttural inhales until the bounce of the cushion startled her awake. Jan sat down.

"Where *were* you?"

Jan held a white powder donut in a napkin, took a bite, and answered between chews, "At the store. Buying milk for coffee. Bought these, too. I know, I know. There's already some little petite fours and fancy pastries and stuff, but powder donuts, aw these were calling out my name. Aren't they just perfect? Want one?"

"I was just getting ready to leave."

"Listen, you can't go yet, it's not over. Don't be mad at me. I just needed some air, that's all."

"Just like old times, isn't it?"

"What do you mean?" Jan noticed her mother listening.

"Come on, let's go outside."

They sat on the front steps. Golden lights glowed from the living room and they heard a car door close, a screen door slam. Jan removed a cigarette from the pack in her shirt pocket.

"You bought smokes?" asked Terri. "Thought you said you quit."

"I know, I know. I needed a break. Something to relieve the tension. My mother."

"Okay, I'll accept that. Give me one."

"I'm sorry, I owe you. You've been really great coming here, putting up with everyone.

It's been a little bizarre for me."

"Bizarre for you? How do you think I feel? I still don't know what I'm doing here and why I let you talk me into it. If I wasn't so fucking smashed, I would have left hours ago."

"I know. What did you mean a minute ago when you said it's just like old times?"

Terri inhaled and then exhaled a long stream before answering. "When you left, you just left, didn't tell me anything, just like now for the donuts. You didn't give me any thought at all, stuck here with all these old people? You left the same way you left me when you moved to San Francisco. No consideration for anybody else."

"Well, that may be, but today I'm sort of innocent. I went with Uncle Ned. We both needed to talk about something and we didn't want my mom around. I didn't ask you to come 'cause it might have been awkward for him."

"You still could have told me you were going."

"You were talking to Lorna and Henry, something heavy, so I just ducked out. I really thought it would only be a minute. We were sitting in the car in the driveway most of the time."

"How would I know that? So, what were you talking about?" asked Terri.

"Next weekend, stuff he did, and my Aunt Mandy, what else? He's all broken up. She kind of held things together. He was really close to her. So was I. Matter of fact, so was my mother and Lorna. All of us. But in different ways. Like all these old guys. That's the thing. And now we'll have to get along with each other. She held it together."

Terri rounded her lips and blew a long tobacco stream into the air. Neither spoke for a few minutes. "So, why did you go?"

"To San Francisco? Well, I'd have to say that it didn't *feel* right. Something wasn't working with us. We were arguing too much. It wasn't fun anymore and you weren't going to admit it. One of us had to end it. So I did." Jan took a long drag and then snapped her jaw, ejecting little smoke rings wavering into the air.

"I could never do that."

"I know. That's why I had to."

"No, I mean smoke rings. I can't make them."

"Oh. Not hard. I'll show you."

They leaned against the iron railings of the front steps, mouths open, lips smacking like two fish. "Hold it in, close on it like this."

Terri produced two ovals of smoke.

"You did it girl. All right!"

"You're a bad influence on me."

"That's why I left."

THE REVELATION

Lorna, Barbara, Terri, and Jan were left cleaning up. Ned
went to bed. The men left promising to return the following weekend.

"I'm glad this is over with. No offense, I really don't like
funerals," said Terri.

Jan said, "You think I do? You think anyone does?"

"Well, some people do."

"Yeah, but they're weird and very lonely. Terri, know why
you were invited?" asked Jan.

"No, I don't."

"It was my aunt who invited you, in that letter she wrote
to my mother. You were on the list." Barbara glanced at
Lorna and announced, "We're going to clean up in the living
room."

"What? Your aunt wanted *me* here?" Terri asked. "I only
met her once."

"I'm telling you, she invited you specifically."

"That doesn't make any sense. Why me?"

"She remembered you," Jan said.

"Is that why you laid such a big guilt trip on me to come
with you?"

"Don't put it that way. She really liked you, asked how
you were and all."

"You told her that I was married, didn't you?"

"Well, no, not exactly. It never came up. She really liked you and I think she thought that well, that you lived in San Francisco with me and that—"

"Why did she think that? You told her that we broke up a long time ago, didn't you?"

"Never came up."

"Why? Why didn't you set her straight?"

"Very funny."

"It wasn't meant to be funny. Why didn't you *say* something?"

"I couldn't. My aunt had this 'thing' about marriage. She wanted everyone to be paired off, even me. Used to say it didn't matter so much who you were with so long as you weren't alone. Maybe 'cause of what happened to her. I didn't want to disappoint her, especially toward the end."

"So, you never told her we broke up, that I got married, have kids, that I'm straight? Why?"

"Told you. It was easier not to say anything. I mean, I was just as surprised as anybody when my mother read me the letter listing all the guests she wanted. She wrote something like, 'Be sure that Jan invites Terri, that nice friend of hers.' That's what she wrote, I swear. You can ask my mother."

"No. It's too bizarre. Probably true."

"What's the big deal anyway? I mean, I had to invite you. It was part of her last wish. It wasn't so bad, was it?"

"Would you have invited me if she hadn't mentioned it?" Terri asked.

"Um, probably not. What's the difference, anyway?"

"Well, that makes me feel really good."

"You're blowing it all out of proportion. She died happy thinking I was in a relationship. Leave it alone."

"It *is* a big deal! She died thinking I was with *you*! That's wrong and you know that's wrong."

"Is it so wrong? I was probably just a game to you. I was probably just a phase you were going through."

"It wasn't like that and you know it. But it does matter what people think. Even your aunt, even dead people."

"You only met her once. She wasn't your aunt. It's not as if she was someone significant in *your* life. She mattered to *me*. I wanted to make her happy. What's so bad about that?"

"You used me. I've been here all day. Most of it waiting for you."

"I'm sorry. I'm sorry about all of it. I wanted to see you," Jan said.

"You did?"

"Yes. Aunt Mandy gave me the excuse."

"But you said—"

"I couldn't just call you. Needed an excuse. She gave me that."

WAITING FOR THE ASHES

Three days later, Jan and Terri waited in the lobby of the crematorium until Mr. Pyle, a slender man in a dark blue suit, came out. He said they weren't quite ready yet and motioned to the couch in the alcove where they could wait. He began to walk away but then spun around like a dancer on his shiny black shoes, winked at Jan, and said, "You can watch if you like."

"Nah, we'll wait here for the vase. I mean, urn."

"Suit yourself then," he said with a smile, turned away and strutted down a long glassy corridor.

"He wasn't serious, you know. He was just kidding," said Terri.

"Really? I thought he was serious. I bet some people like to watch," said Jan.

"Yeah, Nazis. Jan, do you really think anyone *normal* would *want* to watch? I mean, even if they did, I bet the people who run these places don't *really* want you to watch. Maybe the ashes get all mixed up with other people–people you don't even like. I mean, how do you know that the ashes you're getting aren't somebody else's? How do you know?"

"I guess you don't know. Does it really matter?"

Terri was aghast. "Of course it matters. I mean, why are we waiting here? Wouldn't you be mad if the ashes weren't your aunt's ashes?"

"Well, like you said, as long as I don't know about it, it won't bother me. Look, I've never done this before. I'm only doin' it because my aunt asked me to. Now, do me a favor and change the subject, okay? It gives me the creeps."

From there, they began an awkward conversation, trying to catch up on the last eight years of family, friends, where they lived, and what work they did, avoiding touchy subjects and wrong words until both grew exhausted by the pretense and satisfied with the silence.

The lobby had a glossy blue-tiled floor and there were high ceilings and echoes. The women wore their coats because it was cold. Two chairs and the sofa they sat on were upholstered in purple velvet and had gold-painted claw feet. It grew late and the mid-afternoon sun suddenly began to flood through an enormous stained glass window before them that depicted the crucifixion of Jesus.

Jan was engrossed in the newspaper so Terri decided to look at the entries in her checkbook. Just as she reached into her purse, she was transfixed by the sad, searching brown eyes looking down at her, staring into her own eyes. She heard his raspy voice whispering to her, "Why me? Why me?"

She was horrified. She knew that Jan had not heard or seen him. But she had, thorns digging into his scalp, scratches weeping blood onto his forehead, wooden stakes through his palms thick with dark blood about to drip onto the floor. She could not turn away and he could not move. Jesus blinked and asked again, "Why me? Why me?"

Terri shook her head from side to side and in her terror and pity, began to weep, tears washing her vision to a blur. Groping for a tissue in her purse, she looked down. When she looked up again, Jan was standing before the window, arms folded. "I just don't get it. I never did get it and I never will get it." The lobby grew dim, the window receded, just glass.

Terri wanted to talk about it, but Jan wasn't the right person, Sam was. She would tell him later.

Jan pulled a paper bag from her knapsack. "They need better lighting. Can hardly read my paper. Want some pistachios?"

They cracked the shells and ate the salty meats until their hands, lips, and tongues were red and a few minutes later Mr. Pyle appeared smiling, carrying an urn, and said, "Here you go, ladies."

HER FINAL PERFORMANCE

Everyone stood around the yard. Carlos Chacon stepped outside with his son John and daughter-in-law Marilyn who stood in the doorway calling, "Come on everybody. It's time." And four young children burst into the yard.

Carlos retrieved a ladder from the garage and walked across the yard. He placed it against Mandy's house. Jan followed and gave him the urn.

When Moshe arrived with a full dark beard, his wife wearing large sunglasses like a movie star, everyone turned to stare.

"Mom, who's that?" Jan asked.

"Oh, he made it," Barbara said. "That's Mushie, Mandy's rabbi from New York."

Lorna said, "No, he's not a rabbi. He's a professor at City College. They were friends."

Barbara went to meet them.

"Hello. I'm Moshe and this is my wife Miriam. And you are?"

"I'm Barbara, Mandy's sister. I'm the one who called you. I'm so glad you could make it. Too bad you missed the service last week, but Mandy would be so pleased you're here. We're about to begin. Just stand anywhere and watch up there." She pointed to the roof.

Surveying the yard, Moshe raised his eyebrows to signal his wife. She smiled, pointed toward the row of bag ducks and lawn ladies. They navigated there. Meanwhile, the Chacon kids ran about chasing each other. Ned stood near the wind chimes on the maple tree with Henry by his side. As Carlos began to climb the ladder, Ned removed something from the pocket of his plaid jacket and began to look, catching Henry's attention. "*You* did it! *You* were the one. Her own brother!"

"Shhh. Was me...and she, she looked good... I asked and Mandy said 'sure' but my camra was in gettin' fixed so...so I didn't get photos till after... she died. Don't tell Barbie."

"You let me see those–you owe me that, Ned. Let me see and I won't tell," implored Henry.

"Loved her, didn't ya?"

"Yes, yes I did. I just want to *see* her again, that's all."

"Well. Okay...they're a little... fuzzy. Hurry up, they're gonna do it."

Henry trembled, had to look, even though his eyes were already filling up. He took them, shuffling through, muttering, "Look at that, old but she still looks good. God, I can't...."

"Gonna start, give 'em back."

"Thank you, Ned. You don't know what this means to me. She was..." As he handed the pictures back, he realized that Jan and Terri had been watching. "Oh, oh. Your niece caught you," whispered Henry.

"It's okay. She won't... rock the boat. Mandy was my favorite sister, you know."

"She was everybody's favorite. Look at all these people. This is an unusual occasion and she was an unusual woman." As Henry spoke he noticed Barbara looking their way, and Barbara noticed the reverend noticing her.

Meanwhile, Carlos had reached the pinnacle of the garage roof. He was doing his best to remain steady and controlled before his attentive audience. Leaning against the wooden head, he pointed to the urn, and with great aplomb, poured the ashes into the giant opening.

Carlos came down the ladder, went behind the garage to plug in the extension cord, and was rounding the garage when the seven-year-old said, "Grandpa, nothing's happening! It's not working."

"Wait. You must be good. It happen."

Carlos stood beside Lorna.

Moshe asked Bobby, "I don't get it, what's supposed to happen here?"

He shrugged. "I don't know. We're just supposed to watch Santa."

"Santa? I cannot escape him. Why is that?"

"Hmm?"

"Oh, nothing. It is too personal. Only Mandy would understand."

"By the way, I'm Bobby and this is my wife, Angeline."

Moshe nodded, "I guessed that. She spoke very highly of you, Bobby. It is such a pleasure to make your acquaintance. And this is my lovely wife Miriam."

"How did you know Mandy?"

Moshe sighed. "She was a dear, dear friend. We had wonderful discussions. She helped me a great deal through a difficult time, before I met Miriam."

A few minutes went by. They talked in hushed voices. Finally, Marilyn pointed to the roof and scolded, "Kids! Stop running around and look up. See Santa? See? He's smoking. Santa's smoking his pipe."

"I see it! I see it!" they shouted.

The crowd clapped, whistled, laughed, and hugged.

As the reverend was leaving he told Barbara. "I have to say that you are a marvel. The service, the wake, and this event were the most remarkable of any that I have attended. Your sister would be very pleased."

"Thank you. And you are such a sly devil. You knew who the photographer was all along, didn't you?"

"I have been called many things, but not that," he smiled and kept walking.

Henry tipped his hat. "Goodbye, Barbara. Take care."

"Goodbye, Henry. And please forgive me. I shouldn't have lost my temper."

"No, Barbara, it was quite understandable. Frankly, I'm glad you were angry with me. I needed that."

Lorna turned to Carlos, "Congratulations. You did it."

He smiled, nodded, and rested his hand on her back. She didn't mind.

POSTSCRIPT

It was a Thursday. Sam was home with the kids and her class ended early. Terri didn't feel like going home. She felt like going out.

She drove to downtown New Haven, up Chapel Street, down Park, circled the Green twice and read the York Square Theater marquee to see what was playing. The museums were closed. She thought about going to Claire's for a snack or to hang out at Atticus Books until late and then go home.

But no.

Instead, Terri drove around until she found herself on upper State Street. There were no spaces near the intersection or under the highway. Two women locked their jeep then walked up the street hand-in-hand. They looked at her as she drove by.

The door to the bar was open. Packed. She heard a cackle, then another, could see the crowd, see the dancing and heard, "Da-da, da-da, dah. Da-da-dah. Da-da, da-da, dah. Da-da-dah."

Michael Jackson's "Beat It."

Terri knew that she should go home, turn around, leave; it was late. She almost did.

But at the next block, her brake lights glowed. Jan had to be in the bar. There was the old Rambler. And right in front of it, a space.

CPSIA information can be obtained
at www.ICGtesting.com
Printed in the USA
FFHW010644270419
52041308-57461FF